Praise for *Black* [...]

"Harrison finds new ways to press on the bruise of growing up as an outsider, delivering small-town religious horror with wit as sharp as a ritual dagger piercing through a bleeding core of familial trauma."   —*Publishers Weekly* (starred review)

"Think *The Princess Diaries* meets Dante's *Inferno*. That's *Black Sheep*. Only Rachel Harrison could write something with such fiery playfulness and such stunning acerbic wit. Undoubtedly the most enjoyable and compelling horror novel you'll read this year."
            —Eric LaRocca, author of *Things Have Gotten Worse Since We Last Spoke*

"Vesper's story ruminates on themes that include nature vs. nurture, the legacy of family trauma, and the repercussions of organized religion in its various forms. . . . This subject matter elevates a horror novel to a study in philosophy, even as the bloodletting ramps up."   —*Shelf Awareness*

"No other contemporary author harnesses the humanity found in horror quite like Rachel Harrison. With *Black Sheep*, she warms your heart, then breaks it, then rips it out."
                        —Clay McLeod Chapman, author of *Ghost Eaters*

"A razor-sharp voice full of wit and humor, along with some edge-of-your-seat moments, will have readers clamoring for more."
                                        —*Library Journal* (starred review)

"*Black Sheep* is a devilish good time made all the more compelling with an exploration of the complexities of family dynamics. Compulsively readable."   —Kristi DeMeester, author of *Such a Pretty Smile*

"Once again, Rachel Harrison finds light in the darkness and darkness in the light. . . . [Black Sheep] sits proudly among her family of contemporary horror classics."

—Nat Cassidy, author of Mary: An Awakening of Terror and Nestlings

"Anyone who read Such Sharp Teeth knows that Harrison can absolutely nail thorny family dynamics and blend them with visceral horror, but with Black Sheep, there's something new going on, proving yet again that Harrison is one of the most versatile authors in the genre."

—Paste Magazine

"Surprising and snappy, Harrison catches you on Hellraiser hooks with a ceremony of grim wit and communal dread. Black Sheep makes a firm case for dodging every family get-together."

—Hailey Piper, Bram Stoker Award–winning author of Queen of Teeth

"Vesper is my favorite new antihero. . . . This is, in short, my ideal read and my favorite Rachel Harrison novel yet."

—Anne Heltzel, author of Just Like Mother

"Harrison has molded her own addictive niche of relatable heroines caught in unconventional (and, usually, supernatural) situations. Black Sheep may be the epitome of her brand."

—Fangoria

"With brilliant underline-worthy writing, thrilling page-turning pace, and genuine laugh-out-loud humor, Black Sheep confirms what I already knew: I will follow Harrison down any dark alley, always."

—Claudia Lux, author of Sign Here

Novels by Rachel Harrison

The Return
Cackle
Such Sharp Teeth
Black Sheep
So Thirsty

Short Story Collection by Rachel Harrison

Bad Dolls

BLACK SHEEP

Rachel Harrison

BERKLEY

NEW YORK

BERKLEY
An imprint of Penguin Random House LLC
penguinrandomhouse.com

Copyright © 2023 by Rachel Harrison

ISBN: 9780593545867

The Library of Congress has cataloged the Berkley hardcover edition of this book as follows:

Names: Harrison, Rachel, 1989-author.
Title: Black sheep / Rachel Harrison.
Description: New York: Berkley, [2023]
Identifiers: LCCN 2022060614 (print) | LCCN 2022060615 (ebook) |
ISBN 9780593545850 (hardcover) | ISBN 9780593545874 (ebook)
Subjects: LCGFT: Novels.
Classification: LCC PS3608.A78368 B57 2023 (print) | LCC PS3608.A78368 (ebook) |
DDC 813/.6—dc23/eng/ 20230104
LC record available at https:// lccn.loc.gov/ 2022060614
LC ebook record available at https:// lccn.loc.gov/ 2022060615

Berkley hardcover edition / September 2023
Berkley trade paperback edition / August 2024

Printed in the United States of America
1st Printing

For the bad kids

BLACK
SHEEP

1

As I stood singing the birthday song for the fifth time that evening, I realized I was wrong for not believing in hell. Hell was the birthday song. Hell was Shortee's. Hell was the green polo shirt, the khakis, the whole stupid fucking uniform. Hell was my life.

"And the happy Shortee's happy birthday to you, hey!" I clapped, and I thought, *This must be it. This must be the summit of loathing.* I imagined a climber atop Mount Everest, only bitter instead of victorious, grappling with their dissatisfaction with the view.

Kerri presented the chocolate lava cake to the kid, and when he blew out the candle, we all applauded and whooped and I longed to feel what I typically felt, which was numb, instead of what I felt in that moment, which was miserable.

The kid's parents kissed his forehead, ruffled his hair. His sister asked meekly if she could try a bite. I observed them as I distributed extra spoons and napkins, and for the first time in a long time I thought about my family.

For the first time in a long time I missed them.

Or, if I'm being honest, which I suppose I should be, it was the first time in a long time that I admitted to myself I missed them, and how much. In that moment, I surrendered to the tidal pull of family. Of blood.

My hand found my neck, which was naked, absent the token of my youth, a sometimes coveted but more often resented piece of jewelry.

"You okay?" Kerri asked, ushering me back to the kitchen.

"Sure," I said, unconvincingly.

"Awesome. Yeah, so, I was wondering . . ." she said, trailing off, distracted by a stain on her polo. "Ugh! Chocolate. That is chocolate sauce, right? Shit."

"Wondering what?" I asked, checking the window for table eight's order.

"Do you think you could cover my section 'til close?" she asked, batting her lashes, flakes of mascara falling to her cheeks like ash.

"Why would I do that?" I said, poking my head into the window to see what the line cooks were up to, suspicious they were once again slacking off.

"Because I'm asking very nicely," she said. "And because you owe me."

"I owe you?"

"I pick up your shifts all the time."

I snorted. "When?"

"Last week."

"I was sick," I said. It wasn't a lie. I was sick. Sick of working.

"Please, Ves?"

"Why do you need to leave early?" I said, sidestepping an over-ambitious busser who was barely balancing a tray of precariously piled dishes.

She picked a waffle fry off of a plate in the window. A plate that was not for table eight. "Sean."

"Sean?" I asked, dumbfounded. "Really? That guy? You're ditching work for that guy?"

"You're so judgmental."

"The guy treats you like a travel toothbrush. He'll use you for a week straight, then forget about you for months," I said. "And you either don't care or your self-esteem is too low to do anything about it. Either way, the whole thing is messed up."

Her jaw hung open for a moment, eyes widened like those of a child discovering something new about the world, something brutal. *Your burger was a cow. Moo.* I knew this look. I'd offended her with my honesty. But the truth was the truth, and she needed to hear it from someone. Might as well have been me.

She crossed her arms over her chest. "Will you take my section or not?"

"I don't really want to be aiding and abetting, but sure. I'll do it. But I swear, if I have to sing that goddamn birthday song one more time, it's game over."

"Thanks," she said, turning on her heel. She paused on her way to the back room, looked over her shoulder at me. "You know, you're not pretty enough to get away with being as mean as you are. And you're really pretty."

I almost applauded. It wasn't easy to burn me, and she'd straight up smoked my ego.

"Order up—got eight in the window," yelled one of the line cooks. When I went to retrieve it, I thanked him, and then I heard him whisper under his breath, "You're welcome, *Your Highness.*"

There were worse nicknames, worse insults. Worse things.

After ten p.m. Shortee's turned into a cesspool of drunks and rubes, and some nights I'd have the patience for it and other nights it'd make me want to cartwheel off a cliff.

This night was one of the latter.

"Four top at bar," Amy, the host, told me while snapping her gum. Staff wasn't allowed to chew gum, but she did anyway, and I respected her unwavering commitment to such a small act of rebellion.

"Great," I said, checking the clock. Close was in less than forty-five minutes, and I doubted this new table would be out by then, meaning I'd have to stay late. I cursed Kerri and her bad decisions. I cursed my own.

I peeked over and saw that the party was four dudes, one in a backward baseball cap. If I smiled, feigned effervescence, maybe—*maybe*—I'd improve my chances of a solid tip. But I doubted it. At that point I'd been at Shortee's for three years, and in the food service industry for six, ever since I left home at eighteen. I could tell just by looking at someone what they were going to tip, down to the cent. It was like shitty magic, like an evil fairy bestowed a cruel, useless gift on me. A highly specific power of foresight.

"Hey, how we doing tonight?" I asked the guys, approaching the table, struggling to summon any artificial zest. "My name is Vesper and I'll be taking care of you. Can I start you off with something to drink or do you need a minute?"

"Yeah, uh, I'll take a . . ." was how each of them ordered.

I kept my head down, scribbling in my book, trying to ignore the hot nudge of a stare. I was being scrutinized in a way that was, unfortunately, quite familiar to me. I knew in my gut what was coming. I considered running.

This is what I get for thinking of them, for missing them, I thought. *I've called them back in.*

"Vesper?"

I looked up, instinctively, at the sound of my own name.

"First of all, that's a rad name," the guy said. He was the oldest at the table, about the right age. Mid- to late thirties. Old enough to have snuck into her movies, to have rented the videos. He had a five-o'clock shadow, wore all black. His ears had been gauged once upon a time. A former Hot Topic punk. He'd probably bought her poster, had it up on his wall. I knew the one. In a cemetery she posed provocatively in black fishnets, a chain mail bra, and a signature piece of jewelry that everyone assumed she wore just to be cheeky. "Second, has anyone ever told you that you look *exactly* like Constance Wright?"

"Who?" I asked. It was how I usually responded, because I knew it'd piss her off.

"The scream queen? You know, the chick from *Death Ransom*, *Bloody Midnight*, *Farm Possession*, *The Black Hallows Coven Investigation*?"

I shook my head, deriving devious joy from the lie.

"Seriously? You've never heard of any of those movies?"

"I'm not into horror," I said, another lie. "I should get those drinks in."

"You don't need to be into horror to know Constance Wright. You have the exact same face. I swear to God."

He took out his phone, and I bailed. "Be right back with those drinks."

I'd hoped that by the time I returned to the table they'd have moved on to another topic, but no luck. When I went back to drop off their beers, the guy still had his phone out. He'd Googled her, pulled up her image page.

And there she was. My mother.

"You seriously don't know who this is?" he asked. "She's an *icon*."

"Dude, relax," one of the other guys said.

"I don't see it," I said, shrugging. "I'm sorry."

"Really?" he asked. He seemed disappointed, and I felt a twinge of guilt for deceiving him. But it was necessary deceit.

"Maybe it's the hair," I said. I'd cut it off in an attempt to avoid situations like the one I was in, but the pixie didn't make a difference. It didn't change my face.

The man nodded, retrieved his phone. He stared at the screen, scrolling through picture after picture of my mother.

"Guess you're a little young. You missed the golden age. Get high, go see the latest slasher. Get scared shitless. Everyone's talking about horror now, but nothing's scary anymore. It's all *saying something*. Doesn't need to say anything. Just has to be scary . . ." He was talking to himself at that point. Muttering. "Probably why Constance Wright doesn't really make movies anymore. You know, she lives down in Jersey. She has a farm out somewhere."

"Oh wow. Cool," I said, acting like it was surprising new information. I hadn't inherited Constance's acting talents. "Are we ready to order some food, or are we good with the drinks?"

They ordered the spicy Southwest nachos and boneless wings, and any dream I'd had of getting home before one o'clock died tragically right then and there.

I brought them round after round, each guy chugging whatever drink I'd delivered him within minutes, racking up a bill that, in theory, should have led to a decent tip, but they were getting so hammered that I wasn't exactly optimistic that any of them could do the simple math of calculating 20 percent.

The one guy, the former punk, didn't bring up Constance again, didn't bother me, but the one in the backward baseball cap started to annoy me. He'd had the most to drink, and it showed.

"Vessie," he said when I dropped off the nachos and wings. Only Rosie was allowed to call me that. "Vessie, you make these? You go back in the kitchen and make these for us?"

"Sure," I said. "Put them in the microwave and everything."

When I turned to walk away, he reached out for me, swiping my ass with his palm.

I spun around, and he laughed. "Oh, sorry. My bad. Can I get some more of this cheese sauce?"

I nodded and retreated into the kitchen. It wasn't really Shortee's policy to give out sides of nacho cheese, but I scooped some into a ramekin and nuked it for a minute, figuring it was easier to shut the guy up than try to explain the arbitrary rules of a chain restaurant.

I checked the clock. It was eleven fifty-four. It also wasn't Shortee's policy to kick anyone out. If they arrived before eleven thirty, we had to let them stay, let them finish. *Shortee's prioritizes hospitality*, my manager, Rick, would always say. I had this theory that he was a corporate bot masquerading as a real human. I had a lot of theories about Rick.

Just as I thought of him, he popped into the kitchen.

"How we doing, Vesper?"

In restaurant speak "we" is "you," and if you're asked a question as a member of the waitstaff, the response had better be positive.

"Good," I answered through clenched teeth.

"What we doing?"

"A guy asked for more nacho cheese."

Rick frowned.

"I know, I know," I said. "But customer first, right? I'm prioritizing hospitality."

"Just be sure to charge," he said. "Two dollars."

"Really? Two dollars?"

He frowned again.

"Got it. Thanks!" I said, taking the cheese out onto the floor, eager to get away from Rick, though not eager to return to the rude, handsy, nacho-hungry bro.

I wove between the tables slowly, inhaled the vague lemony scent of the cleaning solution we used to wipe everything down. It smelled like the end of the night. It smelled like *time to go home*. But I knew I wasn't going home anytime soon, and my heart tumbled at the thought of another long, sleepy bus ride in the dark.

I stifled a yawn, stifled the urge to throw the cheese at the wall, rip off my polo Incredible Hulk–style, and set the whole place on fire.

"Here you go," I said, sliding the ramekin onto the table.

"Let me ask you something," Backward Hat Guy said, leaning into me, gifting me with a rancid exhale. "We were just talking about how all hot girls have daddy issues. You have daddy issues, Vesper?"

I laughed. It wasn't polite, or a coping mechanism. It was genuine.

If only he knew.

He must have taken my laughter as a signal of some kind, because he touched me again. This time his hand found my waist, and he pulled me in close. For a moment, I thought of Brody. What it'd felt like to be touched by him. To have his hands on me, hands I wanted, that had permission.

"Hey," I said, snapping out of my memory and stepping back from the table. "Don't touch me."

"Whoa, whoa," he said. "Relax."

I laughed again, but underneath this laughter was a staggering rage. It wasn't fresh; it was there always. A seething I kept stashed away, like a baseball bat behind the headboard. I experienced it in the usual way. A brief flare of blinding, white-hot anguish, followed by a mild chill of despondence, and finally a return to indifference.

"I'll be back with the check," I said, turning to leave.

"We're not done," he said. "You'll do what we tell you. We tell you to bend over, you bend over, or no tip."

I whipped around, stunned by the audacity.

"Who's your daddy now?" he asked, raising an eyebrow. The rest of the guys snickered, shook their heads, said nothing.

He reached for the cheese, and maybe it was his own clumsiness or the result of an overzealous microwave, but somehow the cheese bubbled up.

It exploded, essentially.

And it exploded all over his face.

He didn't scream at first, so at first glance it seemed like an innocent spill. But then I noticed the curls of steam slithering from him like skinny pearlescent snakes. And then I heard it. The sizzling.

Then he screamed.

"*Ah, ahhh!* It's burning me! It's burning my fucking face! *Ah!* Help me!" He fumbled for his napkin. The former punk—a quick thinker—tossed his beer at the bro's cheese-scalded face, but the beer did nothing to mitigate the damage. The guy kept screaming. He had a napkin now and was wiping away the gobs of orange cheese. In their wake, pocks of skin were sunset red and peeling. And I could smell the injury, the burning flesh. A foreshadowing.

It was bad. It was really bad.

This time when I laughed, it wasn't because I thought it was funny, or because I was angry. It was nervous laughter. Doomsday laughter.

And it was not appreciated.

I sat at the bar with Rick. He'd made me the Shortee's signature honey jalapeño margarita, which came in a fishbowl glass, and I knew then that I was getting fired.

He had a glass of water with a lemon wedge.

Rick was the kind of guy who wore his pants just a little too high, a brown braided belt buckled one hole too tight, his green polo tucked in. I had a feeling he relished the polo. I had a feeling he slept in it. He was a "don't think of me as the boss" kind of boss. Kerri would talk about how she felt sorry for him, say he meant well. Even though I'd grown up sheltered, I wasn't naive. I suspected that Rick had a mean streak, or some secret unsavory fetish; maybe he had tortured small animals as a child. Maybe he expected things of the world, and in the absence of what he felt he was owed, he fostered an ugly resentment that would rear its head eventually.

Kerri told me I should try not to think the worst of people.

"I don't," I'd told her. "It's intuition."

She didn't seem to believe me.

"So," Rick said, and cleared his throat.

"So," I repeated, and sipped my margarita. If I was about to be unemployed, I was going to suck every last drop of tequila out of the gigantic glass in front of me. Take whatever I could from Shortee's before it left me with nothing.

"This is why we don't do sides of cheese," Rick said, shaking his head.

"The guy asked. Should I have said no?" I didn't raise my voice. I didn't have the energy to be angry. I rarely did. Constantly treading water really takes it out of you. "You said to charge two dollars."

"I'm not trying to get into a blame game here, Vesper. But we might have a lawsuit on our hands."

"Sure," I said. I licked the salt rim. "I mean, the guy grabbed me multiple times, but sure. Let him sue because he's too uncoordinated to handle nachos."

"He grabbed you?"

"Does it matter?"

Rick sighed, which I took as a no.

Of course not.

"Look," Rick said, "I'm going to have to let you go."

I waited to feel sadness, or relief, or fear, or shame. But I just felt drunk. I could never handle those big margaritas. I gave a little hiccup and said nothing.

"It's not just about tonight, Vesper. There have been several complaints."

"That so?" I asked. "Several?"

"About your attitude," he said, brow furrowed. "That you're not a team player."

"I was covering for Kerri tonight," I said. "This incident occurred in her section. If I hadn't so kindly volunteered to take over, I wouldn't be in this situation."

"There it is," he said. "The attitude problem. The sarcasm. Shortee's is a family. No one's above anyone else."

Your Highness, I thought. I wondered if it was the line cooks who complained.

"I've been here for three years," I said, not certain why I felt compelled to fight for a job I didn't even care about. It wasn't about the money; I'd find another job, another Shortee's. It wasn't about the injustice; I'd known from a young age there was no such thing as fair. I thought maybe it was about getting fired instead of quitting, which I'd fantasized about since my first shift. Or maybe I was just so frustrated with my life, the one I'd sacrificed everything in pursuit of, that I couldn't stand to have fucking Rick lecture me about my attitude. "It's fine. If I'm honest, if I had to spend another day feigning enthusiasm about deep-fried mac-and-cheese bites, I probably would have lain down in traffic. And I hate this polo. I hate this polo so much. We all look like preteen dweebs on a class field trip. It's impossible to get any respect while wearing this shirt. We'd have better luck wearing dunce caps."

I gulped down the rest of the margarita as fast as I could.

"I'll mail your last paycheck," Rick said coldly, clearly offended by my polo comment.

"Cool," I said, sliding off the barstool. "Thanks so much."

"Vesper?" Rick called out to me as I was halfway out the door.

I almost kept walking, but I guess maybe I was curious to hear what he had to say.

"Can I give you a piece of advice?" he asked. He didn't give me an opportunity to answer. "You're smart. You're a hard worker. You're beautiful. You're young. But you're not above the rest of us. You're not special."

"Is that the advice?" I asked flatly.

"You know what? Never mind. Good luck, Vesper. I wish you all the best."

I knew he was lying. He wanted me to fail, so he could be right about something. So he could feel better about himself.

I let the door slam behind me and stumbled out into the parking lot, tequila dizzy, guts twisting. The first eighteen years of my life, all anyone had done was dote on me, tell me how special I was. But ever since I'd left home, my family, the church—ever since I'd entered the "real world"—all anyone did was tell me I wasn't.

I still hadn't quite figured out who I wanted to be right.

I wasn't so drunk that I couldn't take the bus, but I was drunk enough that I probably shouldn't have. I just couldn't bear the cost of an Uber, enough to feed myself for a week, especially now that I was newly unemployed. So I took deep breaths when the motion made me queasy. My stomach lurched at every stop, the driver slamming on the brakes. Vomit loomed in the back of my throat. I held it in until my stop. I toppled off the bus and hovered over a trash can. Spicy margarita's revenge.

There were no witnesses, thankfully.

I climbed the hill up to my apartment building. It wasn't far, about a ten-minute walk, but I was work worn after a double shift, my feet blistered, my head pounding; my back, my shoulders, my neck, my joints all squealing. The exhaustion bore down on me, making the hill seem steeper than usual.

The air was like a membrane—viscous, thick with humidity—and the heat hadn't relented. I soured like milk left out on the counter. My blood curdled in my veins. I felt inhuman, like a collection of chunks. My feet dragged with every step up the impossible incline, and I was tempted to collapse right where I was, plant a white flag, and let gravity win. Lose somewhat grace-fully.

The top of my building appeared over the hill. I could see my apartment, the second window down, on the corner—it was pitch-dark inside, with my cheap white curtains billowing out of the open window, reaching into the night like a longing ghost.

Above, the moon shone silver and pretty, *almost ripe for the picking*, as my father used to say. The glittering sky rested like a crown on the horizon. So many jewels—stars burning, burning, so desperate to be seen, seeking attention over light-years. Easy to forget stars are mortal; they're born, and they die. They shine for legacy.

It was July, and July is always stingy with breezes, a simmering miser. But this night . . . this night seemed antsy. I didn't *feel* a breeze, but I saw it skittering all around me. The trees that neatly lined the street swayed, leaves waving. They caught the orangey light of the streetlamps, which seemed to glow more intensely than usual. Beyond the sidewalk, something rustled the bushes. The flowers, lush and blooming, craned their necks.

The movement, the light . . . these things I maybe could have dismissed. It was the silence that unnerved me, that confirmed the wrongness of the scene.

Yes, I was exhausted, and yes, I was drunk, and yes, I was a bit raw from being unceremoniously sacked. But I had spent years, wittingly and unwittingly, calibrating the alarm inside me that alerted me to danger. Those of us who need it don't have a choice.

So I knew when I wasn't alone. I knew when I was being watched.

Maybe everyone experiences it differently, the sensation of hidden eyes. For me, it manifested like repeated prodding with a sharp stick. Like an itch on the inside of my skin.

Around me, the night remained too beautiful. Too clean. No litter on the sidewalk, another disturbing observation. The scene seemed eager for me to trust it, so, of course, I didn't.

I stood, unsettled, teetering in the middle of the street, searching for evidence, for visual proof of a threat. I waited for the appearance of a figure, a shadow invading the circles of light from the streetlamps or creeping out from behind a parked car. I waited for sound, a noise to disrupt the excessive silence. I waited for an antagonist to emerge from the dark.

The thing about danger is, it always has a face. It chooses whether to show it to you or not.

"Go on—come out," I whispered. "Why delay the big reveal?"

There's something you should know about me, that I've come to learn, that I should probably tell you now, so the rest of this makes sense. Seems I'm the type to pick at a scab until it bleeds, then peel back the skin to see what's underneath. The kind of curious that invites self-destruction.

But I'm also impatient, and after what felt like an hour of nothing but peculiar quiet and the incessant pawing of humidity, I relented, turning back to the hill and continuing my climb. I plodded on—pushing through the dizziness, the ache, the pouring sweat, the lingering burn of margarita and vomit in my throat—and finally, *finally*, made it to the door of my building.

I fumbled with my keys. I peeked over my shoulder one last time, half expecting to see someone standing at the end of the walkway, a lurking stranger. But there was no one. I was alone.

All alone.

I managed to get the door open. I had to climb up three flights of stairs on my hands and feet like an animal. My drunk, trembling legs couldn't hold me.

When I got up to my apartment, the mystery of my suspicion unfurled so perfectly, like the gentle pull of a ribbon flattening a bow.

There was a large red envelope resting on my doormat.

All this time, they'd known exactly where I was. Of course they had.

So, that's why the night was acting so strange, I thought. *It was scared.*

I snatched up the envelope and hurried inside, locking the dead bolt behind me. I shuffled across the floor, kicking off my sneakers, tearing off my polo and tossing it in the trash. I freed myself of my bra and collapsed onto my bed, forever unmade thanks to its position; it was wedged in my small studio apartment's makeshift sleeping nook, originally intended to be a closet.

I turned the envelope over in my hands. It was silky to the touch, and weighty. I never thought I'd describe an envelope as beautiful, but it was.

I also never thought I'd describe an envelope as eviscerating, but it was. It was the sword shining in the sun on the walk up to the execution block. It was soul wrenching, spine crushing, inducing a panic so profound, I felt as though I were levitating above my mattress, abandoned by the laws of nature, which wanted nothing to do with me and the ticking bomb in my hands.

Once again, I chastised myself for having thought of them earlier that evening. For having missed them.

You called them back, said a hissing voice in my ear that did and didn't sound like me.

Part of me wanted to frisbee the envelope out the window and move on with my life. Watch some trash reality TV dating show on Netflix that would reassure me I wasn't such a disaster. Start a job search in the morning, or maybe just start over someplace else, pack my shit and go, a total reset, something I'd often daydreamed about but was too lazy to implement.

But, as I said, I'm curious. And, if I'm honest, I'd been waiting.

I'd been waiting for that envelope ever since I left. Waiting for someone to reach out. Ask me, beg me. Say, *Please come home, Vesper. We miss you. Please.*

Because maybe I was desperate for an excuse, or maybe I was desperate for an opportunity to say no, to reinforce that I'd made the right choice by leaving six hard, painful years earlier.

The envelope didn't say whom it was from, for obvious reasons. No return address.

I thought maybe it was from Rosie, more a sister than a cousin, more a soul mate than a best friend.

Or maybe from Aunt Grace, who was more a mother to me than mine had ever been.

Definitely not from my mother, scream queen / queen bitch Constance Wright.

Maybe from Brody, telling me he was ready now. Ready to run away with me.

No, I thought. The envelope was too official to come from Brody. And the way it felt in my clammy grasp, I understood that whatever news was tucked inside, it wasn't good.

The anticipation mounted, dread's meaty hands tightening around my neck. So I slipped a finger into the seam and tore the envelope open, tipping the contents onto a tangle of sheets. Out slipped several small pieces of luxe stationery, edges gilded. I picked up the largest and held it up to the light.

Together we invite you to celebrate the marriage of

ROSEMARY LEIGH SMYTHE

&

BRODY GIDEON LEWIS

Saturday August 16th, Five o'clock in the evening
Mass & Ceremony
Wright Farm
The Hamlet of Virgil, New Jersey
Formal attire

And at the bottom, scribbled in black Sharpie . . .

Please come home. Stay for the weekend, or forever. We
love & miss you.

I let the invitation fall from my hands. I went straight for the
emergency pack of cigarettes I kept in a kitchen drawer, among
take-out forks and spoons, chopsticks, dull knives. I lit one off the
stove top, sat at the kitchen table smoking it, staring out into
space, arrested by utter shock. I ashed my cigarette on the table,
on the floor, on my lap, wherever.

At some point, I retrieved the invitation, read it over and over
as I chain-smoked. My disbelief would return, and I'd need to read
it again. I might have gone on reading it forever, turned to dust at
the table, had I not been distracted by the blue flame licking up
from the stove top.

Either I'd forgotten to turn off the burner or it had reignited
itself.

For a moment, I just stared dead eyed into the flame, thinking of home. Thinking of Rosie.

Sometimes Rosie's hair looked like gold. Other times, it looked like fire.

A memory slipped through the dam I'd spent years building.

On this afternoon, Rosie's hair was pure fire. The two of us baked under the sun—like a heavy yellow stone directly above us that seemed it might tumble down any second, ending the day or ending us. The grass was prickly at our necks; under our knees, our bare calves. We wore cutoff jean shorts we had made ourselves with a pair of scissors and a dream.

We did this often. Would just lie out in the field gazing up at the sky, talking about whatever. Everything and nothing.

That's how it was with best friends. With sisters. The highest of stakes, the lowest of stakes.

"My lips are so chapped," I said. "They're going to fall off."

"Here," she said, digging into her pocket and handing me a birthday-cake-flavored lip balm. Rosie always had things. Gum. Band-Aids. Lotion. Hand sanitizer. Faith.

I never had anything.

"You're my hero," I said in a funny ingenue voice.

She giggled. "Need those lips to kiss your boyfriend."

I rolled my eyes. "I don't really think of him like that. He's . . . I don't know. He's just Brody."

"You'll get married," she said. "It's obvious."

I wanted to tell her that it wasn't. That nothing about the future was obvious to me. But I said only, "We're thirteen."

She turned over onto her stomach, picked at the grass. "I hope I get to marry someone just as good."

"*Whoever you marry will be very lucky*," I said, *tossing back her lip balm.*

"*Aw, Vessie.*"

"*The luckiest.*"

Go figure. I knew fuck all about luck.

I knew fuck all about anything. I'd thought Rosie and Brody would mourn my absence, not use it as an opportunity to get together. All my years away, they hadn't been pining after me. No. Apparently, they had each other.

I stood up and turned off the burner, killed the flame.

2

I realized, once again, that I'd been wrong about hell. I'd come around to the fact that it did actually exist, but it wasn't the birthday song, and it was far away from Shortee's. I'd found it, for real this time, beneath the bustling, steaming streets of Manhattan.

Hell was Penn Station.

New Jersey Transit, the shadow realm.

I attempted to take refuge in a grimy nook as I waited for my train, but it was impossible to get out of the way. A man slammed his suitcase into my shin, sending me reeling into a nearby trash can. He gave a frustrated grunt, shook his head at me as if it'd been my fault.

"So sorry, sir," I called after him. "The audacity of me to have mass."

He ignored me and kept walking.

I observed my fellow Jersey-bound travelers, strangers, people I'd never know, fiddling with the lids of their coffee cups, dropping their receipts on the floor—brazenly littering. They sat on the stairs beneath signs that said not to sit on the stairs. They conversed loudly, scolded their children too harshly or not at all. I watched a child crawl between the legs of an unsuspecting businessman. I watched a young woman with long blond hair and Louis Vuitton luggage park herself directly in front of a large box fan, hogging perhaps the only source of relief in the entire subterranean sweatbox.

I searched for a pair of eyes to meet mine, some hint of reciprocal existential misery. There were eyes, hundreds, maybe thousands of eyes, but they were all glazed over, eerily still, like zombie eyes, glowing pale, reflecting that iPhone fluorescence. That gentle, stealth-damaging brightness.

I didn't judge them for escaping into their phones; I envied that they could. Mine had died, and I couldn't find anywhere to plug it in. I figured there had to be an outlet near the box fan, but the blonde was sitting right in front of it, her suitcases surrounding her like a fortress. She sprawled out on the floor, watching videos sans headphones, sound all the way up.

In my head I heard Kerri's voice telling me not to think the worst of people. Maybe I'd have been inclined to take her advice had she not ditched work to go hook up with a guy who didn't even like her, which had dominoed into my getting fired. And maybe I'd have been inclined to take her advice had my instincts not been right 100 percent of the time. And maybe—just maybe—I'd have taken her advice had I not been heading to the wedding of my cousin / best friend and my first and only love. Had I not been returning to the home I left with the intention of never, ever, *ever* going back. And had I not been, quite honestly, just a little unhinged.

"Excuse me?" I said to the blonde. I could see the outlet just over her shoulder.

She pretended not to hear me.

I considered giving up then, but as I said, I was a little unhinged.

"Sorry, there's an outlet behind you and I need to charge my phone." I held up my phone, as if I were presenting evidence in a showy trial.

Again, she ignored me. I watched a vague annoyance pass across her foundation-caked face, her only acknowledgment of my presence.

"I'm really sorry to bother you," I said, which was true, but I was sorry *for* me, not *to* her. "I wouldn't ask if I didn't need it."

She rolled her eyes and clicked her tongue. "Go ahead, then. I'm not in your way."

But she was very much in my way.

"Fine," I said, giving up.

Sometimes I would imagine a ledger inside myself, floating in my skull. An ancient-looking scroll where, with quill and ink, I'd tally up the incidents that subsidized my cynicism, my lack of faith in humanity. I had no idea where the visual came from, or what purpose it served. It was goofy. Sometimes it'd make me feel better, other times not so much.

This time, on this particular day, I couldn't be passively jaded, because I was actively upset. It was one thing to have no faith in humanity, to be disgusted, disappointed by the general population. But I was carrying around this fresh resentment for the person I'd always held up as an exception. As the epitome of *good*.

I couldn't get over it, get past the question *How could Rosie do this to me?*

It overshadowed all other questions, including the question I should have been more concerned with, which was *Why was I invited?* Or really *How was I invited?*

I'd left the church, and once you left, you were out; you were done. There was no going back, no coming and going for visits, holidays, anniversaries, birthdays. Weddings. And no one had reached out to me in the six years I'd been gone, so why now? Why this?

I needed to know, and I'd be damned if I let Rosie and Brody get married without having to look me in the eye first.

I'd been stewing in my mess of emotion for weeks, and now that I was at the train station, that I'd purchased my ticket home, that I held it in my hands, all I wanted was to disengage. To fuck around on my phone, get lost in an article about the ethics of cryptocurrency or the legit existence of UFOs or an acrimonious celebrity divorce, or read about fall fashion trends, lament the resurgence of low-rise jeans, or stare at a picture of a disheveled Ben Affleck buying deodorant at a West Hollywood CVS.

But I couldn't do any of that, and I couldn't do it because the inconsiderate blonde and her expensive designer luggage were in the way and she refused to move two inches to help a stranger asking politely for a simple favor. She laughed at something—a loud, trilling giggle—and as she did, she let her head fall back, getting dangerously close to the fan.

What if the blades got hungry? What if they ripped her pretty blond hair from her stupid thick head? Would she be laughing then? Would she regret not moving?

I wondered if it was spending my youth reading religious texts that detailed brutal punishments, savage justices, that had conditioned me to violent revenge fantasies, or if I was just fucked-up. It was impossible to know.

I hoisted my bag over my shoulder and headed toward the bathroom. There was a long, long line.

When I finally got to the sink, I splashed some water on my face and wiped up with a paper towel.

I briefly glanced at my reflection. I'd never liked to linger in front of the mirror, since my face was so similar to the face of someone I couldn't stand, who couldn't stand me. For as long as I could remember, whenever I looked at myself I saw her. I used to wonder if she experienced a similar phenomenon, but after years of contemplation I'd concluded that Constance Wright was too self-centered to see anyone but herself.

When I emerged from the bathroom, the blonde was gone, the outlet was free to use, and I wondered if I had just been impatient. If I was the asshole stranger. If I was perhaps too eager to condemn mankind over a small inconvenience.

"Now boarding on track twelve . . ."

A human wave crashed through the station, sweeping past me.

"Making station stops in Secaucus . . ."

I didn't know if the train being called was my train; it was too difficult to determine from the muffled announcement, and I had no direct view of any of the monitors, thanks to the stampede. I had no choice but to surrender to the masses, or else suffer a Mufasa fate.

I was bullied all the way to track twelve. Everyone was too close, the concept of personal space incinerated in the desperate rush to the train. There were shoulders, knees, elbows, fists, all these confusing extremities that didn't belong to me but seemed attached somehow, tangled, inextricable from me. All these hot mouths, breath scorching the back of my neck. Someone smelled, and I was afraid it was me. I was damp, but unable to determine whether it was my damp or if it was transferred to me. Was it my sweat, or a stranger's?

I looked around and saw mangled expressions, experienced a palpable foulness. A rottenness. I wondered, *Why do we all abso-*

lutely lose our shit when traveling? Is there an evil entity that roams around train stations and bus stations and airports, feeding on our rationality, leaving us rude and stupid and impatient and incapable of following simple rules? What other explanation could there be?

There was a bottleneck at the top of a narrow escalator, the only means to get down to the platform. There was also a bottleneck at the bottom of the escalator, on the platform, where the crowd was stagnant, seemingly ignorant of the throng streaming in behind them. They roamed slowly toward the train, stopping to check and double-check the track number, to look around, admire the scenery. There was a woman at the bottom of the escalator who couldn't step off because the man in front of her blocked the way. She tried to step backward, but there was no doing that either, because there were people behind her, bearing down, propelled by the escalator. She let out an uncanny wail. Its pitch was disturbing.

Fear manifests differently in everyone. It thrives in certain throats.

"Move! Move!" somebody yelled. Then everyone yelled.

It was so zany, so terribly ridiculous, that I started to laugh, only I couldn't really laugh, because I couldn't breathe. There was no inhaling; there was nothing to inhale except the neck of the person in front of me, so close, we might as well have been conjoined. And whoever was behind me, the pressure of their body—bones, muscle, skin, heat—was smothering. I was being crushed. It was a human crush.

I thought, *I am not dying in Penn Station. After everything, I'm not going out in hell.*

And also, *I'm showing up to this wedding if it kills me.*

"Step out of the way! *Move!*" I shouted with as much authority as I could muster.

There was a sudden shift. The crowd parted, the bottleneck shattering. I fell forward, tripping over my feet as I stepped off the escalator. I recovered quickly and hurried on, lest I get trampled.

I climbed onto the train, confirming with a disgruntled conductor that it was the right one. I managed to secure a precious single seat, which I reveled in for about two seconds before the reality of it all sank in. The reality of where I was, and where I was headed.

I wish I could say I hadn't made the decision right away. That I'd spent the weeks after receiving the invitation carefully considering, giving it a thorough thinking over, weighing the pros and cons. But I'd made up my mind right then, sitting at the kitchen table smoking, turning the invitation over in my hands. Yes, it was the Rosie-and-Brody factor. But there was also that one line in particular . . .

Please come home. Stay for the weekend, or forever. We love & miss you.

I couldn't figure out whose handwriting it was. I didn't think it was Rosie's, but I couldn't be sure. Had it been so long that I'd forgotten? What else had the years away swallowed? There was a lot I'd suppressed out of necessity, but I always figured I could get it all back if I really wanted. It scared me that some things I might have lost for good. There was a difference between choosing not to remember and forgetting.

I began nervously nibbling on my fingernails, a habit Constance wouldn't approve of. The thought of being reunited with my mother's disapproval resulted in a calamitous chill.

I turned toward the window as the train pulled out of the station, then rumbled through a dark tunnel to New Jersey marshland.

The night before, Kerri had come by with Shortee's takeout as an olive branch. Or really, for the opportunity to vent to me about Sean ghosting her again, with the takeout masquerading as an olive branch. She'd noticed my bag open on the bed, half-packed, and asked me where I was going.

"My cousin's wedding," I'd said, the short, simple answer.

"I thought you didn't have family."

I'd learned quickly after leaving home that family is an inevitable part of conversation, especially if you volunteer to work holiday shifts as often as I did. I also learned that when you tell people you're estranged from your family, they always assume it's your fault. They assume it's on you that you don't get along with the fam, that it's a character flaw. They see it as a red flag. Even if they, too, are estranged. There's so little empathy and understanding when it comes to family, the cornerstone of society, the root of existence.

I'd tried out different responses over the years. I'd say, *We don't talk* or *They're extremely religious*, or, if I was craving sympathy, I'd lean into a more extreme version of the truth and go for *I grew up in an abusive household*. Still met with suspicion every time. A slight twitch of the eye or tilt of the chin that seemed to ask, *Well, what did you do to provoke the back of your mother's hand?* or *Do you not believe in God?*

Telling people I didn't have a family garnered the fewest misgivings, so that's what I'd been doing. And apparently, at some point, that's what I'd told Kerri.

"It's complicated," I said, casually revising my past self's response while gnawing on a lukewarm Cajun zucchini stick. I'd missed Shortee's mediocre food.

"I thought they were all dead," she said. "I sort of figured that's why you are the way you are."

I shrugged, dunking my zucchini stick in the Shortee's "Dirty South" dipping sauce.

"I guess we all are the way we are because of our family," she said, double-dipping. "Nature versus nurture or whatever."

"Or whatever," I repeated, wiping my hands on a napkin. Nothing killed my appetite faster than talking about my family, than discussing nature versus nurture. The question of my life. Whether it was truly possible to escape, to sever blood ties.

I changed the subject. "So, what was the last thing Sean said to you?"

My attention was returned to my immediate surroundings courtesy of the teacup Yorkie in the seat in front of me. It had sniffed out my presence and started to bark with startling aggression. It shoved its tiny, vicious face through the crevice between the seat and the window.

For some reason, all dogs hated me.

"Shh! Pesto, shh!" the owner said, attempting to wrangle it into its carrier.

The dog refused. It went on yapping, clawing, baring its teeth, trying to get to me. Eventually, the girl got up and moved, eyeing me as she did.

"He's never like this," she muttered to herself as she passed by.

Outside the window, industrial marshland muddled into busy, city-adjacent towns, the tracks lined with mega apartment complexes both shiny and new and old and neglected. Eventually, these gave way to picturesque, uppity six-figure-city-salary, not-a-bad-commute towns with neat lawns and nice houses and with gazebos at the train stations. Then to quiet, quaint towns with significantly less charm, no Wall Street salaries. And finally to greenery. To nothing. To swaths of woods and ambitious puddles identified as lakes.

New Jersey is a strange place—full of oddities and local legends, folklore: the Pine Barrens, the abandoned fort at Sandy Hook, Shades of Death Road. Where I was headed was a particularly bizarre pocket of land a stone's throw from Pennsylvania. Too small to be a town, barely a dust speck on a map. A single famous resident who kept a low profile when she wasn't screaming her head off for the cameras. A devoutly religious community so set in their traditions, in their lifestyle, in their faith. There were so many rules, all so arbitrary. Upon reflection, I found it funny that I left only to end up at Shortee's, a similarly totalitarian environment.

One of the biggest rules of the church was, if you left, you could not come back. I still hadn't fully confronted that the invitation had broken that rule, and what exactly that meant. I'd assumed that Rosie or Aunt Grace or someone else had probably gotten approval, an exception. It wouldn't be the first time I'd received special treatment. If I'm honest, I sort of figured when I left that if I ever wanted to come back, I could. But as the years ticked away, I'd questioned my confidence.

I sat up in my seat, reaching for the envelope in my bag, slipping it out. Removing the invitation. I hadn't RSVP'd. I didn't want anyone to know I was coming—not Rosie or Brody, not Grace, not my mother. I wondered if that was a mistake as the train pulled into my station. The final stop.

I stepped out onto the platform and into the hot throat of August. The humidity was intense, odorous. There were two taxis waiting in front of the station.

I knew the second I got in one that I'd made the wrong decision. That I should have chosen the other. The car reeked of strong cologne and cigar smoke. It had seen better days: stained and peeling upholstery, wind-down windows, a tape deck, no GPS. The driver was older, had a deeply lined, sun-crisped face. Eyebrows wiry and wild. He wore a tweed newsboy cap, a big gold chain with a crucifix that lounged in an overflow of white chest hair. His bowling shirt was unbuttoned one too many.

"Hi," I said. "I'm going to Virgil. It's near—"

He cut me off. "I've been at this a long time, kid. I know my way around."

"Thanks," I said, wrestling with my seat belt. Wrestling with my nerves, which had steadily grown more formidable the closer I got to home. I imagined my anxiety as an amphibian, a slick, nimble creature dancing under my ribs. That's how it felt, this anxiety. Alive. Tricky. Slippery. Quick. Difficult to catch.

I'd wanted to strut back into my mother's house cool and confident, chic and casual, beautiful and unbothered. But I was sweat drenched and carried with me the stench of public transit, and I was unsettled in a way I feared I couldn't shake, that I couldn't play off.

"Virgil, huh?" the driver said. "What's out in Virgil?"

I yanked at the reluctant seat belt one last time before giving up. "Family."

"Huh," he said. "They got a farm?"

A bead of sweat landed in my eye. It stung. "Yeah. It's not operational."

"Mm. A lot of the farms around here couldn't make it. Tough times. Gonna get worse now with the Democrats."

Oh joy, I thought.

The driver turned on the radio. We listened to a baseball game through static. I looked out the window, anticipating familiarity. I didn't want home to sneak up on me. I didn't want to blink and be there.

"Can you turn on the AC, please?" I asked as another bead of sweat threatened entry into my eye.

"It's on," he said.

I hovered a hand over the vent and felt nothing. I cracked the window, ignoring the driver's condemning glare in the rearview mirror.

A breeze wheezed in. I inhaled, and there it was. The familiarity. The smell. It smelled like home. Like grass, tall and sweet, blades so sharp, it seemed as though they might draw blood. Underneath, the soil lush and soft as velvet. Cornfields vast and dense with mystery. The stink of the cows, the chickens, the sheep. Honey. Milk. Sunscreen. Water from the hose. Lye soap. Washing hands before dinner, Rosie and I hip to hip at the slop sink, singing while we worked up a lather, like good little girls, like trained animals.

"Our Lord, our Lord we love, our Lord, our Lord we trust, our Lord is here with us, in all things, of all things, the righteous one."

I held on to my inhale, held the scent inside.

The scent of no elbows on the table, wondering whose turn it was to say the blessing, because we were supposed to want it to be our turn, and Rosie always wanted it to be hers, but I never wanted it to be mine and I couldn't figure out why. For years, I didn't know, and it hurt; it was agony. Insomnia. Bad dreams. I could never sit still in mass. *Why?* I'd wondered. *Why?*

The inhale began to burn. My lungs begged for release.

An epiphany at ten. *Because it's all bullshit. It's all fucking nonsense. I'm not wrong, not crazy. They are. Falling to their knees in worship of an imaginary, all-powerful idol. Building their entire lives around a being that doesn't exist. Around fictional text.*

My body demanded the exhale. The air coughed out of me.

"You all right?" the driver asked.

"Yep," I said, clearing my throat.

Outside the window, the terrain leveled; the trees jumped back from the road. The world got so green. The leaves, the grass. I'd forgotten the vibrance of the hue, so specific to the place. To home.

I worried I was about to get sick.

"Gonna need an address," the driver said.

"Donner Road. Number one. You know where it is?"

He grunted, and I saw him pull up a map on his phone.

I took another breath in, then leaned my head out the window and exhaled my unease, let the wind carry it someplace else. *Cool and confident, chic and casual, beautiful and unbothered. Get it together, Vesper.*

"People don't think of this when they think of Jersey," the driver said.

"Guess not."

"You grow up around here?"

"Yeah."

"Ever been to Imagination Land? That's in Hope."

"When I was little."

It had been a long time since I'd thought of Imagination Land. Grace and Carl took me and Rosie when we were young. I remembered splashing around in a wading pool, climbing on a pirate ship, frolicking through a lollipop forest, a peppermint-striped path lined with glittery gumdrops. I remembered holding hands with Rosie on the carousel, drifting on a tube in the lazy river, waving to a friendly plastic whale spraying bubbles out of its blowhole. I remembered waiting in line for the roller coaster, the train resembling a dragon, its painted scales flashing in the sun. I remembered looking around at all the other kids, who seemed so carefree, so happy, and wondering how much time they had to spend in church. Wondering whether they had to say a blessing before they ate or if they could just dig in. Wondering what it was like to live without the Lord over your shoulder.

"You hear they had a child pornography scandal a few years back?" the driver said, interrupting my thoughts. "Some employee taping kids in the bathroom."

I resented that he felt the need to bring this up, casting yet another shadow on my childhood. I got the sense he was waiting for me to engage him, that he had more to say on the topic, probably about how it was a plot orchestrated by the Democrats. Some people need conspiracies, finding the simple horror of the truth too brutal. Whatever his motive, I wasn't taking the bait. I didn't respond.

He turned up the baseball game and didn't speak to me for the rest of the ride, not until we turned onto Donner Road.

"That it?"

It was. It stood tall on the horizon. The magnificent Victorian farmhouse, three stories, the wraparound porch, the turret. Beside it, scattered across the landscape, the squat stone barn. The big red barn. The coop. The shed. The gardens. The field.

There were cars parked up and down the street. I realized I'd miscalculated. I thought I'd walk into my mother's house and deal with that reunion first. Privately. Rip off the Constance Wright Band-Aid and then move on from there.

I hadn't accounted for a pre-wedding Friday night party. A rehearsal dinner.

I was about to walk into a crowd, have a full audience.

Shit, I thought.

"Here's fine," I told the driver.

"You sure? It's still a ways."

"Yep, this is good. Thanks," I said. "How much?"

"Eighty."

It was steep, too much, but I didn't have it in me to haggle. I threw cash at him, grabbed my bag, and slid out without another word. The driver sped away, bathing me in a dark cloud of dust and exhaust perfumed with burning rubber.

I turned around to be greeted by a gang of mosquitoes, aggressive at dusk, when there's a hint of pink in the sky. I could tell it was going to be a violent sunset, the kind that would scorch your retinas, that would linger in your vision long after you looked away.

I adjusted the strap of my bag and started down the road, eyes on my feet, safe from the sun.

I turned onto the driveway. It was long, always felt like miles to me. I interrogated myself about how I was feeling. I wasn't the desired calm, collected, whatever, but I wasn't nervous either. Not really. Not anymore. I wondered why.

Was this what I wanted? To finally be home?

I caught myself then. I still thought of it as *home*.

Did everyone think of the place where they grew up as home, even years after they'd left?

The gravel crunched beneath my feet, like a song I'd heard a thousand times before. The creak of the porch steps was as much mine as my own voice.

There was chatter inside the house, spilling out from the open windows. I heard faint music, the drag of chairs being pulled out, the soft clang of plates. They were about to sit down to dinner. I caught the scent of shallots, of browned butter. Of black pepper. Of red meat. Grace had made a roast, like she always did for special occasions. Her daughter was about to get married. What could be more special than that?

Longing and bitterness clashed in my chest.

I stood at the front door, my bag slipping from my shoulder courtesy of sweat. It was so humid, I struggled to breathe. The air could have been cut into slices.

It'd been six years, but as I stood there on the porch, the time seemed evanescent. Insignificant. I was a child again, hands sticky with melted Popsicle, scraping a squashed bug from the bottom of my bare foot. Summer on the porch. There were the ghost taste of lemonade, the phantom bites of mosquitoes.

No. The bites weren't memories. The mosquitoes were eating me alive.

Just knock. Get it over with. Go.

I might have asked myself whether the whole thing was a mistake, but I think I already knew the answer.

I stalled, peering into the front window. The house was crowded. There was a series of tables pushed together, creating a megatable. It extended from the dining room into the formal living room, angled into the foyer. The megatable was elaborately set. Lace runners. Floral centerpieces. Shining silverware. The revered crystal.

There was a flit of wings against my cheek, a buzz in my ear. I swatted at the air, at the fly zipping around my head. It landed on the back of my neck, and I whipped around, wheeling it off me.

Did I smell that bad? Was I attracting flies?

"Ha ha! Oh my goodness! My gosh, thank you! Yes, we're so excited." Her laugh danced out of the open window. It gave me gooseflesh. *Rosie*. Her laugh.

It was my favorite laugh, hands down. I used to do everything I could to get it, even if it got me in trouble, which it usually did. Straws up my nose at the dinner table. A vulgar drawing of our scripture guide, Ms. Tate. A long-running absurdist joke about a piece of spaghetti that dreamed of being a snake, which, over time, evolved into an epic that rivaled *Ulysses*, continued whenever we had pasta. Rosie was good, sweet, pious, well-behaved. Sometimes I wondered if she was real, or if she was a doll come to life, the perfect porcelain miracle child prayed into existence by two of the church's most dedicated members. But when I could make her laugh, that was proof to me that she was human, too. That she was like me.

Apparently so like me that she, too, would fall for Brody.

Apparently so like me that he would fall for her.

I wondered . . . how long after I left? Months? Years? Did they ever talk about me? Did they pretend that I didn't exist? That I never existed?

I recalled my final conversation with Brody, out at the playground behind the school, where we'd meet up sometimes after dark to smoke weed and drink stolen liquor and fool around.

"*Come with me,*" I said to him, holding his hands to my lips and kissing each knuckle.

He sat above me on a higher step, silent. Around us, the crickets sang; the fireflies blinked light into darkness; the swings swayed in the breeze; the puddle at the bottom of the slide rippled, disturbed by mosquitoes.

"*Brody?*"

"*You're serious?*" he asked. "*You're seriously telling me you don't believe in the Lord? You're seriously telling me you're leaving?*"

"*I'm serious,*" I said. "*Honestly, I'm surprised you're so surprised. I thought it was kind of obvious.*"

"*I knew you sometimes questioned your faith, but this . . .*" He trailed off. He slipped his hands from my grasp.

"*You really want to get married by twenty-five, have two to three babies, live in your parents' house, live here forever? Mass three times a week? Never meeting anyone new, never experiencing anything else?*" I asked. "*You really want this life?*"

"*You don't?*"

It was a curb stomp, broken teeth, an eyeball free of the socket, a bone poking through skin, a shockingly brutal injury. This person whom I was so madly in love with, who claimed to be in love with me, whom I'd known my whole life, didn't actually know me at all.

"*Vesper. Please don't do this. Don't leave,*" he said. "*You're having a moment. You're not thinking straight. You belong here.*"

"*That's just it,*" I said, rising. "*I don't.*"

The memory burned through me like acid.

I didn't allow myself another moment's hesitation. I opened the door.

3

My toes clipped the threshold, and I tripped, toppling into Bartholomew. He rattled around in his giant bell jar.

"Hi, Bart," I said, staring into the eye sockets of Constance's prized model skeleton, allegedly studied by medical students in the early 1900s, and later salvaged from a Philadelphia estate sale, now a decoration displayed front and center in the foyer, alongside an antique ceramic planter shaped and painted like an old-timey circus clown and used as an umbrella stand.

Bart's rattles echoed throughout the house, and it dawned on me that they were now the *only* sounds in the house. The chatter had quieted. I looked up, and everyone was staring. Someone gasped. Someone dropped silverware, and it *clink-clink-clinked*.

I was typically too apathetic to experience awkwardness. Not right then, though. It was pretty fucking awkward.

Their faces blurred in a haze of burning wax, that milky carcinogen air. There were too many. People. Candles. Flowers. Everything. Too many, too much.

But then there was her. Her stare like an ice cube unexpectedly slipped under the collar. Like a stinging whip of wind.

Constance Wright.

She sat, posture unnervingly perfect, her long glossy black hair flowing down, down, down. As she walked it would swish over her hips, like a velvet curtain I wasn't allowed behind. In the six years I'd been gone she hadn't changed at all. Her skin remained flawless, youthful. Eyebrows meticulously plucked into dramatic arches. Lashes thick and dark, even without mascara, though she could never resist fake lashes. She wore them that night, and they fluttered slightly as she parted her burgundy-painted lips to speak, to break the excruciating silence.

"So good of you to join us," she said dryly. She lifted her crystal goblet full of garnet-hued wine and took a slow sip. "Ah, and you let the dog in."

I turned around to see a flash of fur, a massive Irish wolfhound trotting through the front door, heading down the hall toward the kitchen.

I opened my mouth to apologize, an automatic response, and was overcome with a bone-deep uneasiness, horror at a cellular level, as I realized it didn't matter that I'd left, or how long I'd been gone. The habits weren't broken; the dynamic hadn't changed. My absence made no difference. We were going to pick up right where we left off. Her being cruel and unloving, and me apologizing for everything.

"Vessie?" It was Rosemary. She navigated around chairs, around bodies, on her way to me. She wore a white eyelet romper and a pearl headband, her strawberry blond hair in immaculate manufactured waves. The look of absolute shock on her face confirmed that she hadn't been the one to send the invitation. But if she hadn't, who had? "Is it really you? I can't believe you're here!"

"Hey," I said, the only word I could manage.

She threw her arms around me with such force, I lost my balance, stumbled back.

"Am I dreaming? Are you really here?" She asked the question directly into my ear. "I can't believe it! I'm just so surprised!"

Yeah, I bet you are, I thought bitterly.

But at the same time, it'd been so long since I'd been held like that. By someone I loved, who loved me.

After some initial reluctance, I melted into the embrace. I let my fingers find her perfect hair, rubbed a silky strand between them. It felt like so many sleepovers, French braids, sparkly barrettes. It felt like home.

She let me go so she could look at me.

"Your hair!" she squealed. "And your nose!"

I always forgot I'd gotten it pierced during a spontaneous postwork outing with Kerri.

"You look amazing!" Rosie said. She didn't appear to feel guilty for her betrayal. She just seemed excited to see me.

So then I got to be the one who felt guilty. Because I hadn't come back for her. I'd come back to spite her.

Unlike on Constance, the years were evident on Rosie. She looked . . . different. She'd gotten rail thin. Her cheeks had hollowed. Her teeth were artificially white—the work of drugstore strips or cosmetic dentistry. Her lips had been either injected or drawn on. She wore too much makeup—more specifically, a truly egregious amount of bronzer. Her freckles had faded, and either she was more careful in adulthood, staying out of the sun and using higher SPF, or she'd taken to hiding them under foundation. Broke my heart a little to see her without them. I loved her freckles. Sometimes when we were young, I would steal Aunt Grace's eyebrow pencil and dot my own face, so Rosie and I would look more like sisters than cousins, because we'd always felt more like sisters than cousins.

We never bore a real resemblance, though. Not even with the freckles.

But I guess we looked enough alike for Brody.

"How did you . . ." she started. "How are you . . ."

I knew what she was trying to ask me, but since I didn't have the answer, and because I'm kind of a cunt, I said, "It's your wedding. Of course I'd be here. Wouldn't miss it."

"Vesper?" The sound of Brody's voice saying my name was punctuated by chaos. He fumbled the baskets of bread he was carrying, sending dinner rolls soaring over the table. They landed in wineglasses and gravy boats, knocked over candles. Everyone scrambled to clean up. Except Constance, who dispassionately poured herself more wine, and Brody, who looked at me as if I were a velociraptor, a dangerous creature that might gnaw him to death if he dared to move.

"Brody," I said. "Graceful as ever."

He grinned for a split second. Then he looked to Rosie, maybe for permission. She danced over to him, took his hand. "Isn't this so exciting, babe? I've prayed for this. We both have."

Brody cleared his throat. "Glad, uh . . . glad you could make it." He turned to the table. "Sorry about all this. Let me—"

"I got it, I got it. No problem." Aunt Grace. "Everyone, sit, sit. We'll get started in just a minute."

Our eyes caught each other, and she winked at me. I understood then that our dynamic also remained unchanged. But this realization was a relief, because our dynamic was that she loved me and took care of me and showered me with affection, and I lapped it up.

"Let's get Vesper a chair, Mom," Rosie said. "Can we squeeze her in next to me? Between me and Jane?"

"Of course, sweetie," Grace said.

I began to recognize faces. Jane, a former friend who'd always been closer to Rosie because I found her a little twee and didn't have the patience for it, was aggressively waving at me. Brody's parents, Kenneth and Roxanne, in matching white button-downs, shifting in their seats, uncertain how to respond to my presence. Brody's sisters, twins Birdie and Beatrice, who had an obnoxious habit of constantly whispering to each other. They were doing it right then, right there at the table, and it was fairly obvious they were whispering about me. I smiled at them to let them know that I knew. They promptly stopped whispering, sat up straight in their seats, took sips of water in unison.

Then there was Uncle Carl, Grace's husband, Rosie's dad, everyone's dad. He wore khaki shorts and souvenir T-shirts from places I doubted he'd ever been, since he was raised in the church. He made corny jokes and stood in a wide stance with his hands on his hips, looking around with a sort of nebulous confusion, like he didn't know how he'd gotten to where he was but golly, he was sure as heck happy to be there. He'd tried to be a parent to me, to step in like Grace had. The difference was, I welcomed Grace because I'd wanted another mother. One who was loving instead of cold, one who would hug me, tell me how beautiful and precious I was. But I'd never wanted a father other than the one I had. In his absence, there was only heartache. Carl couldn't ever fill his shoes.

"Hiya there, Vesperino," he said.

"Carl, would you help me?" Grace said. "C'mon."

They were a real comedy duo. They had a sitcom marriage. Carl the clueless husband, Grace the high-strung wife.

My bag was heavy on my shoulder, and I wanted to set it down but didn't know where. I felt in the way, like I had at Penn Station, and it filled me with dread.

All the time I'd been gone, I could fantasize about what it would be like to return home. I was ruining the fantasy with reality. I could never escape into a pretty fiction again.

I'd always assumed that if I ever did come back, I'd be welcomed with open arms. I'd assumed I'd step back into love and adoration—with the exception of Constance's, of course. I worried I'd made a grave miscalculation. The vibe was indecipherable.

There was a great reshuffling, a chair dragged in from somewhere, a place setting that didn't match the rest.

"Come, Star," Grace said. *Star.* Her pet name for me. I couldn't help but smile at the sound of it, at the sweet term of endearment. She took my bag and set it down at the foot of the stairs. I then followed her around the table. She pulled the chair out for me, then kissed me on both cheeks like she did when I was little. "Welcome home."

"All righty," Carl said. "Everyone all settled?"

There was a wave of nods, a general murmur of agreement.

"Well, then. Everyone, the moment you've all been waiting for. The toast."

I caught Constance sighing, pouring herself yet another glass of wine.

"I want to start off by thanking all of you for being here with us tonight, to celebrate this beautiful occasion. . . ."

It was all happening so fast. I wondered how I was sitting at that table, in the house I'd grown up in, with my family, with people I'd known and who knew me, like nothing had ever happened. Like the past six years were a dream.

I looked down at the plate in front of me. Constance's good

china, with a pretty gold-and-silver art deco pattern, one of the few things she owned that wasn't gothic, adorned with skulls or clowns or other morbid imagery, that wasn't related to any of her films. I traced the pattern with my finger.

"We understand this commitment. We honor this commitment. The sanctity of marriage. A promise to walk together not only in this life but in the one that follows. A vow to share in the joys, in the hardships, and in faith of our Lord and Savior. Now, I've known Rosemary a long time. Her whole life, in fact—"

"Dad," Rosie said, rolling her eyes.

"She is sweet, thoughtful, kind, understanding, except when it comes to my jokes," Carl said, grinning his goofy grin. "She is a valued member of our community, a beloved member of our community. A beloved teacher to her students, a beloved friend, a beloved daughter. To know Rosemary is to love her. And I know Brody would agree with me."

He loved me first, I thought, reining in a sneer. It was too much all at once. The mixed bag of emotions from being home. My animosity over the occasion. I didn't know what to confront first, where to start or how. I took a gulp of wine.

It tasted like mass.

"See, my son-in-law to-be, Mr. Brody here—he's a smart man. Brody is an equally valued member of our community. I've also had the privilege of watching Brody grow from a boy into a man. He is compassionate, composed. Sharp-tongued, I'll tell you that. Have to keep your wits about you with this one. He's sharp! I know you all know!"

There was a chorus of mild laughter.

I fucking hate shit like this, I thought.

I drank more wine.

"And he is equally devoted in his worship of our Lord. It is their devotion, their faith, their love of Him, that is the foundation of their love for each other. I couldn't be prouder of them, or more excited for their future together. So let's raise our glasses, and cheers to the happy couple!"

"Cheers!"

Everyone clinked glasses. Mine was already empty.

"Thanks, Daddy," Rosie said. She'd always been a daddy's girl. I was, too, when mine was around.

"Now I've talked enough!" Carl said.

Constance snorted. Everyone pretended like they didn't hear it.

"Who will lead us in the blessing?" he asked.

There was a polite pause, everyone waiting graciously, allowing the opportunity for someone else to volunteer, someone who might want the spotlight more than they did.

"How about Vesper?"

My eyes darted to my mother, who raised one of her epic eyebrows with malicious precision. With this small gesture, this minuscule shift of expression, I was reminded exactly where I'd gotten my pettiness from.

"Vesper?" Rosie said. At first, I thought she might object. After all, I was a heathen. I'd strayed from the path of the Lord.

I supposed it both was and wasn't the right time to specify that I was back only for the wedding, not to rejoin the community and recommit myself to the faith. As everyone at the table stared at me expectantly, I was reunited with an explicit form of discomfort, like the vicious twist of an arm. The pressure to pretend I believed in something I didn't believe in.

I opened my mouth to speak. Part of me considered doing it. What did I care? The blessing was just words, words I'd regurgitated without meaning, without feeling, thousands of times before. But then there was the small voice in my head saying *Don't you dare*. Reminding me that this stupid fucking religion was the bane of my existence.

"I'll do it," Brody said. He reached for Rosie's hand. "May I say it?"

I knew then that he still loved me. He was saving me.

A mischief awakened in my chest like the stirring eyelid of a long-slumbering dragon, a patient fire crackling beneath its scales.

Rosie and Jane, who sat on either side of me, each grabbed one of my hands, threading their neat, manicured fingers between my scrubby ones.

"As it was in the beginning, as it will be in the end, truth everlasting," Brody said.

Everyone repeated. I mouthed along but didn't expend any volume, a fine compromise. "As it was in the beginning, as it will be in the end, truth everlasting."

"May you hear our prayer of gratitude for these thy gifts which we are about to receive, and look deep into the red of our hearts, and know our devotion."

Call and response. "May you hear our prayer of gratitude for these thy gifts which we are about to receive, and look deep into the red of our hearts, and know our devotion."

Faith is so time-consuming. You sit there spewing nonsense for five minutes while your food gets cold.

I thought about Shortee's. I thought about the birthday song. At least it was quick.

Never thought I'd long for the birthday song.

I wondered if my whole life would be this way, comparing bad to worse. I wondered if I'd ever be anything but resentful of perspective.

"Oh Lord, be with us, your faithful servants, as we savor these blessings. In your name, of your name, for your name."

Such enthusiasm. For such bullshit.

"Oh Lord, be with us, your faithful servants, as we savor these blessings. In your name, of your name, for your name."

Faithful servants. Such fucking bullshit.

And yet there was a strange vibration in the air, an electricity rippling through the room. A palpable excitement. I looked around and saw elation. The Lord was on the edge of their lips, divinity at the tips of their tongues, and the taste of it was intoxicating to them. His name brought them pure joy.

It brought me pure dread.

"Praise to Him."

"Praise to Him."

Their god. Not mine. Never mine.

"Hail Satan!"

"Hail Satan!"

"Hail Satan," I muttered, infusing my tone with sarcasm to curb my nerves.

The words left a sour taste in my mouth, a heat in my throat. It'd been so long since I'd last spoken them. I didn't want them to have any power, to hold any weight, but they did. They held an entire childhood. They held guilt, shame, absurdity, exasperation.

I reached for Jane's wineglass, pretending I didn't realize it wasn't mine. I drank.

"Let's eat!" Carl said.

Then it was the clanking of silverware, the sawing of knives through meat, the slurping of gravy, the wet smacking of lips, the grinding of teeth. Words garbled, spoken with mouths full. Grace and Roxanne debated the use of mayonnaise in chocolate cake. Carl and Kenneth engaged in a passionate discussion about the current Yankees roster.

The reason I'd never told anyone that I was raised in Satanism was because I knew it'd be impossible to continue the conversation past the assumptions, to escape the misconceptions. One thing I'd learned out in the world was that nobody's so different. We all buy toilet paper, contemplate the ply. Request help at self-checkout because something always fucking goes wrong, doesn't scan. We all spend too much money at Target, stand there in the parking lot going through the receipt, brow furrowed. We forget to take our vitamins, to take out the trash. We microwave leftovers. Set our alarms. Waste time on the internet. Forget our passwords.

We worshipped gods of our choosing. Satan. Christ. America. Celebrities. Capitalism. Clean living. The New England Patriots. La Croix.

I failed to see how Satanists were any different from Catholics or whoever, whatever, though I knew if I stated this publicly, I'd likely be stoned in the streets or burned at the stake, so I kept my mouth shut.

I grew up in Satanism. It wasn't weird to me.

"You know, I really prefer sour cream," Roxanne said.

"Anything but Greek yogurt," Grace said.

"Vesper," Jane whispered to me in her meek baby voice. "Vesper."

"Hey, Jane," I said, skewering a roasted potato and shoving it into my mouth. I was starving.

"We've all missed you so, so much."

I turned to her. She was a perky blonde with small, pointy teeth. She wore a bow in her hair every day, color coordinated with her outfit. There was something childlike about her, even as an adult. I found it off-putting.

"I'm married now," she said, showing me her rings.

"Congrats," I said, and again drank from her wineglass.

"You remember Ant Alberts?"

"Sure," I said. A quiet kid, all shoulders, who read scripture during lunch. I used to look at him across the cafeteria and wonder whom he would end up with. I used to think, *As long as it's not me.*

"He's my husband now," she said. "And I know you're probably thinking, where's the baby? Soon. We're trying. We're hoping soon."

She crossed her fingers and smiled so wide, her lips curled over her teeny goblin teeth.

I didn't know what to say. One of my primary beefs with Hell's Gate Satanism was the church's insistence that its followers marry within the religion and promptly produce more Satanists. Replacements for when they eventually died and went on to spend eternity frolicking in the fires of hell or whatever.

I decided to change the subject.

"Where's Lily?" I asked, innocently enough. Lily was Jane's older sister. Lily, Jane, Rosemary, and I all hung out growing up. Sleepovers, day trips, school, sports, church. In my eyes, bonds in the church weren't really significant. It was a small community; you didn't have much of a choice in friends, much of a selection. You spent time with whoever was around because they were there, not necessarily because of any genuine connection. Jane and I had been friends out of proximity. But with Lily, the friendship had been real.

Jane's smile didn't fade, but her left eye began to twitch. It was the slightest display of agitation, but it's all I needed to know that Lily had left. She was gone. She, too, had left the church.

Interesting, I thought.

Jane clapped her hands together, then unfolded her napkin across her lap. "It's going to be a beautiful wedding tomorrow. Beautiful couple, beautiful wedding."

And I might have been projecting, but she seemed a little smug. Kind of wanted to stab her with my fork.

"Yeah, sure," I said coolly. "Beautiful."

She started to say something else but then recoiled suddenly, shrieking. Her chair tipped back, butting against the china cabinet behind her, its contents clattering.

The Irish wolfhound I'd accidentally let inside thrust his head between us, wriggled his snout up to her plate, and began to lap up some gravy.

"Prince," Constance said in a firm tone I recognized. It was the same one she'd used to discipline me. "Prince."

I had assumed that the dog belonged to my aunt. Grace once told me that she and my mother had Irish wolfhounds growing up, and they both loved them, which I found hard to believe. My mother didn't seem like a dog person. Grace was. She'd had a shepherd, Charlie, when I was born, but he had apparently tried to eat me. There were no more dogs after that. Not until I left, I guess.

"Prince," Constance said again, snapping her fingers. The dog lumbered off, but not before giving me a quick growl. "Grace, control your beast."

"Sorry about that," Grace said.

"Oh," Jane said, blushing. "No worries, no worries."

She fetched her napkin from the floor. Grace got her a new plate.

"Vesper," Roxanne said, leaning across the table to get closer to me. "Vesper, welcome home, darling. It's so lovely to see you."

"Hi, Roxanne."

Brody's parents had always loved me. Spoiled me. Roxanne gifted me family heirlooms. An emerald necklace, an opal ring.

I felt a twinge of guilt for having pawned them after I left.

"Your hair looks amazing. So fashion-forward."

"Thanks," I said. I wondered if Brody's parents treated Rosie like they'd treated me. I wondered if she was an adequate replacement.

I turned to my cousin, who was cutting a scrawny green bean into thirds. I wondered if part of her had been glad when I left, had been eager to take my place.

Rosie, clocking my gaze, playfully nudged me with her elbow. "It's so strange. It's like you never left."

"It is and isn't," I said. "A lot's changed."

"Let's find a moment. Sneak away," she said. "After dessert. Meet me outside. Porch swing."

"Porch swing, huh? Guess I should have gotten a tetanus shot."

She laughed. "It's not *that* bad."

"It's a rusty death trap. It has been since we were kids."

"Well," she said, slipping a third of the green bean between her lips, "we've survived it this long."

"You're not hungry?" I asked her.

She didn't get a chance to answer. Carl, a few glasses of wine in, started telling everyone a story about his and Grace's wedding. Some high jinks with misplaced rings.

I tuned him out, realizing I was also a little wine drunk, or a lot tired. And that I really had to pee.

"Excuse me," I mumbled, shimmying out of my seat, behind

chairs, out to the foyer. I went to pick up my bag and caught Bart staring at me with his big empty eye sockets.

"Don't give me that look," I whispered to him, heaving my bag over my shoulder, taking a deep breath, and starting the perilous climb to the third floor. The stairs were steep, uneven. Typical of an old house.

I was winded by the time I got to the third-floor landing, my former reading nook.

It was as I remembered it. The built-in shelves were jammed with familiar books, only it seemed the spines had frayed over time, and were now covered in thick layers of dust and cobwebs. On the ottoman sat a tea tray, also sheathed in dust. The tea set was black, rat themed. The handles of the small, delicate cups were crafted to look like pink rat tails. The teapot had rats painted on it. Flowers, too, but they were secondary to the rats, the real stars.

The tea set was a gift from a prop master Constance befriended on the set of *The Black Hallows Coven Investigation*. Well, I guess "gift" was a generous term.

I found it ironic that my mother was the only member of Hell's Gate who resembled something close to the general public's idea of a Satanist. A horror icon with a love of the macabre. But she was an outlier. Most Hell's Gate Satanists were Disney fanatics, preferred Mickey Mouse to Michael Myers.

One of my earliest memories was of Constance returning from a shoot, bringing me a souvenir. She'd presented it to me in a small silver box tied with pink ribbon. I'd thought it might be a gemstone, or jewelry, barrettes. Something sparkly. It was a glass eyeball. A prop from the movie. I was five.

"You don't like it," she'd said, without inflection, without feeling.

"I do! I *love* it." I'd wanted to please her. To make her happy. To make her proud that I was her daughter, that she was my mother.

"Don't bother to lie, Vesper," she'd said. "You're not any good at it."

I shuddered at the memory and stepped through the door in front of me into the bathroom. My bathroom.

It, too, hadn't changed, other than the cobwebs. There was the claw-foot tub, a dated green toilet, a pedestal sink. A big oval mirror etched with flowers, the glass smudged, scratched. The walls were papered with illustrations from old medical journals. Wedged awkwardly in the corner was a small vanity that Constance had found in an antique shop in Santa Monica. She'd claimed it belonged to Jayne Mansfield. I doubted it.

I dropped my bag to the floor and the tiles danced, loose like baby teeth. I went to the bathroom, washed my hands with waxy violet-scented soap that had most definitely been there since before I left, and splashed some cold water on my face.

I looked up, and for some reason, that was when it really hit me. I was *back*. I was *home*. Something about seeing myself in that bathroom mirror, with my short hair, with my nose stud, the version of me I'd created outside of that house, that place, my new self transported against the old, familiar backdrop. It was unmooring.

"Why are you here?"

I heard myself ask the question, my own voice in my ear, but my lips didn't move. My reflection was jarringly still.

"What do you want?" Again, I heard my voice, clear as day. But my lips didn't part; my mouth didn't open to speak.

I stepped back, rubbing my eyes.

"Uh, what?" I said. Now the mirror reflected me speaking.

I leaned in closer, pressing my hips into the sink, bone against porcelain. I looked a little out of it. Delicate red blood vessels threaded the whites of my eyes. Bizarrely, my pupils were dilated. Just a little. I blamed adrenaline.

My cheeks were flushed from the wine, from the heat. My hair was damp with sweat. I reached up to unmat my baby bangs from my forehead, but once again, my reflection did not follow the movement.

And once again, I rubbed my eyes. I took a deep breath that snagged in my throat, entered my lungs in tatters. I gripped the sink, expecting the porcelain to be cool, but it wasn't. It was hot.

I noticed the singing of pipes. Their voices hideous, loud.

It was an old, old house. It had always made noises. Groaned as if it were being tortured. I'd just forgotten how unsettling it could be. Like living above a dungeon.

I was out of sync. With the house. With myself.

Adrenaline. Wine. Exhaustion. Emotion, maybe. Whatever.

I took my face in my hands, and my reflection followed suit.

"You're fine," I told myself firmly, ignoring the questions snaking around in my brain, the echo of my own disembodied voice.

Why are you here?

What do you want?

I opened the bathroom door, kicked my bag out onto the landing toward my bedroom, and then descended the steps.

The banister felt smooth and familiar in my grasp. I listened to the cadence of my steps on the creaky stairs, and the fading croon of pipes. I inhaled, smelled something heady and rich. Incense. Musk. My mother's perfume, a distinctive scent that I'd always loved despite the association.

My shoulders fell, rolled back. I hadn't realized how tense I was until the tension left me, fleeing like a wounded soldier.

That moment on the stairs, nothing else mattered except being where I was. Someplace not necessarily safe, but intimate, known.

So it goes. There's no place like home.

I paused at the bottom of the stairs, a memory materializing. It performed itself for me like a sad little play.

It was my birthday. I was dressed for mass. Black patent leather Mary Janes, a frilly black dress with lace and organza, dark ribbons tied in my hair. I must have been younger than six, or maybe turning six. I didn't have my necklace yet. I would have remembered. It was heavy on my neck, especially when I was young. It took some getting used to.

I tripped at the foot of the stairs, likely distracted by all the red balloons, or maybe I'd been saying a quick hello to Bart, or maybe I'd been looking up at the front door, hoping to see a tall shadow interrupting the sunlight streaming in through the glass. Hoping he'd come.

"Vessie, you okay?" Rosie came up beside me. She'd been chasing me, I think. Or we'd just been running around, burning off our party excitement.

I'd scraped my arm. I observed the injury with cool curiosity. I thought the pattern of missing skin resembled the lace on my dress.

Years later, there'd be another mishap at the foot of the stairs. But I wouldn't let myself think about that.

"Does it hurt?" Rosie asked.

I'd shrugged.

"You never cry," she'd said. "You never cry at all."

She was right. I never did.

I wasn't sure if that meant I was strong, or that I was broken.

4

I watched the thrash of translucent wings around the light, the beauty of such stupidity.

"You're all going to die," I told the moths. "You dumb fucks."

The rusty screech of the porch swing seemed to scold me. Seemed to say, *You're no different.*

Strange how within all of us is a compulsion to run both away from and toward danger. Survival instinct and self-destruction. Curiosity, deviousness, boredom, desire . . . They can all override evolution. What did those cavemen run for, anyway? What was the point?

To save themselves, I guess. Not for us. Not to embed some common sense in their descendants' DNA.

"You're deep in thought," Rosie said, sitting next to me on the swing and handing me a flute of champagne. I'd slipped away after dessert—three ripe red raspberries atop a neat scoop of vanilla mousse with perfect swirls of dark chocolate. I figured Rosie would notice my absence and come find me. It took a little longer for her to follow than I'd anticipated. My arms and legs had been ravaged by the mosquitoes, and without the stimulation of the party inside, my sleepiness began to assert itself.

"Me? Never," I said. "Never had a thought in my life."

I pulled my knees up to my chest. Drank the champagne, drank in the night, the honeyed summer air. The sun had long set, and the moon was out, bone white, brooding among ravenous stars. Out on the farm, night was a different beast. The dark was merciless. It swallowed the edges of the world, leaving the house, the barns, the coop, the shed, and nothing else. Nothing beyond. Night took the fields, the road. Everything. It wasn't just the illusion of isolation. It *was* isolation.

"What were you thinking about?" Rosie asked, bringing her flute to her lips but not taking a sip.

"Evolution," I said. Satanists didn't believe in evolution. "Not trying to be controversial. Just honest."

"You've never needed to try to be controversial," she said, grinning. Her teeth gleamed under the porch light. She looked like she belonged in an advertisement for mouthwash. She looked a little crazy.

"Someone invited me," I said. "I got an invitation."

"Oh! Oh. I mean, I wanted you here," she said. "Of course I wanted you here. I asked. I just didn't think it would be possible. I went to the High Priest on multiple occasions. He never gave me a direct answer. I thought . . . I'd given up hope. About you coming to the wedding, not about you coming home. I never gave up hope for that. For you."

It made me salty that my return gave her satisfaction, that it likely further confirmed her belief in prayer. I was tempted to tell her that I had come back like a vengeful spirit, like a Shakespearean ghost, to remind her that he had loved me first.

"I've missed you so much," she said, her voice sad and wispy. I looked at her, and she was staring out into the darkness, fixated on a point concealed in shadow. I wondered what had caught her attention. She was peach sweet, would stop to admire a rainbow, marvel at a praying mantis. I squinted, tried to see what she was seeing. And there it was. A lightning bug. "I think about you all the time. There's so much I've wanted to tell you. Talk to you about. There's been a void."

I could have told her I felt the same. I probably should have; it's not like I was opposed to lying. But I'd worked too hard to bury my feelings. I refused to exhume them for a fleeting sentimental moment. And besides, even if I had allowed myself to miss her all those years, to fully experience the weight of her absence, any wistfulness for our relationship would have been macheted by the fact that she was marrying my ex. The only guy I'd ever loved.

She rested her head on my shoulder. She was a few months older than me, but she was the little sister.

"This feels like a good dream," she said. "I thank the Lord for bringing you here."

"New Jersey Transit brought me here," I said. "Sorry."

She sat up straight. "Vesper."

"I'm here for your wedding," I said. "Not because I changed my mind about any of the reasons why I left."

She bit her lip. "I was afraid of that."

There was a fluttering in my gut, a quick flare of nerves. I decided it was best to change the subject. "You know what's weird? My taxi driver today brought up Imagination Land."

"Oh gosh! I remember that place. We begged my parents to take us. *Begged*."

"There was, like, a pirate section and a candy village or some shit."

"You won the beanbag game. You knocked over all the cans and got a plastic crown with pink rhinestones. I was so jealous."

She went stiff beside me and made a mousy noise. A quiet, distressed squeak. She was suddenly on the verge of tears. "You didn't want to leave. You wanted to hide there and stay forever. You said we could live in the gingerbread castle. You didn't want to come home."

"Really? I don't remember that part."

"I never knew how to help you, Vessie." She took a breath, then downed her champagne. "If you don't want to talk about your relationship with the Lord, that's okay. You can think on it. Pray on it. Come around in your own time."

"Okay," I said, unsure how my attempt at a pleasant trip down memory lane had circled back to my relationship with Lord Satan.

"Also . . ." she said, and swallowed. "I'm sorry I never got a chance to tell you about Brody. To ask. I thought because you left . . . I mean, not that I wanted you to leave, not that I didn't want you to come back. It just happened. It was a good match. *Is* a good match. I love him, Vessie. I love him so much."

I asked myself if that was what I wanted, to hear her grovel. To get an apology. But it didn't make me feel better. It didn't change anything.

"I missed you, too," I said, for some reason.

"Sometimes, maybe you did," she said. "Don't forget. I know you, Vessie. You're more like Constance than you like to think."

"Hey," I said, surprised she'd go there.

"I'm not saying it to upset you. I'm saying it because I know you can shut off your feelings in a way I never could. I doubt you ever cried missing me. I cried myself to sleep for months. Years after you left."

Until you found comfort in Brody, I thought. But also, *Aww, my Rosie.*

"I'm not my mother," I said. "I do have feelings. I love you, Rosie. You know that."

"But you're mad. About me and Brody," she said, tapping her empty champagne flute with a French-manicured nail. "I knew you would be if you ever found out."

"I'm not mad," I lied. I'd forgotten how thrilling it was to be known by someone. And how inconvenient.

"Bullshit."

"Rosie!" I gasped. She *never* cursed. "Dollar in the swear jar."

She giggled.

"The scandal."

"Oh please," she said.

"What would the Lord think?"

"Don't," she said, and smacked her lips the exact way Grace always did.

I wondered where it lived, how deep it was. The part of them that instructed this gesture. Could it be extracted? Was it a habit to be broken? Or was it in their DNA, in their blood, embedded marrow deep?

Nothing terrified me more than this. The notion that without a choice we inherit parts of us that we cannot change. Cannot cut out.

"Since when did you start swearing?" I asked her. "What else? Do you smoke cigarettes? *Weed?*"

"Gosh no," she said, squeezing my knee. "I haven't changed. Promise."

"Rosemary? Rose, you out there?" Grace called from inside the house.

"Coming!" Rosie yelled.

"Is Vesper with you?"

Rosie looked to me. She was checking to get my approval before revealing my whereabouts. I found it moving that after all this time she was still loyal to me. Aside from the whole Brody thing, of course.

"I'm here, Aunt Grace," I said.

"Oh goody. You two come on in now, yeah?"

"She's not going to recruit me to dish duty, is she?" I asked Rosie.

"You know she is," she said, standing. "Not me, though. I'm the bride."

She did a little spin.

"Cool," I mumbled. I finished my champagne and swung myself to stand.

The porch wrapped around the entire perimeter of the house. We went in through the back, entering through the sliding doors into the kitchen, where Grace was waiting.

Next thing I knew, I was elbow deep in soapy water, which flooded the bright yellow dish gloves I was wearing. I wasn't sure where they'd come from. There was no way in hell they belonged to my mother, who would never wear yellow, even just to wash dishes.

"Whose are these?" I asked Grace when she returned to the kitchen with even more dishes. I'd worked in several restaurants and was still overwhelmed by the number of dishes.

"Oh, they're mine," she said. "I keep a pair here. Your mother's are too small. Thanks again for helping out, Star."

"You didn't give me a choice," I said.

"We always have a choice." I sensed a lecture, but then Constance clicked into the kitchen. She wore stilettos even at home. I didn't mind. Helped me track her movements, anticipate her.

Still, the threat of her presence was taxing, adding unnecessary pressure to a simple chore. I scrubbed vigorously, knowing that if I left even the tiniest speck it would be noticed and invite criticism.

She came up behind me. Her disapproval would have been imperceptible to the untrained eye, but it wasn't to me. Her disapproval was my sixth sense. Couldn't say if I was born with it or if it had developed over the years.

"What?" I asked her.

"You're not using enough soap," she said. "The whole point is to clean them, you know."

"Aware, thanks," I said.

She scoffed.

"Is that all of the dishes, sis?" Grace asked Constance.

It was hard to believe they were sisters. They did have the same lips, high cheekbones, pointy ears. But Constance was tall, beautiful, regal. Grace was stocky, with all the elegance of a bowling ball. Temperament-wise, too, total opposites. Grace approachable, eager to laugh. Constance an ice queen. They were alike mostly in their penchant for gardening, and their radical devotion to Satan.

And the smell of them. Their natural scent, without perfume. It was the same. Genetics.

"No. There are more. Many more," Constance said, leaving the kitchen with a wave of her hand.

"She's not happy to see me," I said to Grace, handing her a plate to dry.

"That's not true." Grace had always lied to me about my mother. It wasn't malicious. She might not have even known that she was lying. She might have really believed that her sister loved me. Or she might have just been trying to make me feel better.

"If you say so."

"I do," Grace said. "Another plate. *Merci beaucoup.* I like the hair, by the way. Only you could pull it off, with that face. Well, your mother, too."

"A few weeks ago some guy asked me if anyone had ever told me that I looked like Constance Wright."

"Goodness me," Grace said, smacking the towel against the counter as she let out a raucous laugh. "What did you say?"

I checked over my shoulder to make sure Constance wasn't approaching. "Said I'd never heard of her."

Grace laughed again. Then she leaned close and whispered, "Did you see her last one? *Cannibal Dinner Party?*"

Shamefully, I had. I'd seen every one of my mother's movies. I nodded. Grace made a face, and the two of us snickered for a moment.

"You must get that a lot. Out in the world."

"Get what?"

"People must tell you all the time. That you look like her," she said. "I always forget she's famous."

"She's not that famous," I muttered to myself, just as Constance strode back into the room. She stood beside me at the sink and watched me wash for a second.

Then she said, "Vesper, I think that's quite enough *help* from you."

"A pity," I said, removing the dish gloves and handing them off to Grace. "Good luck to you."

I sauntered into the hall, grateful to have been relieved of dish duty though not exactly thrilled with the circumstances of my removal. What did she expect? For the dishes to glitter? To reflect the light of a thousand suns? To have a little animated sparkle like in a cartoon or detergent commercial? And why did I care? Why did I still care?

"Ves."

I'd been too caught up in my thoughts to pay attention to my surroundings, and I'd walked straight into Brody. Most of the guests had filtered out by then. I hadn't realized he was still around.

"Brody." I scrutinized him. He was clean-shaven, his hair combed back tidily, held in place with gel or pomade. He used to leave it wild, even for mass. It got him into trouble. It got him my respect, inspired hope that maybe he felt the same way about Hell's Gate that I did. That he, too, thought it all was bullshit. That Satan was bullshit.

"I'm sorry," he said.

"For what?" I asked. It was a loaded question.

"Uh, bumping into you," he said.

"You should be sorry. How dare you? An outrage."

"I know, I know," he said. "Please forgive me."

I sucked some air through my teeth. "I'll think about it."

"It's good to see you, Ves. I'm happy you're home," he said. He surprised me by pulling me in for a hug. The embrace itself was disappointing. He kept his distance from me. It was technically a hug but more the equivalent of a pat on the shoulder. Then he surprised me again, whispering in my ear, "Are you good? You look good. Sorry. Seem good."

I bit down on my lip to keep from grinning. "I'm good."

He pulled away, flustered. "Good. Good. The Lord delivers us many blessings. Hail Satan."

"Yeah, sure. Hail Satan."

"Vesper, are you in need of directions?" Constance asked, appearing behind me, seizing my arm. "And, Brody, you're getting married tomorrow, aren't you?"

"Yes," he said, nodding. He was terrified of my mother. Everyone was.

"Ah, so you remember. Suppose you'll need some rest," she said, opening the front door for him. "Good night."

"Good night, Constance," he said, leaving hurriedly, tripping over his feet.

She slammed the door shut and dragged me to the foot of the stairs, digging her long nails into my skin.

"That's fine. I didn't like that arm anyway," I said. "Had no use for it, really."

"What are you doing here?" she asked me, her tone particularly chilling.

"Attending the wedding I was invited to."

"You don't expect me to believe that." She whipped me around, got hold of my other arm, too. I was in her clutches.

"Are we going to hug?" I asked bravely. I rarely summoned the courage to get sassy with my mother. She'd never shied away from discipline, from punishment.

"You don't believe that yourself, do you? Or are you completely deluded?"

"I'm not sure what you mean."

"You don't truly want him, so it can't be Brody."

"What isn't Brody?"

"You clearly have an ulterior motive," she said. "Don't bother to lie, Vesper. You're not any good at it."

I remembered the glass eye. She'd said the exact same thing to me then, when she'd gifted it to me and I feigned enthusiasm.

"I'm not lying," I said. "I have no ulterior motive. I don't have the patience or energy for some Machiavellian scheme. I was invited and took the opportunity to come back and see my family. Is that so hard to believe?"

She smirked. Her makeup was immaculate. Her skin. For a fraction of a second, I felt grateful to be her daughter. To have her genes. To have inherited her face.

Then she said grimly, "You shouldn't be here. You shouldn't have come."

"I—"

"Reconsider. You've already proven you know how to leave quietly. I trust you can see yourself out."

She turned on her six-inch heels and clicked away.

"Thanks for the warm welcome," I said under my breath. "Bitch."

I looked to Bart for solidarity, but he just stared.

I guess technically he wasn't staring. Can't stare without eyes.

I took a deep breath and trudged up the steps. If I'd had any hesitation, any doubts about attending the wedding—which I don't think I did, at least not that I can remember—they were vanquished right then and there. My mother's suggesting I leave only fortified my resolve to stay.

When I got to the second-floor landing, I glanced down the hall to her bedroom door. It was shut, of course. Locked, I knew. She valued her privacy, didn't like me touching her things. I had an early memory of accidentally knocking a perfume bottle off her vanity, the sound of it shattering, the shards of thin painted glass in my tiny palm as she forced me to clean it up, no dustpan or broom, just my hands. When I was done, I had to get my own Band-Aids.

Another time, I'd decided I wanted to play dress-up and let myself into her closet without asking permission, knowing if I did, she'd have said no. She found me there, draped in one of her premiere gowns, admiring myself in the mirror, and she flew into a rage. "Can I have nothing for myself?" she'd said as she chased me out.

After that, the door was always locked. I couldn't be trusted not to break something, not to root through her drawers, steal a tube of lipstick or pair of earrings. I couldn't be trusted to honor her boundaries, her rules, which were almost always at the expense of my needs. If I ever had a nightmare when she was home, I couldn't go into her room to seek comfort, climb into my mother's bed and have her soothe me back to sleep. Nah. It was tough luck.

When she was away filming, which was 75 percent of the time, I'd occasionally try to pick the lock, break in. Without success. I'd told myself that I wanted in to spite her, but the sad truth was that I just wanted to be close to her. And also maybe some lipstick. A piece of jewelry. An heirloom. A non-gruesome prop or accessory. Something that mattered to her that could matter to me.

There was the temptation to try again as I stood there on the landing. A prodding curiosity. A prickly vindictiveness.

Though I hadn't expected my mother to be happy to see me, I also hadn't expected it to hurt that she wasn't. With all the scar tissue I'd built up, I forgot how easily I could be split open. All the shrapnel of her casual cruelty embedded in me, and now I had more damage to add to the collection. Cool, cool, cool.

I flipped off her locked door and continued up the steps to my room.

I might not have magically won over my mother, but it seemed I still had some sway over Brody. He'd been so nervous, letting a compliment slip.

Something wriggled uncomfortably in my gut. Maybe guilt. I wondered if I still felt loyal to Rosie, despite her not extending me the same courtesy re Brody. Or . . .

You don't truly want him, my mother had said. I hated her to be right about anything.

I sighed, kicked my bag into my room, and followed it inside. I felt around the wall for the light switch, flipped it on.

"Oh hell," I said to myself.

It was exactly the same, as if it'd gone untouched for six years. Walking into the room, it almost felt like I was time traveling. Not the good, fun kind of time travel, the kick-in-the-teeth kind, the "don't touch anything or the future will be fucked" kind.

Someone must have come in to dust every once in a while, because it wasn't dirty. It maybe smelled a little musty, but the top note was *me*. It was sandalwood candles. It was the watermelon-flavored sour gummies I'd smuggle up from downstairs, let sit out and harden. It was the amber-vanilla perfume that I used to shop-lift from the kiosk at the mall. There was a bottle of it on my dresser. I'd left it out but forgotten to pack it. It was still there, beside a birthday-cake-flavored lip balm and a friendship bracelet that Rosie had made for me. I hadn't forgotten that. I'd chosen to cut it off, leave it behind. I didn't want to carry her around on my wrist, or the irony that I'd rendered our friendship impossible the second I defected.

I collapsed onto my bed, a hard twin made up with a black quilt embroidered with pentagrams. A gift from Grace. She was a big-time quilter. If only there'd been a wider market for Satanic quilts.

I leaned down and sniffed the bedding. It'd been washed recently, which I found curious. Either someone had known I was coming, whoever sent the invitation, or all this time someone, likely Grace, had been prepared for me to return at any moment. A spontaneous homecoming.

I found that a little moving, a little pathetic, but mostly satisfying. To know that I'd been missed. To know that I was wanted somewhere. Even if it was here.

I thought about Rick. *You're not special,* he'd said.

Not to you, I thought, *but what about in the eyes of the Lord, King of Hell?*

I laughed to myself, then broke into a hearty yawn.

It was hot in the room; it always was. There was a single window, with a view of the front yard, the ancient, mangled oak tree whose branches cast menacing shadows on my walls. The window refused to open for me; it required strength I didn't have. I used to recruit Uncle Carl or Brody for help. That irritated my mother.

If you want to go running off to a man every time you face some small adversity, it's going to be a long life, she'd said.

She'd rather I suffocated in humidity, sweat myself to death.

I stared longingly at the window, aching for a breeze.

I was distracted by the subtle *tick-tick-tick* of the clock. The Kit-Cat Klock perched over my antique dresser. The dresser was the worse for wear—mismatched knobs, bottom drawers protruding slightly, like an underbite. The clock I'd had since forever; I swore I had hazy memories of staring up at it from my crib.

The clock's eyes roamed side to side; the tail wagged. It was a kitschy little gem. I swung my legs off of the bed and looked at it, permitting a momentary swell of nostalgia.

I could blame the nostalgia, the emotion temporarily ejecting me from reality. Or it could have been just one of those weird things. The clock's tail went on wagging, but its eyes stopped dead center. As if it were looking at me. As if it recognized me. As if it remembered me.

I blinked. It didn't. It couldn't. The happy cat, whiskers and a bow tie, no choice but to smile because that's how it'd been built, how it was made. Bulbous white eyes with vertical slits of pupils black as voids.

I stood up and walked over to it, gave it a light tap upside the head. It whirred, and then its eyes began to move again as they were meant to. Back and forth, back and forth, on and on.

"Nice to see you, too," I said.

I yawned again. I decided I was too tired to shower. I undressed, rummaged around my bag for the giant Black Sabbath T-shirt I slept in. I got my phone charger out and went to plug it into the outlet next to my bed. That was when I discovered the new addition.

A femur-and-human-skin lamp featured in *Cannibal Dinner Party*, Constance's latest film. Also her worst reviewed. For good reason.

It might have been the most disgusting prop she'd ever brought home, which was saying something. She'd positioned it on my nightstand, which I took to mean that she knew I'd be coming home someday, and that when I did, she didn't want me to be too comfortable. She knew I'd hate the lamp. She knew.

I didn't want to look at it, but I didn't want to touch it either. I debated whether I should bite the bullet and move it somewhere. Hide it under the bed or in the closet. Somehow that seemed worse. Like I couldn't trust it out of sight, like it'd come crawling out in the night while I was asleep. Like the shriveled lips sewn on the shade would open up, reveal teeth.

It was unfortunate that the prop person or whoever had made it had paid such attention to detail. I didn't know what it was constructed of. Maybe soft leather? Curiosity getting the better of me, I reached out to touch it. It felt distressingly like skin. And the stitches felt like . . . like . . . I don't even know. Wrong. They felt wrong.

"I hate it, I hate it," I said, gagging, shaking the feeling from my hands.

I unplugged the lamp so I could plug in my charger and finally—finally—charge my phone. I thought about the girl from Penn Station, the blonde who wouldn't move to give me access to the outlet. It wasn't worth being annoyed about, but whatever. I hoped wherever she was, she was having a shitty time, had an itch in a place she couldn't scratch.

It was a little after ten, and though my body was exhausted, I was too worked up mentally to pass out. I turned my phone on. I had a text from Kerri that I contemplated ignoring, about whether she should try reaching out to Sean again.

I decided to respond. I just said, No.

I set my phone on the nightstand.

The decision wasn't conscious. Next thing I knew, I was opening the drawer, checking to see if they were still there. My necklace. And the photo.

My fingers found the necklace first. I was surprised that the silver hadn't tarnished.

It was a beautiful piece of jewelry, but I couldn't divorce its beauty from what it symbolized. It was a pentagram encrusted with rubies, flanked with emerald-cut diamonds, on a thick glittering chain. The necklace had been gifted to me on my sixth birthday, as was tradition in Hell's Gate. It was sort of like a Satanic rosary, or dog collar. At six, everyone got one and was required to wear it to mass. Mine was more elaborate than most, and it had drawn a lot of attention. Sometimes it had embarrassed me. Other times, I had felt proud to wear it, to own such a beautiful thing. I felt it suited me.

I put the necklace aside and found the photograph. The only picture I had of my father, the only tangible evidence of his existence.

I took a deep breath and stared at the photo. It wasn't even of him. It was of me standing in the foyer, wearing a summer dress. His arm was around me, his hand on my shoulder. He wore rings. Many rings. I wasn't looking at the camera; I was looking up at him adoringly. Maybe he was looking back at me, but I had no proof, because he was cut off. It was only his arm in the picture, only his hand.

I closed my eyes and attempted to paint an image of him from memory. He was handsome. Square jawed. Silver haired. A heavy brow, warm eyes. Perfect nose, centered in his face, a slight curve I'd run a skinny finger along while he'd laugh. A wide mouth, pretty lips for a man, naturally pink. Movie-star teeth. Movie-star aura.

I ached at the thought of him still. I hated myself for it.

I shoved the picture back into the drawer, threw the necklace on top, and slammed the drawer shut. I pulled the sheets over my head and made a devil's bargain with sleep.

⛤

I dreamed of him.

Of waiting for him.

I dreamed of tracing patterns of sunlight across the floorboards, pretending I didn't know how late he was. Pretending I didn't already know he wasn't coming.

Pretending my sit bones didn't hurt from the hours spent bouncing excitedly on the steps, staring out the front windows hoping to see him coming up the driveway. Any second. Any second.

Pretending I'd forgotten all the days just like this one. Pretending I'd forgotten how it felt, my tiny, grubby fingers clinging to the windowsill as I watched. As I hoped. As I prayed.

Please, Lord. If he comes, I'll be good. I'll believe. I'll sit still in mass. I'll read scripture. I'll memorize every word. Just let him show up this time. Let him come.

I felt my body shudder violently, felt the pillow slip out from under my head, but I couldn't free myself of the dream. Of the past.

Of how I used to hold my eyes closed for a long, long time, telling myself that if I waited a little longer, when I opened them, he'd be there on the porch, making a goofy face, pressed up against the glass.

Sometimes I worried that I might keep my eyes closed forever, clinging to this hope. I worried I'd be lost in the darkness. I worried I wouldn't even care. Because I would never love anyone the way that I loved my father. His presence was like pure light, his energy euphoric, his attention a coronation.

"He isn't coming," Constance said, appearing in the dark behind my eyelids. *"You're smart enough to know that by now."*

"He'll be here," I said. *"He'll come back for me. He'll come back for me."*

Then I heard his voice. Clear as day.

"Hey there, Princess."

And I thought, *Okay. This is a good dream.*

5

My eyes peeled open.

It was startling, waking up in my childhood bedroom. There was a moment of acute disorientation before it all came back to me, and even then, I couldn't quite trust my surroundings, couldn't calm my nerves or center myself in the space. I felt untethered. I floated out of bed and over to the window. The glass was fogged with humidity.

It was a thousand degrees.

I rubbed the sleep from my eyes with my thumbs. It was dark still, very late or very early; I hadn't been out for long. I inhaled sharply, and my throat alerted me to my thirst. It was urgent. I needed water. I needed to crush ice between my teeth.

My shirt was stuck to me. I'd sweat through it.

Without much thought, I stumbled out onto the landing, heading down to the kitchen for a glass of cold water. But it was waiting for me.

Fear, greeting me like an elbow to the back.

Any old Victorian has a creep factor, especially one in a remote location. But of course my mother's house was also brimming with morbid decor and horror memorabilia. Though I'd grown up there, I'd never quite gotten used to it. Because knowing that Blood Thirst's mask from *Bloody Midnight* is displayed on a bust in the hall on the second floor doesn't sufficiently prepare you for the experience of seeing Blood Thirst's mask. Promise that. Doesn't matter how many times you've seen it.

And it's not like it was a Party City mask. It was the real deal. Extremely detailed, camera ready. In my opinion, Blood Thirst might have been Constance's scariest movie adversary, though there was much debate about it on Reddit.

Not that I frequented those subs or anything.

I continued down the steps, wondering what other horrors awaited me. Constance was always adding to her collection, always rearranging, so there was no way ever to prepare yourself.

I arrived at the bottom of the stairs and turned into the hall, where I came face-to-face with the cursed portrait from Constance's episode of the horror anthology series *Cemetery Tales*. It was of an old man, done in the abstract. He was midscream.

It was hideous in a way that begged to be looked at. I paused in front of it. Someone had left the light on in the kitchen, and it was bright enough that I could see the agony in the man's eyes, the red gape of his mouth.

In the episode, Constance's character finds the portrait in the attic of her new house and is rightfully disturbed. She leaves it on the curb for trash pickup. She watches it get taken away as she sips a cup of coffee at the bay window.

Later that day, she finds it on the wall, hung up over the fireplace. It's a well-executed scare. The shot of her walking through the living room, not paying attention, the background not quite in focus. The close-up of her face as she senses something's not right. The slow pan. Her eyes glancing over. A fast cut to the portrait in its new place, scored with an equally brief screech of violins. Constance's reaction is one of pure terror.

I'd only ever seen her emote on screen, her vulnerability behind glass. She was more human to me when she was pretending to be someone other than herself.

She trashes the portrait a second time. The second attempt doesn't take either, and it reappears over her bed. Then she takes it out back, chucks it in the fire pit. Douses it with gasoline. Defiantly lights a match and drops it with a sigh of relief, or maybe compassion? There's an artsy shot of her watching it burn, her face through the yellow flames.

Then the man starts to appear in the flesh. At first, as a smear in the periphery. One we, the viewers, always see before she does. He gets clearer and clearer. Closer and closer. Until, predictably, he kills her, dragging her into the frame. At the end of the episode, she, too, appears screaming in the painting. Wow. Gasp. Fade to black.

The episode actually wasn't that bad. Nothing revolutionary, but not bad. You could buy prints of the painting on Etsy, both with and without my mother's tortured face.

I shrugged and continued on to the kitchen.

I guess I should admit, I did imagine the man from the painting following me. I did hear footsteps interrupt the quiet of the house, a slow approach, a cadence that didn't match my own. I did feel the creep of a cool shadow just over my shoulder, a hovering. An awareness of observation, a needling suspicion.

I dismissed it.

The kitchen, thankfully, was more "goth-lite" than "house of horrors." Coffin-shaped cutting boards, a collection of cast-iron cauldrons of varying sizes, a planchette spoon rest, a fruit bowl that stood on bronze chicken legs. I retrieved a black highball glass out of the cabinet beside the sink. It had a spiderweb pattern etched around the rim. I filled it with cold water from the fridge, chugged it down, then got some ice. I tipped a cube into my mouth and let it dissolve on my tongue.

I rested my arms on the counter. The quartz was cool and smooth. I let my palms spread across it, traced the veins with my fingers. Through the kitchen window, I could see a figure standing out in the field. Its back was to me, I knew. Soon the wind would spin it around, and its red eyes would slice through the darkness. It was scarier positioned this way, because it looked like a person, like a lurker alone in the field in the middle of the night, when in fact it was the evil scarecrow from *Farm Possession II: Revenant Sickle*, considered one of the best horror sequels of all time. It'd been out there for a while. Since I was about fourteen, I think.

The scarecrow definitely came sometime after the intruder, because Constance was away filming *Farm Possession II* when he showed up. A rabid member of her fan club she'd left me alone to contend with.

Suddenly my skin felt too small.

I refilled the glass and roamed into the parlor, where I said a quick hello to the life-sized animatronic Mr. Ransom from the franchise that made Constance Wright a star. When I was younger, I was eager to demean my mother's legacy because I felt I was collateral damage. As an adult, I realized circumstances wouldn't have changed how she treated me. I forgave Mr. Ransom.

I sipped my water and stared at him in his black trench coat and fedora, his face wrapped in bloodstained gauze, features concealed. I gently tapped a naked toe on one of his big boots. When I was really little, I wondered if he was my father. If the face beneath the gauze belonged to the man who would come to visit me sometimes.

When I was old enough to Google, I realized it wasn't. Rob Logan wasn't my dad. Just a B-list actor with a solid villain laugh.

I leaned in close. Whispered his catchphrase, the line most associated with his character, though he says it only once, and in the second film. In the original franchise, anyway. I hadn't seen the reboot. "Welcome to your nightmare."

I'd barely finished speaking when there was a rapping at the window. I slapped a hand over my mouth to stifle a scream as I watched a shadow slip by. Again, I thought of the intruder. Again, I felt in danger of being suffocated by my own skin.

"Ves," I heard. Someone was calling my name through the open window. "Ves."

"Brody?"

His face appeared, peeking in from the porch.

"Meet me out here," he said, his voice hushed.

I went out through the front door, closing it softly behind me. The last thing I needed was to wake my mother.

"You scared the hell out of me," I said, clutching my chest, feeling my heart pound against my hand. "What are you doing here?"

"I had to see you," he said. He was in a white undershirt, basketball shorts, and Adidas Slides. He was sweating, just as flustered as he'd been earlier. "I need to know you don't hate me."

"That's why you snuck out to my house the night before your wedding?" I asked, crossing my arms, tilting my head to the side. "To ask me if I hate you?"

He ran his hands through his hair, a nervous habit. "Come on, Ves. Would you rather bullshit? Talk about the weather?"

"Sure is a hot one."

He laughed, then shook his head. "I still can't believe you're here. It feels like a dream."

"Funny—Rosie said the same thing."

He leaned over the banister, shifted his weight from leg to leg. I wanted it to be more satisfying than it was, watching him squirm.

"You were gone," he said. "You left. I didn't think you'd ever come home. And even if you did, after everything you told me, after everything you said . . . you know it doesn't work."

"What doesn't work?" I asked, sitting in one of the rocking chairs, pulling my legs up under me.

"When one person is a follower of the Lord and the other . . ." He trailed off.

"Is a wretched heretic?"

"I didn't say that."

"Not in words," I said, leaning forward and then back to get the chair going.

"You're mad."

"What was your plan? To throw rocks at my window? Sneak up to my room like old times? What would you have done if I wasn't already awake and downstairs?"

"Hadn't really thought it through."

I raised an eyebrow.

"Should I have drawn something up? Played through multiple scenarios with dolls?"

"Do you have dolls?"

"Of course. You don't remember my extensive doll collection?"

"Must have suppressed it," I said. "I'm good at that, you know."

He turned to me, chewing on his thumbnail. "I missed you."

"That's exactly what I thought when I received your wedding invitation. I thought, he misses me so much."

"What was I supposed to do? Never move on?"

"With Rosie, though?"

"Who else?" he asked. "Jane? Dana Cunningham?"

He had a point.

"We were both so lost after you left," he said. "It just happened. Over time the relationship changed. Developed. We're a good match, Ves."

Whatever I'd felt when I first read the invitation—shock, rage, resentment, malice—I didn't feel it anymore. I was back to indifference. I'd thought that my apathy was a defense mechanism, and maybe to an extent it was, but I worried then, sitting on that porch, that maybe I was just incapable of sustaining feeling. Maybe I really was as callous as my mother.

"I am sorry, Vesper. And I've meant every word I've ever said to you. I swear to Satan."

"I bet you do."

"I still pray that you find your way back to the Lord."

"Then you've wasted a lot of time," I said, standing. I didn't like where the conversation was headed. "I don't hate you, Brody. In all honesty, I'm not sure I ever loved you. We were kids. And what do I know about love anyway?"

"Everyone loves you, Vesper," he said. "We all love you. The Lord—"

"Okay," I said, cutting him off. "All right. Is this resolved now? Can you walk down the aisle free of guilt or whatever?"

"This wasn't about guilt."

"Sure."

He brought a fist to his forehead, pounded it lightly.

"What?" I said.

He came toward me, took my face in his hands, and kissed me. His lips were so familiar to me, his hands. Mine found their way into his hair. It was sticky with product, damp with sweat. His tongue was cold. He tasted the same.

The kiss was so good, I thought about asking him again. *Run away with me.* But my ego was still bruised from his first rejection, even though I knew it had nothing to do with me. It was about Satan. About Hell's Gate. The promise of eternity delivered by hellfire. The binds of family and religion, beliefs he was raised with, as intrinsic to him as breathing.

"Do you believe me?" he said, pulling away, his palms still cradling my jaw. "Do you believe that I loved you?"

"Past tense," I said, tapping his hands so he'd release me.

He looked at me, big brown eyes like a lost dog's.

"This is all so Shakespearean," I said. I laughed to myself. "'Hell is empty, and all the devils are here.'"

"What?"

They don't study Shakespeare in Hell's Gate. Only scripture.

"Never mind," I said, turning toward the banister, leaning forward to get a view of the stars. "Actually, you know, something that always got me about Satanism—the Hell's Gate sect, anyway—was this idea that we the chosen would be absolved of all sin because of our faith, but everyone else? No redemption for them. They'd get to burn for eternity in hell, while we inherit the flaming remains of the earth post-judgment. Rebuild. Create a utopia from the ashes. Because why? Because we worshipped the right god, and they the wrong one? Seemed so arbitrary. Unjust."

I saw a streak of lightning in the distance. A thin shimmering threading the sky.

"There are people out there who believe in things just as strongly as you believe in Satan." I paused to sigh. "It's a complicated world. What's a mistake, what's bad luck, what's a shitty hand, what's evil?

Why does the devil get to decide who deserves what? And what exactly are his criteria, other than total devotion?"

I reached out a hand and felt the soft trickle of rain.

"The Lord is all knowing. He alone knows the truth of the universe. We trust in him. It's trust, Vesper. Trust."

"Well, can't blame me for having a hard time with that," I said, turning back to him with a solemn grin.

"Did you find him?" he asked. "Your dad?"

"I tried," I said, my voice breaking against my will. "I didn't have much to go off of. You know my mother; she's refused to tell me his name, give me any information. I did one of those stupid spit-in-a-tube DNA tests, and somehow even that got fucked up. They refunded me because my saliva was corrupted, which . . . There's a joke in there somewhere."

"I'm sorry, Ves," he said, reaching for my hand and kissing it.

I almost asked him if he planned on telling Rosie about what had just transpired, but I figured he was smart enough to keep it to himself. Let it remain between us. Or between him and the High Priest in confession. Or between him and his god.

"You should get back. Big day tomorrow."

"Yeah," he said. "Yeah."

His eyes got wet; his lips inverted. He looked as though he was about to cry. He kissed my hand again. Both my hands. The right, then the left.

"I wish things were different," he said, and then he turned, walked fast into the dark of the front yard. He didn't even flinch at the rain.

I lingered on the porch for a few minutes, waiting until Brody was completely out of view, waiting to see more lightning. But none came. It wasn't a storm, just a spritz. Nothing exciting.

Still, I liked the smell of it. I liked the eerie quiet.

I wondered if things could've been different if Brody had come with me, but I struggled to romanticize this alternate timeline, because I knew it wouldn't have ended well. He would have resented me. We likely both would have ended up at Shortee's, experiencing adjacent misery over two-for-one appetizer specials and bottomless chicken-and-rice Delecta-bowls.

I took one last look at the sky and went inside, locking the door behind me. I searched in vain for my water glass, which I'd set down somewhere but couldn't remember where. I turned off the kitchen light and headed upstairs. I went around through the parlor to avoid the portrait in the hall, which I feared might be empty, the old man having left the frame to terrorize me.

Nah, I thought, yawning as I climbed the steps. *I'm probably going to have a boring death. I'm going to die of heart disease in a shitty nursing home. Arteries clogged from eating too much chain-restaurant food. Or maybe it'll be my liver, courtesy of that goddamn fishbowl honey jalapeño margarita.*

I arrived at the third floor tired, ready for sleep. When I stepped into my bedroom, I didn't notice anything was amiss. Not for a few seconds, at least. Not until I smelled the rain. I looked over to the window, and saw it was open. Not just a little. All the way.

I knew I hadn't opened it, and I knew Constance hadn't opened it. We were both physically incapable of prying it from the sill.

I whipped around.

If it's the fucking anguished man from the portrait . . .

There was no one wedged in the corners of my room, no one creeping in the shadows under my bed or in my closet. I checked quickly but thoroughly. I poked out onto the landing and into the bathroom.

There was no one there.

Had Brody been inside the house?

I went back into my room and shut the door. Locked it this time.

I sat down on my bed, literally scratching my head.

I was ready to shrug it off, but then I saw my glass of water on the nightstand. The one I'd just been looking for downstairs, that I thought I'd misplaced.

I hadn't brought it up, but someone must have.

It confirmed that someone else had been in my room.

Had been in the house. Someone other than my mother and me.

And the photograph, the one of my father's hand—I was certain I'd put it back in the drawer, but it was waiting for me, placed neatly on my pillow.

There was a sudden flare of light, followed by a staggering crack of thunder. The rain turned violent. It pounded against the house, came in through the open window. I went to close it and had to put my entire weight on the pane to get it down. It got stuck about a quarter of the way. I kept pulling, desperate to shut it so I could pretend that nothing was awry. So I could convince myself that maybe I had opened the window, brought up the glass, left out the picture.

I had been out of sync with myself earlier, with my reflection in the bathroom mirror. Maybe it'd happened again. Or maybe there was another version of me hiding in the walls of the house, the ghost of my former self, forever trapped in a shitty childhood.

It wasn't like me to entertain the paranormal. I blamed the house. I blamed my mother.

I took a deep breath and gave the window a hard tug, finally getting it shut.

Just then, a white smear caught my attention. A small something scuttling under the oak tree.

A lamb.

It wasn't unusual to see lambs on the farm. Or in Virgil generally. They were always around to be sacrificed at wedding ceremonies, at christenings, at the monthly Black Mass. It was—by far—my least favorite Satanic ritual, the slaughtering of the lamb.

"Better get going, my dude," I whispered to the lamb, which of course couldn't hear me. Or see me as I drew a finger across my neck. "It's escape or execution."

6

The sunlight was unbearable. I groaned in protest, rolled over, smashed my face into my pillow. The day was already sweltering, and it had barely started. I'd been mercilessly woken by a great ruckus downstairs, by the hot slivers of sun coming in through my window, by the kneading of heat.

Sleep slipped away, and I knew I'd lost it for good. I turned onto my side and glared at the Kit-Cat Klock, which informed me it was nine forty-five.

With a grunt, I tossed my feet onto the floor. I staggered over to my bag, grabbed a clean bra and pair of underwear, and went into the bathroom to shower.

I was rudely reminded of the aggressive water pressure, the finicky temperature control. The shower experience was either tiny ice daggers or scorching hot spittle. I oscillated between the two, lathering myself quickly to end the suffering. I emerged tense but clean.

While searching my closet for something suitable to wear—since I'd forgotten to pack an outfit for the day of the wedding, as I'd been focused more on the wedding itself—I stumbled upon my old school uniform. Black pleated skirt, black vest, black blouse with embroidered red pentagrams on the collar, black-and-red-striped pentagram knee socks. A real dream come true for anyone with a goth schoolgirl fetish. I shuddered at the sight of it. How many days of my life had I been forced to wear it? How many mornings did I wake up and have to put on a costume? Too many. It was bad math.

I shoved the uniform to the back and selected a baby blue smock dress. I braved a look in the full-length mirror that hung on the back of my closet door. I looked fine. Rested. I moved in unison with my reflection, which should have made it easier to dismiss what had happened the day before, but there was this persistent discomfort, a reluctance on the part of my body to co-operate with my mind's rationalizing. *Adrenaline. Wine. Exhaustion. Emotion.* Yeah, maybe I'd had some adrenaline. Maybe I'd had too much wine. Maybe I'd been exhausted, emotional. But my emotions hadn't opened my bedroom window. Hadn't carried a glass of water up the stairs and set it on my nightstand. Hadn't taken out my father's picture and set it on my pillow.

I didn't want to think about it; there was so much other shit going on. I did my best to suppress my suspicion, which manifested as subtle queasiness.

Toast was my solution. I wanted toast.

I started down the stairs, pausing on the second-floor landing to dodge bridesmaids. Jane, and Brody's sisters, Birdie and Beatrice. They all wore matching robes and wielded hot tools—curling irons and straightening irons and hair dryers. They carried big bags overflowing with eye shadow palettes and dry shampoo. They giggled and squealed indiscreetly. I stood perfectly still, like a gazelle before a lion, hoping they wouldn't see me. They didn't. They danced down the hall, into my mother's room.

It wasn't entirely surprising that my mother would open up her space to Rosie and her gaggle of bridesmaids. Living in the biggest house in Virgil—and spitting distance from the cathedral—Constance felt a sense of obligation, a duty to her community and to her god, to offer up her home as a gathering place. She wasn't a particularly warm or enthusiastic host, but she never complained, and never seemed as irritated by anyone else's presence in the house as she did by mine.

So yeah, it wasn't surprising, but it was fucking annoying. I wasn't sure what bothered me more: Rosie being allowed to barge in, or the bridesmaids, who weren't even family. Rosie, probably. I always suspected my mother liked her better than me.

"Star!" I heard.

Grace was in the foyer, wearing a frilly apron, a spatula in one hand and her phone in the other. "Come on down. I'll make you some breakfast. You want coffee?"

"Uh, sure," I said. It'd been a long time since anyone had offered to make me coffee, make me breakfast. I wasn't particularly hungry, but I wanted the comfort of being fed.

"I was going to make myself some toast," I said, following her into the kitchen.

"Nonsense. You're getting my famous chocolate chip banana pancakes."

Over the years, I'd attempted to re-create Grace's special pancakes, but I never could get mine to taste like hers, as good as hers. I'd resigned myself to never having the pancakes again. I'd mourned the loss of my all-time favorite breakfast. I'd wished someone had warned me, or that I'd been smart enough to intuit when I left home—it was the small comforts that were the hardest to lose.

Grace moved around the kitchen like it was her own. It had been, once. She and Constance had grown up in the house; it had belonged to their parents, and their parents' parents, and on and on. My great-great-great-grandfather owned the land that eventually became Virgil. My great-great-grandfather built the farm, and the house of worship hidden underneath it. My family had been deeply rooted in the faith for generations. I was born of Hell's Gate elite, and on top of that, Constance poured the majority of her Hollywood income into the church, and it increased her status, and my own by association.

Constance inherited the house after Grace married Carl and moved in with him and his family, who lived in a triplex just off the town square. I wondered if Rosie and Brody would stay there, or if they'd move in with Brody's parents, who lived in a little stone house in the woods at the edge of the village.

I could picture them in either place. It was easy to picture them together, not because I'd seen them at the rehearsal dinner but because they made sense for all the reasons that Brody and I had made sense, and then some. His family was also rooted and well-connected in the community. *A good match,* as both Rosie and Brody had said. He'd said it right before he kissed me.

"You okay, Star?" Grace asked. "You're out in space."

"Still waking up," I lied.

"Ah," she said, pouring coffee into a skull mug for me. Constance had a collection. "Stevia and a splash of vanilla creamer?"

I nodded, surprised she remembered.

"You just missed the girls," she said. "Rosie didn't want pancakes. I think she's nervous. To be expected."

Or she's just not eating, I thought.

"You should go up after breakfast. I know they'd all be thrilled to have you. Especially Rosie. She always pictured you as her maid of honor—I'm sure you know that."

"Was it you?" I asked, sipping my coffee. It was perfect. "Did you send me the invitation?"

She didn't look up from the mixing bowl. She took a beat. "I'm grateful to whoever did."

"Huh," I said. "A real mystery."

"No, Vesper. A miracle."

Maybe Satan himself sent it, I almost said. I was smart enough to bite my tongue, though I did enjoy the image of a red horned devil licking an envelope with his split snake tongue, slipping it through a mail slot with one hand, the other holding a pitchfork.

Of course, Satanists didn't believe their Lord looked like a devil cartoon. But I wasn't a Satanist.

"We're grateful you're here," Grace said. "Back home."

"For the wedding," I said, clarifying. "Back for the wedding."

Her eyes darted over; her wrist neglected the whisking. "Sorry?"

Constance swept into the room in a black silk robe with ostrich-feather trim, matching feather slippers. "Is there coffee?"

Grace continued to stare at me, her brow furrowed. Her lips capsized into this horrible frown.

"Grace," Constance said, snapping her fingers. "Coffee. I'm in urgent need of caffeine."

"Oh. Sorry, yes. I'll put on a fresh pot," she said. "Star got the last of it."

Constance huffed. She eyed me as I took a slow sip from my skull mug. I resisted an exaggerated, Folgers-commercial *mm mm.*

"Tell me you brought something decent to wear," Constance said, disgust rippling across her face as she took note of my current attire.

"Are culottes acceptable?"

"You can't be serious."

"I'm not," I said. "I brought a wedding-appropriate dress."

Not entirely true. I'd brought a revenge dress, purchased the day after I received the invitation, when I was freshly angry. It was red satin, tight, strappy, with a low neck, high slit. To call it wedding appropriate was a stretch.

"And for mass? You will be attending mass," Constance said. "To attend the wedding is to attend mass. That is something you comprehend, correct?"

"Correct," I said.

"Connie, you want some pancakes?"

My mother winced. She hated—*hated*—to be called Connie. Only Grace could call her that and walk away unscathed.

"When have I ever wanted pancakes?" she asked. "I imagine arsenic would be better for my digestion."

"Wouldn't taste as good, though," Grace said, finally shaking her frown.

"Well, next time I'm tempted to poison myself, I'll come straight to you."

"Looking forward to it," Grace said, winking at me. She was a big winker. Rosie was, too.

"Very clever, Grace," Constance said, getting a hard-boiled egg and a container of raspberries out of the refrigerator. She was a creature of habit. Every morning, a hard-boiled egg, six raspberries, and black coffee. If she was feeling really feisty, maybe a soy cappuccino.

"We need to be ready for pictures at four," Grace said, adding a slab of butter to the skillet. It sizzled.

"Mm," Constance said, cutting her egg with a knife and fork instead of biting into it like a normal person.

"You, too, Star."

"Me?" I said, nearly snorting my coffee out of my nose.

"No," Constance said, shooting Grace a look. Grace shot one right back.

"I do or I don't?" I asked.

"You do," Grace said, at the exact same time Constance said, "You don't."

"Hmm," Constance said, dabbing the corner of her mouth with a napkin and turning to me. "Vesper. Don't you think it's best you sit out the photos? Considering your history."

"With Brody?" I asked, my stomach churning at the memory of our kiss.

Constance raised an eyebrow. "With leaving."

"Ah."

"Nonsense," Grace said, angrily flipping a pancake. "You're very, *very* important to all of us, Vesper. You're an integral part of this family, and this community."

"Okay," I said, craning my neck to see if the distribution of chocolate chips in the batter was to my liking. Seemed sufficient.

While Grace was focused on the pancakes, Constance glared at me and I mouthed, *Fine. No pictures.*

She plucked her raspberries from the container, washed them, and put them in a crystal dish. When the coffee was ready, she poured herself a cup and left the kitchen without another word.

Grace was quiet, too. I sat in silence drinking my coffee until she served me the pancakes.

"There you go," she said. "Bon appétit."

"Thank you, Aunt Grace."

"You're welcome, sweet girl."

She might have been the only person on the planet ever to describe me as sweet.

I took a big bite of pancake. It was good, but it didn't taste the way I remembered. I wondered what had changed, my palate or Grace's cooking skills. Or maybe I'd just overhyped the pancakes in my memory, made them wondrously delicious in retrospect.

It occurred to me then, mouth full of chocolate chip banana mush, that our past is not the truth. It's warped by time and emotion, inevitably muddied by love and resentment, joy and shame, hope and regret. I couldn't trust my own memories. Good or bad.

Great, I thought, squirting some syrup onto my plate. *My grasp on reality has been deeply shaken thanks to a subpar breakfast.*

"Mom!" Rosie screamed from upstairs. "Mom! Can you come here? Now, please!"

"Oh boy," Grace said. "Must be a bridal emergency."

"High stakes," I said, stabbing a banana chunk.

"You know it. You need anything else, lovey?"

"I'm good. Thanks again for the pancakes."

"Of course," she said, squeezing my shoulder. She kissed me on the cheek, then lingered there at the side of my face and whispered, "This is your home. This is where you belong. With us. We love you. We need you."

She ran a hand over my head, my cropped hair. "Be down for pictures at four."

I cleared my throat, shook off the pressure. Played it cool. "If I show for pictures, can't imagine Constance will be too pleased."

"Is she ever?" Grace asked. Another wink, and she was lumbering out of the kitchen. "Be right up, Rosie!"

I sat alone at the counter eating my pancakes. I poured myself another cup of coffee despite knowing the excessive caffeine would make me jittery.

Chaos unfolded upstairs. Heavy footsteps, moaning floorboards, chittering conversation, the whirring of blow-dryers. Rosie could be uptight, and she was also a bit of a perfectionist. I figured she wouldn't be much fun to be around, and I thought maybe I'd just hide out in my room until it was time for the wedding. Having kissed the groom was likely a contributing factor.

I didn't feel remorseful. I wasn't concerned about guilt. Guilt I could handle. Swat away, crush like a bug. I felt volatile, and that was rare and scary. My emotions were elusive, my mood unstable. They weren't in my jurisdiction. Any moment, I anticipated insurrection. A coup. I was in danger of losing control. Getting reckless, causing damage. More than I already had.

The wedding was mine to destroy.

Whether the thought brought me satisfaction or horrified me, I couldn't say.

I stood up and tossed the rest of my pancakes into the trash. I considered just leaving the dishes but wanted to see if I could possibly wash them to my mother's standard of clean. I knew I couldn't, but I also couldn't walk away from the challenge.

I ran the water hot, got a fresh sponge out from under the sink. I scrubbed with all my strength. With the water running, I could no longer hear the pandemonium upstairs. Without the sounds of people, I was alone.

My gaze floated up from the sink full of soap suds and dishwater. I looked out through the window, and instead of seeing the field behind the house, I saw myself. My reflection. A shadowed outline of me. And behind me, someone standing in the doorway to the kitchen. Someone tall, broad shouldered. Just standing there.

I turned around.

The doorway was empty. The hall beyond it empty.

"Hello?" I said.

No one answered.

But it wasn't because no one was there. Someone was. Only I couldn't see them.

At least, that's how I felt in the moment. Convinced of an invisible presence.

I looked back to the window, and I was alone in my reflection. No second figure loitered over my shoulder.

My suspicion metastasized. A worm of a thought wriggled its way around my brain. *What if they're watching me?*

The question spawned.

What if someone was tasked with keeping an eye on me, and they're the ones who were in my room last night? What if they saw me with Brody?

Who put them up to following me? And why?

I sighed, turned off the faucet, left the plate and skillet in the sink, wiped my hands on a dish towel.

Despite the general public's conjectures about Satanism, I'd never once thought of Hell's Gate as a cult. It was a church. No one was forced to stay. But if you left, if you chose to forsake Satan and live among the unchosen, you were essentially dead in the eyes of the community. That I'd been invited back was a big exception. I'd assumed I got special treatment because I'd received special treatment my entire life, because of my family, because of my mother, who had also gotten special treatment by not being kicked out when she procreated with an outsider, a nonbeliever.

But I began to wonder if I'd been smug in this assumption. If maybe I'd better watch my back.

I pivoted to the empty kitchen.

I heard the bridesmaids singing along to Taylor Swift upstairs, and I felt stupid for thinking I was in any danger.

"She wears short skirts. . . ."

My paranoia was quelled.

On my way up to my room, I reconsidered staying sequestered. I'd gone through the hassle of coming home; if I'd wanted to sit by myself mindlessly scrolling through my phone, I could have done that back at my apartment.

Also, if I joined in the festivities, I could hang out in my mother's room, a real treat for my rebel spirit.

I turned onto the second-floor landing and beelined for the door at the end of the hall.

It was wide-open.

I felt like a Polly Pocket standing in a Barbie Dreamhouse. Maybe the room seemed so massive because it was, or maybe the second I crossed the threshold, I'd reverted to a childlike state, transformed by nostalgia and awe. It was just as glamorous as I'd remembered. There was a colossal four-poster bed draped in red velvet. The windows were also dressed in velvet, thick curtains tied back with tasseled ropes. The walls were papered with gold damask. Everything extra. Big sconces with half-melted candles, red wax spilling over. On the far wall there were bookshelves overstuffed with heavy tomes of Satanic scripture.

Above, centered in the high ceiling, was a pentagram chandelier dripping with crystals.

"Vessie!" Rosie screeched. She sat with hot rollers in her hair at my mother's enormous antique vanity. She wore a white robe with *Bride* embroidered across the back in cheugy pink script. "You're here!"

"I'm here," I said, with much less enthusiasm.

"Are you going to get ready with us?"

"You have to!" Jane said, popping her head out of the bathroom. Her face was half-contoured, and she looked fucking crazy.

"Pretty please!" Birdie and Beatrice whined in unison. Birdie pointed a curling iron at me in a vaguely threatening manner, so I said, "All right, sure. I'll stick around."

I approached my mother's nightstand. On it was a small lamp—notably not a disgusting prop from a film about cannibals—an opalescent prayer book, and an empty picture frame. I picked up the frame and flipped it over. I wondered why she had an empty frame beside her bed. Had there been a picture inside it once upon a time? If so, who was it of? Me?

My father?

In my quest to find him, I read a lot of gossip about my mother. Supposed affairs with costars, her mysterious quiet life on the farm. None of it led me to my father's identity, which my mother wouldn't disclose, for whatever selfish reason—religious or personal—but I did get to discover some fun alleged details of her sex life, which I'd since scoured from my memory.

I wondered if one of her former hookups had occupied the frame. It made me pretty nauseous.

The pancakes had been a mistake.

"Hey, Vesper?" Birdie said, still brandishing the curling iron. "Do you have a dress?"

"Yeah," I said.

"What color?" Beatrice asked.

"Red."

"*Oooh,*" the twins said.

"Okay, okay, we can work with that," Jane said, rummaging through her makeup case. "Like, what shade?"

I opened the back of the frame to see if there was a picture hidden inside. There wasn't.

I wondered then whether my mother had locked me out because I was a nuisance, or if she'd locked me out because hidden in her room there was something that she didn't want me to find. Something about my father.

"Vesper? What shade?" Jane repeated.

"Uh, like . . . red? I don't know. It's red."

"Hmm," Jane said, hands on her hips. "Like, an orange-red or a blue-red?"

"Jane," Rosie said, her voice tight. "Are you going to . . ." She gestured to the rollers in her hair.

"Oh, sorry! Got distracted."

Rosie smacked her lips. She was annoyed.

"Spotlight is on you, Rosie," I said, reassuring her. "I'm just a doting fan."

She rolled her eyes.

"I mean it. Honest truth."

"I'm trying to stay present and just savor every moment of the day," she said, staring at herself in the big vanity mirror. "But there's *soooo* much going on. And what if they sent the wrong flowers, the wrong number of chairs? So many things could go wrong."

"Nothing is gonna go wrong," I said, thinking, *Other than me kissing your fiancé last night.*

It was hard not to think about the kiss. It was such a good one.

We'd always had amazing chemistry. I wondered if Brody touched Rosie the same way he'd touched me. Maybe. But she didn't touch him the way I had. That, I knew.

I sighed, refocused on snooping while Jane took the rollers out of Rosemary's hair and Birdie and Beatrice primped and sang along to an obnoxious love/wedding-centric pop playlist. They were all too distracted to pay any attention to my sleuthing. Still, I tried to be discreet.

I discovered a stack of manila envelopes on the floor, slightly obscured by a giant palm plant. I opened the envelopes, heart hammering with radical hope, but they didn't contain long-lost letters from my father. They contained scripts. I held in my hands *The Haunting at Ghost River*, adapted from a book of the same name. I'd never heard of it. Curious, I thumbed through, read some of it. It actually wasn't bad. Eventually, I stuffed it back into its envelope.

I sat there on the floor batting away stray palm leaves. I scanned the room, admiring my mother's oasis. I noticed the door to the bathroom was open and saw an opportunity.

"I'm going to the . . ." I started, before I realized no one could hear me over the music. I slipped inside the bathroom, locking the door behind me. It was essentially the same as mine upstairs. Claw-foot tub, pedestal sink. No wallpaper, though. The walls were a stark white, and there was a stained-glass window above the toilet. And the tile on the floor had a pentagram design. *The devil is in the details,* I thought.

Beyond the tub and towels, there was another door. The closet. I tried the brass knob, anticipating that it would be locked, but it wasn't.

Her closet was huge. A whole other room. Racks and racks and racks of clothes, bags, shoes. Gowns she'd worn to premieres. Vintage skirts. Faux-fur jackets. I went straight for her costumes. Her dress from *The Black Hallows Coven Investigation*, in which she played an ancient witch. It was black velvet, with dramatic sleeves and a corset top. Beautiful. The black ribbons that tied the corset were embroidered with symbols. Details missed on screen.

Then there was her blue gingham romper from the original *Farm Possession*, with the square neckline and eyelet trim. The black cutoff jean shorts and silky cowl tank and cropped cardigan from *Death Ransom*, the look that had made her famous. It had the belt with it, black leather with the oversized silver buckle. I searched for the shoes, the high-top Chuck Taylors with the thick lugged platforms, and the skull hairpin—the character's signature accessory.

My first Halloween out of Hell's Gate, I was working at a small café that stayed open late, had poetry slams and open-mic nights. For Halloween, they put on some sort of ghost story reading. It was chaotically busy, and at some point, I saw her. Everything went still, went quiet.

It was my mother.

Rather, an exceptional imitation. Kristal Link, the heroine of the *Death Ransom* franchise.

I almost fucking passed out.

Over the course of the evening there were more Constance clones. More Kristal Links. Prudence McDonalds, in the blue gingham. Lady Veronas, in black corset dresses. Dr. Ava Night, from *Bloody Midnight*, in cracked cat-eye glasses and white lab coats spattered with fake blood.

How appropriate, I thought. *It's Halloween and I'm being haunted.*

"What do you think you're doing?" It was her. My mother. The real deal, behind me in her closet.

I flapped my lips for a moment, startled, stammering. I was a child again, caught playing dress-up without permission. "I thought I locked the bathroom door."

She flipped her hair over her shoulder. "Apparently not."

"You just walk into a bathroom even if the door is shut?"

"It's my bathroom," she said. "And my closet."

"I was just . . ."

She approached me, narrowing her eyes. "Just what?"

"Looking," I said.

"For?"

"Nothing."

"Right," she said, swiveling away from me, turning her attention to a series of garment bags hung on the back of the door. "Are you going to continue to look for nothing, or are you going to help me carry these dresses?"

I took a final look at her costumes, a final feel of them, and then grabbed the rest of the garment bags, helped her carry them out to the bridesmaids, to Grace, and to Rosie.

"Is it too early to put on our dresses?" Jane asked.

"Maybe, but . . ." Rosie started. A devious grin split across her face. "I've been waiting my whole life for this! I don't want to wait any longer."

It took Constance, Grace, and the entire team of bridesmaids to get her into that dress, which was surprisingly simple. Mermaid silhouette, sweetheart neckline. Pure white. The fabric had a sheen to it.

It suited her. She was a perfect bride.

"I can't wait to marry Brody in this dress," she said, admiring herself in the vanity mirror.

An ugliness snuck up on me from the inside.

She was so happy, glowing like a pearl. About to marry someone whom I had been with first, the only serious boyfriend I'd ever had. She was about to live happily ever after in a life that could have been mine, if only I could have stomached it. I was jealous that she got to be a dumb, giddy sheep, never questioning anything. Showing up to mass thinking she'd live forever because she was among the chosen, not caring that everyone else in the world would burn for eternity in the torturous flames of hell for the simple sin of not worshipping Satan.

I bet she thinks I'll burn, I realized. *I bet she thinks I deserve it.*

"Vesper, you're the only one who hasn't seen my dress," she said, turning toward me. "What do you think?"

I knew what I should say. I knew the only appropriate response was effusive praise. But in that moment, I couldn't let go of my animosity.

So I looked her up and down and said, "It's . . . nice."

What followed was total silence. The look on her face made me feel like a monster, and I swung from petty glee to genuine remorse. I wanted to say something else, tack on a compliment, though I knew the damage had been done.

"I mean . . ." I started.

"You look *gorgeous,*" Jane chimed in.

Rosie's expression melted into absolute despair.

Grace furrowed her brow, puckered her lips. "Oh, honey."

Birdie and Beatrice exchanged a tense look.

"Vesper. You should go get ready," Constance said. "Show us this supposedly appropriate dress."

"Fine," I said, grateful for an excuse to get out of the room, escape the bad situation I'd just created, like stepping off of an elevator after dropping a fart.

"You're a beauty," Grace said, holding Rosie's face. "The most beautiful bride."

"I'm not," Rosie said in response. "That's just it. I'm not."

There was something in her voice that made my heart wrench, and as I walked through the door, I had this vision. A flashback so intense, it was as if the past had bitten into me.

It was a perfect autumn afternoon. Rosie was sprawled across the floor of my bedroom, still in her school uniform. I'd taken mine off the second I got home, changed into a pair of shorts and one of Brody's T-shirts.

"Take this candy away from me," she said, gnawing on a licorice rope. "I'm going to eat it all."

"So eat it all," I replied, browsing my nail polish selection. I kept the bottles organized in a plastic ice tray.

"I can't. You don't understand. Sugar makes me break out. I'm not like you. I'm not naturally beautiful. I have to try."

"You're beautiful. What are you talking about?" I asked. "What do we think of Electric Ballet?"

I held up the neon pink shade.

She gave a nod of approval. "Not beautiful like you. You're so lucky."

"Pssh."

"You are! You're dating Brody," she said. "You're the most popular girl in school."

"Out of, like, fifty kids," I said, shaking the polish.

"Still. Everyone loves you."

"Yeah, except my parents," I said, plopping down on my bed.

"My parents are basically your parents," she said. "And they love you more than me."

I sat up. "That's not true."

"It is. It's okay. You're special. Everyone thinks so. You know I'm right."

"Aren't we all special in the eyes of our good Lord Satan?" I asked flatly, muting my tone to conceal my sarcasm, something I did so often, I would eventually go on to lose all inflection, developing a signature monotone. A voice void of emphasis, of feeling.

"I wish I looked like you."

"No, you don't," I said. "I've been cursed with the face of someone who is supposed to love me but can't stand me. I'm not lucky. My life is fucked."

"I'd trade," she said.

"I'd take you up on that, except I couldn't do that to you. Love you too much to let you into my shoes."

"I guess me, too."

"Oh well," I said. I held up the nail polish again. "So, yes to this pink?"

"Always yes to pink!"

We painted each other's nails, and as the polish dried we laughed so hard that our sides ached, our cheeks went numb.

I couldn't tell you what we laughed about. Probably nothing. That's what's special about adolescent laughter. So much, so big, over so little. You lose the ability to laugh like that as you get older. The more you know, the less funny it all becomes.

I longed for a simpler time, for ignorance. For how easy it'd been to love her when little else mattered. Before the church came between us, before Brody came between us. Before the years turned us into different people, adults with incompatible values. It made me bitter to think about how she worshipped what I blamed for our downfall. I imagined us as two flies drowning in honey, and while I struggled to get free, she was content, thinking, *Isn't it sweet?*

Maybe I'd have gone on contemplating the callousness of change, of loss, had I not looked up and been face-to-face with Blood Thirst.

"Goddamn it!" I shouted, scurrying past, imagining the bust swiveling, the mask turning to watch.

7

When I got back to my bedroom and to my phone, I found I had multiple missed texts from Kerri.

OMG you'll never believe what just happened . . .

JK I guess you will.

Rick got fired.

No one knows why but there's a rumor Sonya found him jerking off in his office.

But Kenny says it has something to do with him lying to corporate about the #s???

Who knows. But he's gone.

Maybe u were right about him.

Of course, I was right, I responded.

How's the wedding btw?

I sent a gun emoji next to a smiley-face emoji.

LOL.

I set my phone down on my bed and changed into my dress, as instructed.

It was even less wedding appropriate than I remembered. Wearing it for a night out at a club would have raised some eyebrows. The red satin clung to my figure. It stopped just above the knee, but the slit came up midthigh. The neck was low, square. I couldn't wear a bra with it. If the straps could be categorized as spaghetti, they were angel-hair. They crisscrossed at the back.

I stood in front of the mirror on my closet door, wondering if I was brave enough to walk out in the dress.

I sent a picture to Kerri, who responded with several fire emojis.

I turned around, looking over my shoulder into the mirror, studying my exposed back. I searched for a cardigan in my closet and pulled out a cropped long-sleeved one that Grace had made for me. It had a loose knit. I tried it on. It ruined the whole aesthetic, but it did make me look more church ready.

I took it off and stuffed it into my bag, along with my phone, tinted lip balm, and pentagram necklace, which I knew I would have to wear to be permitted inside the cathedral to attend the mass/wedding but didn't want to put on a second early.

I applied some mascara and worked a small dab of pomade through my hair. I checked the time on the Kit-Cat Klock. It was somehow already past three. The day had flown by, and the wedding was so soon, approaching with all the patience of an avalanche.

I thought about the kiss the night before.

I thought about hearing my own disembodied voice asking me why I was there, and what I wanted. The truth was, I really didn't know.

I leaned into the mirror, wiping a smudge of mascara from my eyelid. I noticed that, same as the day before, my pupils were dilated. I looked like a shark, or an evil doll.

"You're both," I heard myself say. Again, my image in the mirror was still as I spoke.

I stumbled back, away from myself, slamming the closet door shut to escape the mirror.

My hands trembled as I slipped on my shoes, a pair of brown sling-backs with kitten heels. I walked out of my room and down the stairs on Bambi legs.

I was so unsettled, I didn't know how to be in my body, what to do with the unease frothing in my gut. Part of me wanted to bolt out of the house, to run and run and run until I couldn't anymore, until I collapsed, numb to everything, even the earth beneath me. But I knew I was just being stupid. Weak. Irrational. So I returned to Constance's room, where everyone was essentially where I'd left them. Rosie gripped Grace's hand tightly, and the bridesmaids circled around. My mother stood nearby, her back to me.

They were in prayer.

"Please, Satan," Rosie said, "let today be filled with your glory. I am so blessed by your gifts, my Lord. All that is, is by your glory. My greatest blessing is that today I get to join my life with one of your most devoted servants."

I was more careful this time, about controlling my destructive impulses. Otherwise I might have let out a feral scream.

"Together we will worship you every day," she continued. "We will build a home in your name. We will bear children in your name. In your name, of your name, for your name. Please bless this union, Lord. Please be with us today, righteous one. Please guide Brody and me as we walk the path of eternity forged by your fire. Guide us here, now, and forevermore. Glory be. Hail Satan!"

"Hail Satan!" everyone repeated. "Hail Satan!"

The chant went on and on, as loud and ruthless as a jackhammer. Just when I thought I couldn't take it anymore, they broke into song.

"Glory, glory to the faaaa-ther. Glory, glory to the faaaa-ther! Our Lord is hell's true king."

I'd lived long enough to know that it's possible to experience a moment so unbearable, you feel like dying, just evaporating into the ether, escaping into nothingness. I'd felt that way sometimes at Shortee's, wearing that fucking polo, singing the birthday song. And I felt it then, listening to them warble joyfully about Satan.

They swayed from side to side, smiling at one another, and I really thought I might liquefy or spontaneously combust, leaving only a small mess in my wake. But then Constance turned around, looked up, and saw me. To my surprise, she started to laugh.

That got everyone's attention. Hearing Constance laugh was jarring. I think I probably could have counted on my fingers the times in my life I'd heard my mother laugh.

"Oh, Star. You look beautiful," Grace said. I could tell that she meant it. I could also tell by the stunned expressions of the bridesmaids that they did not know how to react to my dress.

Rosie's eyes went wide. I thought about that afternoon when we'd painted our nails. *I wish I looked like you,* she'd said. I was purposely exploiting her insecurities on her wedding day, only I couldn't fully commit to my villainy because part of me still loved her.

"Oh, Vessie, that's such a great color on you," Rosie said, her sincerity annihilating. "You look amazing."

"You intend to wear that to the wedding?" Constance asked through laughter. "That is your idea of a wedding-appropriate dress?"

"I have a cardigan," I mumbled, feeling like the biggest, stupidest piece of shit on the planet.

"Mm. The picture of modesty," she responded, twisting her hair into a long rope.

"Why should I be modest?" I asked, shifting to defiance. "'The gifts of the Lord to his chosen shall be the true gifts of the world.'"

It startled me how easily I was able to recall and recite scripture.

"And is she not a gift?" Grace asked, beaming.

My mother scoffed. I found the hypocrisy pretty rich, that she would attempt to shame me for my attire when a generation of teenagers had beat off to a poster of her posed seductively wearing chain mail and fishnets in a cemetery. I wouldn't dare point this out to her, though.

I sat on the bed while the bridesmaids sprayed perfume and makeup setter and hair products. I choked on the fragrant chemical cloud. Grace and Constance got dressed. Grace wore a navy mother-of-the-bride gown with her pearl-and-pentagram necklace, Constance a high-necked black dress with a black lace overlay, chandelier earrings, a bejeweled pentagram barrette. Her necklace was all black diamonds.

We went down for photos. I hid in the parlor while everyone else went out to the porch. Luckily, Rosie had wanted the first time Brody saw her in her dress to be when she was walking down the aisle, so I didn't have to stand there grinding my teeth while they had a first look, while they kissed and doted on each other.

I flipped through some of Constance's coffee-table books to distract myself. I wished she had normal ones with artful photographs of diners and cute labradoodles getting into mischief, instead of mummified corpses and the world's most notorious haunted places.

"Vesper," Grace called in through the window. "Come, come. We need you."

"Need," I repeated under my breath as I stood up and went outside.

"Look at you, there!" Carl said. "Snazzy dress."

He shot me with finger guns.

"I want one with me and Vessie and our moms, and then one with just the two of us," Rosie said, apparently holding nothing against me, which only made me feel worse.

Constance scowled in protest. We reluctantly allowed the photographer to pose us next to each other.

"Get in closer," said the photographer, whom I recognized as Ben Goodwin, a boy who had been a few years older than us at school and had a penchant for nose picking. "Closer."

I heard Constance groan as if in physical pain.

"Smile! Big smiles. Or just any smile. Happy to be here."

He snapped a few pictures and looked at them on his camera. I could tell he wasn't satisfied with the shots.

"Okay, now just me and Vessie," Rosie said, waving me in. "Careful of my dress."

"I'm careful," I said. My guilt pressing, I added, "You look gorgeous. Like a princess."

"You're the princess," she said, slipping her arm around my waist and pulling me in close.

"Good, good. Beautiful," the photographer said.

"You really went with Booger Ben as your photographer?" I whispered in Rosie's ear.

She burst out laughing. She whispered back, "He's the only one in Hell's Gate."

Ben cleared his throat. He'd probably heard us.

After photos, Rosie and the bridesmaids went back inside, and I sat in a rocking chair watching cars pull up, guests arrive. They headed toward the barn, which was typically where church functions were held. Outside the barn there was an area set up for the cocktail hour. A bar, antique couches and tables and chairs, string lights, a vintage food truck. All very rustic chic.

Had an outsider driven by, they'd have seen an ordinary wedding, nothing Satanic, nothing suspicious. Hell's Gate had always hidden in plain sight. Virgil was isolated, hard to come by if you didn't know it existed, and if you did, it had a reputation for being a devout religious community, which was enough of a repellent without specifics. No one wants a lecture, a stranger to attempt to recruit them into a mystery faith. We kept to ourselves, were self-sustaining, smart and strategic and secret. And, supposedly, we had Satan on our side.

Constance approached me, smoking an electronic cigarette. "The audacity of you not only showing up but wearing that dress. I almost respect it."

"Almost," I said.

"I trust you're surviving out there," she said, gesturing beyond the farm.

"I'm surviving." I figured I wouldn't get another opportunity to have the conversation, so I said, "I looked for my father."

"Did you?"

"Hard to find someone when you don't even know their name."

"Mm," she said. I noticed a tightness in her jaw. Otherwise she kept her cool.

"You shouldn't keep him from me."

She laughed again. Twice in one day, a true spectacle.

"Why can't you just tell me who he is? I get that he couldn't be around, that it was complicated because he's not Hell's Gate—"

"Is that what you think?" she asked, laughter ceasing abruptly.

"There's nothing in the way of us having a relationship now," I said.

She cocked her head to the side. "Except me, I suppose."

"Why do you have to be like this?" I asked, gripping the arms of the chair.

"You've never trusted me. The first time I held you, the way you looked at me . . ." She trailed off, staring out at the yard. The brilliant blue of the sky had started to marble ominously, a darkness snaking through. Rain clouds. "I don't expect you to start trusting me now, so I won't ask. If you want to know your father, you'll know your father. I'm done discussing it."

She turned on her heel and clicked away, disappearing into the house.

The fury made my bones creak, strained my skin. I felt like a screaming kettle, and no one was coming to pour me out. A blister longing to burst.

The sky made good on its threat of rain. It poured. Guests hustled toward the barn, seeking shelter. I imagined Rosie somewhere upstairs, panicked and devastated at the turn of the weather. Brody, too, probably.

Oh well.

Maybe they could pray the sky blue again. Hail Satan.

People dressed in all-white ensembles ran around throwing tarps over the couches and chairs in the cocktail-hour area. *Save the liquor,* I thought, fearing the bottles would get lost in the squall and I'd have to endure the reception dead sober. Watch unanesthetized as Rosie and Brody slow danced to Ed Sheeran.

I shuddered at the thought.

Thankfully, the rain passed quickly. A summer shower.

"Better get on going," Carl said, stepping onto the porch. I'd missed it earlier, but he wore a pentagram-and-polka-dot bow tie. "Gotta snag yourself a good seat in the cathedral."

"Sure," I said.

"And, Vesperino . . ." he said, gesturing to my neck.

"I'll put it on."

He gave me a double thumbs-up.

I sighed, rocking myself out of the chair and stepping off the porch onto the lawn, which was muddy. My heels sank in. I made my way, gracelessly, to the barn.

It looked incredible inside. I'd never seen it decorated so ornately. Branches wrapped in strands of twinkling lights hung from the ceiling. Glass orbs holding tea-light candles seemed to float midair. A giant crystal chandelier glimmered over a marble dance floor, surrounded by tables topped with white linens and towering centerpieces. The most extravagant flower arrangements I'd ever seen.

Gauzy jewel-toned fabric draped along the walls, held in place by more glittering branches and flowering vines. The whole room glistened. It was an ethereal dream.

My eyes found their way to the door. Well, it wasn't a door exactly. An inconspicuous wooden panel that slid over to reveal a hidden passageway to an underground Satanic cathedral. To the Hell's Gate House of Worship.

I took a deep breath, dug my necklace out of my bag, and swiftly clasped it around my neck. My skin went hot on contact, aflame with itch. It wasn't tight but it felt tight. I got out my cardigan, too. Draped it over my shoulders.

I walked toward the door, but something stopped me from passing through it. A sudden hesitation. It struck me.

What the hell am I doing?

The whole reason I ran away was that I didn't fuck with Satanism, and here I was, about to be a willing participant. I'd been so focused on my presence at the wedding being deservedly uncomfortable for Rosie and Brody, I never properly stopped to think about how painful it would be for me.

"Second thoughts?"

Constance stood behind me, eyebrows raised, insufferably self-satisfied.

"Nope," I said, and went straight through.

A dank, narrow passageway led to an equally dank, narrow winding staircase lit by medieval-looking torch sconces. These stairs were tricky enough in flats, but descending them in heels was a death wish. I clung to the iron railing.

Constance managed no problem.

At the bottom of the winding staircase was an enormous arched doorway, carved from stone, etched with Satanic symbols.

A dark, gaping maw in the earth, a red velvet curtain flapping like a giant animal tongue.

"Say it," Constance said. "Say it and go through. Or don't and turn around. Leave again."

I huffed. My mouth was dry, and my voice sounded funny. Farcically high. Cartoonish. "Here I enter the House of the Lord. Here I cross the threshold into the realm of divine fire. Praise Him. Hail Satan."

Constance made a clucking noise. She nudged me through the doorway.

There was a second staircase, a few wide steps that led down to the entrance of the cathedral.

A crowd loitered there. Among them, the High Priest in his dark robes, cylindrical hat. He was old, had immense jowls that shook when he spoke. He looked like a human basset hound. He'd always taken an interest in me, stopping me before and after mass to have a chat, ask how I was doing, assure me of the Lord's love.

He must have had a radar for me, because he turned to the stairs, made eye contact, and waved, like he'd anticipated my arrival, knew exactly when I'd be coming.

I wondered if he'd sent the invitation. At the very least, he would have had to approve it. Otherwise he wouldn't have been so happy to see me.

His attention gave me instant heartburn, like I'd just chugged Tabasco sauce.

"Vesper," he called out. My name echoed. Everything echoed down there. It was a cave. "Vesper, child of Satan, daughter of the Kingdom of Hell, He welcomes you home."

Everyone stared.

I gave a little nod of acknowledgment, then put my head down and shouldered my way through the crowd. Whispers erupted around me.

"She's back?"

"Praise be, it's Vesper!"

I'd been in obscurity for so long, I'd forgotten sometimes it's harder to be around people who know you than people who don't.

I passed through the cathedral doors, approached the pews. I ducked into an empty row, slid all the way over. I angled toward the wall in hopes no one would see me, but from the volume of whispering, I knew that everyone had.

I leaned closer to the wall, to the giant piece of stained glass depicting the fires of hell burning heathens, their faces contorted in agony. There were pieces just like this all around the cathedral. Forests full of Harpies. Skulls on sticks. The great fiery apocalypse, the blood-soaked final judgment. Even as a kid I'd had the awareness to wonder, *Should I be seeing this?*

No. The answer was no. It's a cruelty of life that we can never protect our own innocence. We can only watch ourselves lose it in retrospect. Scream at memories.

The cathedral was beautiful, in the way most cathedrals are. Grim and mesmerizing. Interspersed between the stained glass were pentagrams and wall torches, statues of Baphomet—horned goat head atop a muscular humanoid body with giant wings—cast in bronze or carved from stone. Baphomet acted as a sort of Hell's Gate mascot, like Gritty for the Flyers. Just as creepy, less fuzzy.

There was a massive baroque pipe organ toward the back. Golden, several stories tall, wide as a house. We were taught in school that it was the largest in the world, though I'd since come to realize there was no way to validate that claim. No one in the world knew about it except for us.

It began to play, and the whispering ceased. The pews filled quickly.

The wedding was happening. It was no longer something happening in the future, in the abstract. It was actively occurring. Panic swam through my veins.

There he was. Standing at the end of the aisle. Brody. In a black suit, white shirt, red tie. He looked so handsome, and I thought, *Goddamn it.*

I thought about the first valentine he'd ever given me. He'd slipped it to me after school. A heart cut from construction paper, folded in half. Inside, he'd written, *Next year I'll get you chocolate.* We were eight.

He'd made good on his promise. I got chocolate every year after that. Up until I left.

I wondered if I would ever find someone outside of Hell's Gate who could make me feel the way that he did, who would love me as much as he did. I knew the answer was probably yes, but then again, as far as I knew, my mother had never had any serious relationships after my dad. I worried. Maybe some of us get only one love, have it in us to do it only the once.

The organ music changed, and the High Priest appeared beside Brody. Grace and Constance walked down the aisle. Then the bridesmaids. Then everyone stood. I had to use the pew to help me stay upright.

Rosie appeared in the doorway to the cathedral, and I looked to Brody, anticipating the sting of his gazing lovingly at someone who wasn't me. But while everyone else in the place was fixed on Rosie, he was fixed on me.

This is all so fucked, I thought as Rosie glided down the aisle, graceful on Carl's arm.

When they arrived at the altar, Carl pulled back her veil and kissed her on the forehead, and then the ceremony started.

"So the Lord giveth us the strength to stand and grant us respite from weary legs. You may be seated. Praise be to the Lord."

"Praise Him."

"Glory be to the Lord."

"Glory be to Satan."

"We gather today in worship and in gratitude, and to witness the most sacred union of two of the Lord's chosen . . ."

I'd forgotten how long Hell's Gate services were, and how horribly boring. I wanted nothing more than to set my head down and take a nap. Snooze through it.

I played with the pentagram around my neck. It was both familiar and violating. The clasp scoured against my vertebrae.

The High Priest droned on and on. My sit bones ached. I was freezing.

"Brody, on the day of your holy commitment to the Lord, did you pledge to Him eternal faith?"

"I did," Brody said.

"And as part of that commitment, did you promise to enter a loving union and bear children in His name?"

"I did."

"And do you hold to your commitment today, before your family, your friends, your church, and your Lord?"

"I do."

The High Priest turned to Rosie and asked her the same questions.

I must have dissociated, defaulted into numb mode, because I don't remember feeling anything throughout the rest of the ceremony except tired and bored as shit. It wasn't hard for me to disconnect. Maybe it was my nature, or maybe I'd been forced to adapt. To free myself of weariness and confusion and skepticism as a child enduring long masses and ceremonies, Satanism in general. To cope with my parents, minimize the damage of my mother's coldness and my father's absence. I'd never know which parts of me were *me*, versus the traits I'd inherited, and what the family I'd been born into had done to me—how it had bent and shaped me when I was young and malleable.

"Do you, Rosemary, take Brody to be your husband, to bind your life to his here on earth?" the High Priest bellowed.

Her smile was so bright, I could see her teeth gleaming across the cathedral. Her eyes like sequins and her cheeks round, pink, and shimmery. She glowed. And I thought maybe I should just be happy for her. Forget the chip on my shoulder. She hadn't done anything I wouldn't have if I were in her position. Brody either.

"I do."

It wasn't her fault. It wasn't his. It wasn't mine. I looked around the cathedral, at the stained glass, at the multiple Baphomets, at the High Priest, at the pews—people crammed in shoulder to shoulder. Why were they so willing to believe in something so ridiculous? To shirk science and logic for imaginary idols? Was it really such a hard pill to swallow that the universe was just random, that there was no higher power?

"Will you walk hand in hand with him into the hellfire that shall deliver you beyond?"

Could they not accept that our existence wasn't ordained? That it just was.

"I will."

Or was it death that drove them to faith? Were they not brave enough to accept its inevitability? Did they need to believe they could transcend it in order to live?

"Now we come to the slaughtering of the lamb, a gift to show the Lord your devotion, your commitment to Him and to each other. Do you commit to this sacrifice?"

"I do."

"I do."

Or did they believe because the faith was all they knew? Because their parents taught them it was right and true, like their parents had taught them. Brainwashing, but with holy water. Spanning generations. Centuries.

"Blood of the lamb. May its red river flow from earth into hell," the High Priest said. A clergyman dressed in black robes walked in from the wings leading a lamb by a rope. A noose, really. I wondered if it was the same lamb that I'd seen through my window the night before. I hoped not.

Brody took out a dagger from inside his suit jacket, and Rosie took the rope from the clergyman. She pulled it tight, steadying the lamb. Its sweet, dark eyes bulged.

"Blood of the lamb," Brody said, and I looked away. Hunched over. Held my breath. Plugged my ears. I stayed like that, counted down from ten.

When I finally sat up and opened my eyes, removed my fingers from my ear canals, the High Priest was saying, "Before the Lord, I now pronounce you husband and wife."

They kissed. It was a dull kiss. A dry peck on the lips. Everyone cheered, jumped to their feet, applauded wildly. There was this radiant joy, a sense of purpose that I could see in all of them. But I couldn't understand it. I couldn't reach out and take some for myself.

How could I? There was a dead animal on the floor, its blood pooling around it. And no one gave a shit except for me.

I was home, but I was still alone.

In that moment, I missed my father so badly, I thought it might kill me. I thought about the last time I saw him. I was nine years old. His visits had always been sporadic, rare treats. He'd come to the house; we'd stay at the house. Never go anywhere. Never see anyone else. I didn't ask questions, because I was young and never knew any different, and because even then I could sense how fragile it all was. I was afraid that if I breathed the wrong way he'd disappear, never return. That I'd have my father privileges revoked and it'd be on me, by my mistake.

I wasn't wrong to fear it. Because the one time I was bold . . .

"Daddy," I said.

"Yes, Princess?"

"Can I tell you a secret?"

He leaned down, rubbed his jaw, his silver stubble. "A secret?"

I nodded.

"Well, I would think so. I'm your dad, after all. And I'm a great secret keeper. Best in the world, as a matter of fact."

"Really?"

"Oh yeah. I've got some secrets you wouldn't believe."

"Like what?"

"Nice try."

I giggled.

We were sitting on the rug in the parlor, Mr. Ransom looming in the corner, wielding his fake hatchet. We were playing cards. Gin rummy. My father wore a suit, as always. For work, he'd told me. He loosened his tie.

"What's this secret?" he asked.

"If I tell you, will you promise not to be mad?"

"How could I ever be mad at you?"

I shrugged.

"Hey," he said, reaching out and lifting my chin. "Look at me. I could never be mad at you. You're my favorite person."

"You're mine," I said.

He clutched his chest. "I'm glad. I am pretty cool, aren't I?"

"Humble, too."

He laughed. "All right, Vesper. What's this secret?"

"I want you to take me with you. I don't want to live here anymore. Mom's never here, and she wouldn't mind anyway. And I . . . I don't like church. I don't like school. I don't . . . I don't care about it."

"About what?" he asked, shuffling the deck.

"Satan."

He nodded calmly. "That so?"

"I know I'm supposed to, but I don't. I stopped saying my prayers at night. I just go right to bed."

He was silent. Kept on shuffling.

"I'm sorry," I said.

"You don't need to apologize for thinking freely, Vesper. I'm proud of you. You're a leader, not a follower. You have a mind of your own. But," he said, dealing the cards quickly. One for me, one for him, one for me, one for him. "I can't take you with me. I wish I could."

"Oh," I said.

"You do believe me, don't you? If I could . . ." He trailed off. "And you're wrong, about your mother. She would mind if you were gone."

I looked at him. "You can tell me the truth."

"I am." He finished dealing. "Your turn."

I picked up the cards, examined my hand.

"We both love you, Vesper. You're the most important thing to us. More than you know. You trust me, don't you?"

"Yes, Daddy."

"Good," he said. "Now let's play."

The organ was wailing again, and the smell of incense was oppressive and nauseating, and the cathedral walls seemed to inch closer and closer. It was claustrophobic. A tomb pretending it wasn't a tomb. A statue of Baphomet seemed to stare at me, glass eyes reflecting flickering candlelight.

I knew that it must have been my fault. That what I had said during that last visit caused me to lose him.

No, I thought. *I never lost him. The devil took him from me.*

8

I took full advantage of the cocktail hour, trying both signature drinks, Rosemary's raspberry gimlet and Brody's bourbon fizz. The sun was out again, and the staff—church teenagers dressed in white pretending they weren't sneaking drinks when no one was watching—had wiped every surface dry of rain, returning the scene to picture-perfect.

I sequestered myself at the bar, perched on an end stool, my back angled to the mingling crowd. I had my phone out, which was rude but effective in keeping people away. I wasn't in the headspace for small talk. I knew no one would ask me about my life outside, so I wouldn't have to explain that I'd spent the last few years in an unglamorous part of Westchester County, sporting a polo and serving plates of baby back ribs I was fairly certain were generated in a lab. I knew people would ignore that I ever left, ignore that a world existed beyond Virgil. That's just how it was. Instead, they would tell me what they'd been up to. What their children were up to. *Sarah's in the second grade now—I can't believe it! She's singing in the choir.*

I'd have to nod along, feign interest. Well, I wouldn't *have* to. Being an asshole was always an option.

Being honest.

But it was easier to keep to myself, slurp my bourbon in solitude. I rarely drank bourbon, because the taste of it always reminded me of Brody. He'd come over sometimes after school with a bottle when Constance wasn't around. We'd drink and make out and talk. Brody was the only person I'd ever confided in about my father. I remembered this one time. . . .

Brody was behind me, kissing my neck as I thumbed through records.

"You're distracting me," I told him. "I take this seriously."

"I know you do," he said.

"This one was one of my dad's favorites." I paused to look at the album cover. It quickly became too painful, and I went on browsing.

"You don't talk about him much anymore," Brody said, hugging my waist tightly.

"What's there to talk about?" I asked, pretending my wounds didn't exist, that I was whole and unaffected. "He's not here. I am."

"'Trust in the Lord, for He shall ignite the flame that lights the dark,'" he said.

I shook him off. He didn't usually quote scripture around me—I think because he could sense I wasn't into it—but every once in a while he'd let something slip.

"If it weren't for the Lord, my dad would be here. He'd come back. I know he would."

"We need to have faith," Brody said. "Things are as they're meant to be. We just might not understand why yet. It'll make sense someday. I promise it will."

"Maybe." I was so tired of being told that faith was the answer to everything when it never seemed to solve anything. I wondered what the difference was between being told to have faith and to be quiet. I suspected there wasn't one.

"Never mind," I said. "I don't feel like listening to music. Let's do something else."

I kissed him, just to feel something different. Something good.
He tasted like bourbon.

I downed my drink and wished for a distraction as I sat there alone at the bar, mourning the life I could have had if only I'd been born into a family of atheists.

"Vesper," I heard. A woman I didn't immediately recognize was touching me, hand on my shoulder. "It's Mary Beekman. Remember? I was your preschool teacher."

"Sorry," I said, shaking my head. I did remember her, but I didn't want to entertain her.

"Oh, that's okay," she said. "I just wanted to tell you I'm so, so delighted that you're home."

"Thanks," I said. I threw her a "Nice to see you."

She leaned in, squeezing herself between me and the man on the stool next to me. He grunted, looked back. When he saw me, he bowed his head and smiled, the tip of his tongue peeking out between his teeth. It was Tony Alberts, Ant's dad, Jane's now father-in-law. He was the village accountant.

"So," Mary Beekman said. Her breath was rank. "Is he coming?"

"Is who coming?" I asked.

"He must be, if you're here," she said. Her head swiveled as if it were loose on her neck; her eyes went big and round in a way that shouldn't have been possible.

"What?" I asked, leaning away from her. The stool teetered beneath me. I was in danger of falling. Hot sunshine flowed over me, and I felt sweat crack like an egg at the crown of my head. It dripped down, alarmingly viscous. A consuming, dangerous nausea possessed me, and I thought, *Ah shit, am I about to pass out?*

I turned to the bartender and asked for a water.

"Mary," Tony said, his voice stern. "Mary."

He yanked her back with such violence, I could hear her bones crack. She squealed.

"Forgive me," she said, her arms dangling strangely. "Forgive me."

She was ushered away by two older men I recognized as Nate Adams, the blacksmith/plumber, and Jacob Sterling, Jane and Lily's dad.

"Must've had too much to drink," Tony said, laughing heartily. "Open bars, am I right?"

The bartender set a glass of water down in front of me, and I had to use both hands to lift it to my lips. I was shaking, and I felt so woozy. . . . Was it the heat? Heatstroke? Was it the alcohol?

I drank the water. It sloshed around inside me, provided no relief. I set both palms flat on the counter, took a series of deep breaths.

"More water," I called to the bartender. "And a ginger ale. With lime."

The only thing I'd eaten all day was a few bites of the pancakes. I waited for my drinks. I chugged the water, and carried the ginger ale with me as I slid carefully off the stool and went to chase down some food, hailing a cater waiter like a cab.

"What's this?" I asked before shoving a pastry-puff-looking something into my mouth.

"Potato knish."

"Cool," I said, mouth full. "What else is there?"

Shrimp, bruschetta, mini meatballs, bacon-wrapped dates, stuffed mushrooms. I went weaving through the crowd, sampling everything, hoping something would settle my stomach, settle my nerves.

"Hungry, Star?" Grace asked me. I stood alone at a high top, and she'd come up behind me, placed a cool hand on my back. "You look a little pale. Are you feeling okay?"

"Not really," I said.

She frowned. "What's wrong?"

"Queasy. Probably the heat. Maybe I'm dehydrated. I don't know."

"Need some electrolytes?"

"Yeah, I guess," I said. "Does anyone know what electrolytes are? Or did everyone just sort of decide they were a thing and that we need them?"

Grace shrugged. "I got some pills in my bag, in the house. Why don't we get you inside? Cool ya down. Still another twenty minutes 'til the reception starts."

"All right."

"We'll have you feeling better," she said, walking me toward the porch. "Have to enjoy the party!"

"Yep." I never really liked parties, especially ones not for me.

She led me inside, sat me at the kitchen counter. She disappeared upstairs, returned a few minutes later with a small white packet. She tore it open, tipped out the contents. Two tiny circular pills.

"Swallow them," she said. "Don't let them dissolve."

It was nice to be taken care of.

"Sure thing," I said, then popped the pills into my mouth and swallowed with my saliva.

"What was Mary up to?" Grace asked me. She pulled a compact mirror out from somewhere, opened it, fixed her lipstick—which was slightly smudged at the corner of her mouth.

"She asked me if someone was coming. She seemed a little . . ." I spun a finger at my temple.

Grace smacked her lips.

"What?" I asked.

"Oh, no. Nothing," she said, snapping the compact shut. "I should be getting back. Need to make sure it all goes smoothly for our Rosie. The ceremony was beautiful, don't you—"

She cut herself off. Worry eclipsed her face for just a moment.

"Look at you, my Star," she said, holding my chin. "So gorgeous, I can hardly take it!" She kissed me on both cheeks and then released me. "Okay, lovey. I'll see you in the barn."

"Okay . . ."

She was acting strange. Something felt off with her, with everything. My internal alarm was chirping, but I didn't know why, what it was for. I'd made it through the ceremony. Rosie and Brody were married. The hard part was over, and I wasn't even that bothered by it.

Right?

Then why this ambiguous warning? This intense physical worry.

I got up and went to the bathroom. The downstairs powder room was small, painted emerald. It had a gaudy gold toilet, a gaudy gold sink. A roaring-lion's-head faucet. Black-and-white photographs of cemeteries in ornamental frames covered the walls.

My urine was distressingly dark, and as I washed my hands, I confronted my reflection and found that my pupils were still dilated. They might have even gotten worse, the black of my eyes threatening a takeover.

There was a knock on the door.

"Vesper." It was Rosemary. "Vesper?"

"Just a second," I said, shutting off the faucet and opening the door. "Hey."

"Hey," she said, smiling. "You okay? Mom said . . ."

"I'm fine," I lied. "What's up? Oh, and congratulations."

She threw her arms around me, gave me a quick squeeze. "Thank you, Vessie."

"Rosie, we're on a timeline . . ." Jane called down from the second-floor landing.

"I came in to use the bathroom," she said. "Group effort with this." She gestured to her dress.

"I bet," I said.

"And thought I'd check on you," she said, tilting her head to the side. "You sure you're okay?"

"Actually, do my eyes look weird to you?"

She put her hands on my shoulders and brought her face close to my face, furrowed her brow.

"Look beautiful, as usual," she said. "You have the prettiest eyes. The shape. The color."

They were my only facial feature that wasn't a direct copy and paste from my mother. Maybe they were my own, or maybe they were my father's. It'd been so long since I'd seen him, I couldn't be sure.

"Thanks, Rosie. I'll let you get to it."

"Right, right," she said. "Promise you'll dance with me?"

"Ha. No chance," I said, grinning. "Death before 'Cha Cha Slide.'"

I shot her a peace sign, then turned around and walked out the front door.

"Boo!" she called after me.

When I stepped out onto the porch, I was met by the chitter of birds and a swift, cool breeze. There'd been an altering, a change that occurred in my absence. The sun had absconded, despite it being just shy of seven o'clock. The heat had withered, and while it wasn't cold, I couldn't say it was warm either. The air had a bitterness to it. An unpleasant feel, an unpleasant scent.

I inhaled deeply and identified the smell as sulfur. A vague tinge of sulfur.

Once I was aware of the odor, I couldn't ignore it. I wasn't sure where it was wafting in from, which direction. I moved toward the barn, hoping it would dissipate, but it only got stronger.

"What *is* that?" I asked no one, because no one was around. Everyone had filtered into the barn; the cocktail area was abandoned. I stood alone under the oak tree, and something compelled me to look up at my bedroom window. Maybe it was that I realized I was standing in the same spot as the lamb I'd seen the night before, and I wondered if it could have somehow sensed my presence, the way I was sensing a presence now.

My heart felt like it was being wrung out. My bedroom light was on, and there was a shadowy figure standing in the window. A person. Someone. Perfectly centered. Looking down at me.

I took a step back for a better view and tripped over a root. I fell through a curtain of branches, barely catching myself before spiraling into the trunk. Air wheezed in and out of my lungs.

And when I crept forward, peered out from the branches, I saw that my room was dark. The light was off. There was no one standing in my window. At least, not anymore. Not that I could see.

My chest was so constricted from the scare, I could barely move, barely get myself out from under the tree. I wondered if I'd gone delirious.

"Vesper." It was my mother. She strutted across the lawn in a new dress. This one was short, above the knee. Strapless. Leather.

She had on a black lace bolero with a frilly collar. Her hair was piled up on top of her head. "I'd ask what you're doing, but . . ."

She kept walking. She'd changed her shoes as well. Her stilettos looked like murder weapons.

I followed her. "Why the outfit change?"

She ignored me.

"What happened to wedding appropriate?" I asked.

"You tell me," she said, holding the barn door open for me. "You're at my table."

I stayed behind her as she slithered between tables and clusters of people in conversation. We turned heads, the two of us. Or maybe just she did.

She looked stunning. Like the movie star she was. The epitome of glamour.

Though most of the other tables were long and rectangular, ours was small. A little circle. There were three place settings.

"Who else is sitting here?" I asked.

My mother downed a glass of champagne that I assumed was meant to be saved for the toast. She tapped her long nails on the crystal, something I'd never seen her do before. She wasn't a fidgeter. I'd only ever known her to hold perfectly, eerily still.

"Vesper, if you want to stare at me, I'm sure you can find a picture on the internet," she said.

I thought of the guy at Shortee's who'd pulled up her Google image page. I thought of what had happened later, the nacho cheese incident that lost me my job, that lost that jerk bro a layer of skin from his face. His voice echoed in my head. *"You have daddy issues, Vesper?"*

"All right, all right, I'd like to welcome you all here tonight. . . ." There was an obnoxious DJ on the microphone. Might have been

Connor, Brody's cousin; I couldn't tell. A pale, lanky dude in his mid-thirties wearing sunglasses that had LEDs around the rims. They flashed different colors. "Are we ready to get this party started?"

No, I thought.

"Lord," Constance muttered under her breath, reaching for my champagne.

"Hey!" My objection was ignored. She drank it in one gulp.

"I'd like you all to make some noise for our beautiful brides-maids and handsome groomsmen. Let's welcome to the dance floor . . . Birdie and Jeff!"

From behind a curtain, they emerged dressed in feather boas and plastic fedoras. They did a bit of choreography, then lined up around the dance floor. This repeated for the next set, and the next set, until I was on the verge of madness, until finally . . .

"And now, the moment we've all been waiting for. Your bride and groom, the new Mr. and Mrs. Brody Lewis!"

They spun into the room, arms up in victory. They took to the dance floor as an indistinct popular ballad started to play. They must have taken lessons; they performed a coordinated waltz. I noticed Rosie had some lamb's blood on her dress, along the hem. I wondered if she'd freaked about the spatter, or if she saw the blood as a badge of honor.

Watching them, I felt not an iota of jealousy, of hurt. In that moment, I accepted the reality that the chasm between their be-liefs and my own always had been and would be too wide to jump. I couldn't long for a life with them in it, because they were indivis-ible from the church. They'd just murdered a lamb. It was impos-sible to wish myself a part of any of it, to long for ties I'd already severed, having been reminded it was for a good fucking reason.

As they waltzed, carefully following the choreography, concentrating, all I could think was, *Nah, all set.*

"Could this song go on any longer?" Constance whispered, more to herself than to me.

"What are you anxious about?" I asked her.

She sighed. "You'll know soon enough."

"Thanks for the cryptic update," I said, my patience wearing thin, my own anxiety mushrooming, becoming unruly. "That's exactly what I was hoping for when I asked. A vague nonanswer."

She snapped her head toward me, and I anticipated a sneer / verbal berating, but her expression was almost sad. Wistful.

The song faded out. There was emphatic applause. The DJ announced the father-daughter dance. Carl jogged out onto the floor, waving like an Olympian crossing a finish line. He and Rosie swayed back and forth to an irritating country song, and I thought about how I used to dance on my father's feet. The only time I ever danced was with him. He was so charming; I would have done anything he asked.

After Carl and Rosie finished their dance, I thought there was hope for dinner, but then Roxanne and Brody had a dance. It seemed an endless parade.

I sipped my water. I noticed my fingers were slightly pruned. I was shriveling up. If something happened to me, I wondered if Constance would display my desiccated corpse in the foyer next to Bart.

"All right, give it up for your groom and his mama, Roxanne," the DJ said. "And . . . sorry?"

The High Priest whispered something in his ear.

Constance smoothed her hair, took a breath, raised her chin, and ran her tongue across her top teeth. She was readying herself for something.

"We who walk the path of fire shall not perish in the flames," the High Priest roared.

I figured he was launching into another sermon, so I stopped listening to him. Instead, I listened to the heavy drumming of my heartbeat, its pace growing faster, faster, faster, faster. My queasiness intensified. My body was frenzied, and I still couldn't understand *why*—why was I so sick with panic? It felt like a coin flip if I was going to pass out or throw up.

And then the screaming started. For one disorienting second, I thought it was me. That I was screaming. But then I realized I was actually the only one who wasn't. It was everyone else. Wild, wild screaming. Primal. Unhinged.

I looked around and saw people sliding from their chairs to the floor, falling to their knees, flailing.

It was fucking pandemonium.

I turned to my mother. She remained upright in her chair. She stared out onto the dance floor. I followed her gaze.

A man stood alone in the middle of the floor. He wore a dark suit. I couldn't see his face; my mother obscured my view. I felt too sick to lean around her for a better look, too sick to move.

"Who is that?" I asked her.

She didn't answer. I thought maybe she couldn't hear me over the screaming.

"Who is that?" I repeated.

A chant broke out. "Hail Satan! Hail Satan!"

It was so incomprehensibly loud. A ringing seared my ears.

My eyes rolled back, up to the ceiling, where the lights twinkled, branches glittered, tea-light candles blushed in their glass orbs—a magical scene contrasting with the ugliness below. The utter chaos.

Summoning strength from some deep pocket of my being—an all-powerful "just get the fuck out!" instinct—I shot up, ready to make an eager dash for the door. But I didn't get far.

The man stood in my peripheral vision. He wasn't a hulking figure, but he had a presence that demanded my attention. A charisma that radiated off him in amber waves. I smelled sulfur, even stronger now, and then a burning, and then something citrusy and woody and curiously familiar.

I pivoted slowly on my heel. Between me and the man was a valley of bodies, stooped, scrambling. They clawed like animals at the floor, at their own faces. Their limbs twitched. They shuddered and sobbed and whimpered and prayed. "Hail Satan," they said. "Hail Satan."

The man raised his hands, and the crowd ceased making any noise. The silence was immediate and absolute. It lasted a long, long time.

I was the one to finally slice it open.

"Dad?"

9

It was him. My father.

"Look at you," he said. "My girl."

"What are you doing here?"

"I'm here to see you," he said. Then he gestured around the room. "And my friends. To join the party."

"Praise be!" someone shouted. "Hail Satan!"

"Uh . . ." I looked over my shoulder to my mother, who blinked rapidly, fake lashes aflutter.

"Everyone," he said. "Please, rise. It is so good to see you all. It's been too long. I . . . have been busy. Very, very, *very* busy."

The crowd buzzed. People began to peel themselves off the floor, return to their seats.

"But I am so grateful to be here tonight. It is because of your unwavering faith and devotion that I can appear before you, and we can celebrate together. The marriage of Rosemary and Brody— an exemplary young couple, don't you think?"

He paused to give everyone the chance to nod, applaud. Agree.

"And, of course, the return of my beloved daughter. The relationship between a father and daughter is sacred, no?"

Again, he paused to receive his approval. His praise.

"Now, if you'll excuse me, she and I have some catching up to do. It's been . . . what? Ten years? I look forward to speaking with the rest of you later in the evening. Please, enjoy the party. In my name, of my name, for my name."

He waved his hand, silver rings catching the light.

"Fourteen," I stammered, my tongue clumsy. "It's been fourteen years."

He approached me, put his arm around my shoulder, and led me outside.

"Can I tell you a secret?" he said. Maybe he was referencing our last visit. Maybe not. Maybe he didn't even remember. "I hate weddings. Mediocre food. This false sense of importance. DJs. Between us, that DJ is burning in hell regardless. No amount of worship, no penance, will save him from the fire."

I was speechless. Stunned. For as long as I could remember all I had wanted was to be around my dad, to be with him. To see him again. And here he was next to me, but it was all wrong.

"What the fuck are you doing here?" I asked him.

"That mouth," he said. "You're quite skilled with profanity. You get that from me."

He leaned against the side of the barn. Casual. Unstressed.

"You're not Hell's Gate."

"Who said that?"

I wanted to respond but couldn't, because I realized no one had ever explicitly told me that my father wasn't in the church. I'd assumed. It was how I made sense of his absence. Why my mother never spoke of him. Why no one in the church ever spoke of him. It was a logical conclusion—either he was an outsider or he'd defected. I never considered . . .

"I . . . I don't understand. . . ."

"I'm not *in* Hell's Gate, Vesper," he said, and lit a cigarette with a match he ignited by pulling it fast between his thumb and index finger. "I *am* Hell's Gate."

I felt my guts knot. "Dad?"

"You were so curious to know my name," he said, exhaling. He offered me his pack of cigarettes. "Sorry, did you want one?"

"Uh, okay." I took one and he lit it for me.

"Good girl," he said as I took my first drag. "So. Do you want to know it? My name?"

"Um . . ." I didn't. I'd changed my mind.

"It's Lucifer," he said. "It'll all make sense. You'll just need to think on it. It wasn't my idea to keep it from you. That was all your mother. She thought it'd be too much pressure if you knew who you really were. Had to eat her words when you left, but I knew you'd be back."

I could almost hear myself break. Hear the lid blow.

"What the fuck are you talking about? You left me. You . . . you abandoned me. And now you show up, and you're telling me— you're really telling me—that you're Satan? That you think you're Satan? As in, the devil? Lucifer."

He took a long drag of his cigarette, appeared contemplative. "It was always interesting to me that you hadn't come around. I know it isn't stupidity. Denial, perhaps? A form of rebellion? This punishing skepticism you've committed yourself to for years now. This refusal to put your faith in anything. So logical . . . it's almost illogical."

I interrupted him. "I have no idea what you're saying. You could be speaking Elvish."

"Elvish?"

"Some nerd language. I don't know."

He laughed. "Are you calling me a nerd?"

"Are you an adult man who calls himself Lucifer?"

"That's my name."

"Sure."

"It is," he said, ashing his cigarette on the lawn. "If you'd stuck around until you were eighteen, we could have been formally introduced at your confirmation. That's when I meet all my followers."

"I'm your daughter. I'm not a follower. I'm your daughter." My voice broke and I was ashamed. He'd been wrong when he said that I'd refused to put my faith in anything. I'd once put my faith in *him*. In a father who loved me. And what a grade A idiot I was for that.

"Vesper . . ."

"You can cut the bullshit with me, Dad. Just tell me the truth."

"I am."

My mother emerged from the dark in silence like a goddamn phantom. She stood beside my father, and he handed her his cigarette. She took a drag, exhaled the smoke out of the side of her mouth. Then they kissed.

They weren't shy about it. It was long and passionate and truly disgusting. I saw tongue.

"Yeah. Don't mind me," I said, covering my eyes.

Is this really my life? I wondered. *How the hell did I get here?*

Then I remembered the invitation.

"It was you," I said to my dad. My parents finally ceased sucking face. "The invitation. You sent it. You invited me to the wedding."

He nodded. "I knew you'd come. Not just because it was Rosemary and Brody, all the history there. But because you were waiting for a reason. Because in those bones of yours, in those veins, is the truth. And it doesn't matter where you go, how far. Doesn't matter what you do. If you work at Shortee's or for the UN. If you pray to me or to another god or to no one. You are who you are. You're my daughter. Nothing will change that."

"Wait. How do you know about Shortee's?"

"I know everything, Vesper. I'm Lucifer. Satan. King of Hell."

I hunched over, hands on my knees, ready to vomit. "No. No, no."

"The devil himself," he said, arms wide. A presentation.

I retched.

"Vesper," my mother said. "Calm down."

I retched again. It was violent, a full-body revolt.

"And if I'm Satan, and you're my daughter, that makes you . . ."

"A fucking tragedy," I said, spitting into the dirt. "So, let me just . . . My mother is a horror icon, and my father thinks he's the devil and secretly runs a faction of Satanists. I should be entitled to free therapy, right? I have to be."

"Vesper," my father said, coming closer. I wobbled back.

"I thought . . . Never mind," I said, again embarrassed by the emotion threading my voice.

"I was your favorite person. You're still mine," he said. I looked up at him, and the way he was looking back at me . . . It was exactly as I remembered. His attention, his energy, his gaze. It was everything. "If you don't believe I am who I say I am, what difference does it make? I've missed you, and I know you've missed me, too. We've been waiting years. Why deprive us of this time?"

I stuttered.

"If you want to go, you're of course free to do whatever you like. But I hope you'll stay. I have no right to ask, but please do not leave me to suffer this reception alone."

"Alone?" my mother said. "Is that right?"

My father raised an eyebrow at me, his mouth darting to the side of his face. It was a signal, establishing a camaraderie between us. Yes, my mother existed, but not really, because she existed outside the bond my father and I shared. She didn't understand us, but my father and I understood each other, in part because we understood what it was to know her. And also because we just did. I got him. He got me. There was this ease. It transcended everything.

I still loved him. He still loved me.

He reached out his hand. "What do you say? Come on. You're too curious to leave now."

He was right. Of course he was right.

"If Satan says." I slipped my hand into his. I couldn't resist, as much as I wanted to. I really wanted to. But it was him. My dad. My favorite person. I'd waited so long to see him again. . . .

"Let's go back in," he said. "Constance."

He offered my mother his free hand. She took it.

The three of us walked back into the barn together.

Everything felt strange, so nothing did. The absurdity of it all somehow blunted itself.

All happy families are alike, I thought. *Every unhappy family is unhappy in its own way.*

Upon our reentering the barn, no one put in any effort. They blatantly stared. We were gawked at through the salad course.

"We should serve this in hell," my father said, stabbing at some watercress with his fork.

"With alfalfa sprouts," I said.

"Yes," he said. "Yes."

"They're good for you," my mother said. "Vitamin K."

"Nothing good for you is ever any fun, is it?" my father asked. He'd somehow acquired a bottle of red wine and poured a glass for my mother, and then for me, and finally for himself. "Cheers."

We clinked glasses.

There were dueling murmurs in my brain. *That man sitting next to you, with whom you share genes, thinks he is the devil. He is gravely delusional, and he is your father.* And then, *It's him, it's him, it's him. He's right there. You're right here. You're together again. You're together.*

"There's no point," he said, shoving his salad plate away. "Life here is so short, and so easily wasted."

"Nihilist," I said, and sipped my wine.

"Who taught you that word?"

I snorted. "Not you, if that's what you're getting at."

We both turned to my mother, who was cutting a cherry tomato in half. "Don't look at me. She was too stubborn to ever learn anything from me."

"Well, where do you think she learned to be so stubborn?" he asked.

Constance shot him a flirtatious grin.

I couldn't tell if I was happy or horrified. The situation felt both completely unnatural and totally normal. The kind of normalcy I'd always craved. A mother and a father and me. Together eating dinner.

Only . . .

With the eyes of a hundred-plus people on us. We were being observed. My father in particular. Because they all thought he was . . .

What are you doing? I harangued myself. *Just sitting here eating*

*salad? Fucking salad? When everyone in this room believes you're literal
Satan spawn.*

The epiphany I had then came down like a guillotine blade.

When I was younger, I'd had this confidence, this attitude of *I
can do anything because someone dumber than me has figured it out.* I
used to tell myself that when filing my taxes, acquiring renters'
insurance, building IKEA furniture, freezing my credit.

But sitting there in the barn, I realized that no, I was actually
the dumbest person. There was no one dumber than me.

Because my whole life everyone had treated me like I was special. Fawned over me. Tried to appease me. And it wasn't because
they loved me or selflessly yearned for my happiness. It was because they believed I was fucking Lucifer Junior. It was Satanic
nepotism.

I chugged my wine, shocked by my own stupidity. Heartbroken
by my obliviousness.

I looked around. I saw Grace and Carl. Rosie and Brody. Everyone. Had they all known?

Was it a giant conspiracy?

"What is it?" my father asked, pouring me more wine.

"These people all know you," I said. "They recognized you."

"As I said, I meet all my disciples at their confirmation ceremony."

"But . . ." I started. It was too much to speak it out loud. Hu-
miliating. "So everyone knows you're my dad. Like, is this common
knowledge?"

"Vesper. Is it really necessary to ask these questions?" my
mother said, taking the bottle of wine from my father and refill-
ing her own glass to the brim.

"Yeah. I'd say so."

We were interrupted by dinner. Plates of pinkish meat, mounds of lukewarm mashed potatoes, pale asparagus.

"Lamb," my father said, unfolding his napkin across his lap. "My favorite."

He cut into it and took a bite. He chewed. I watched the angle of his jaw shift. What was more human than eating? And yet there was something about his movements I found strange. Unordinary. He was so elegant, it was almost awkward. But I figured it was by design. He looked like he didn't belong. He had this aura of exceptionality. It made him fascinating.

"Aren't you hungry?" he asked me.

I shrugged.

"Vesper prefers her food from the microwave," my mother said.

"I do love that microwave flavor," I said. "Delicious radiation."

My father laughed. "Whatever you like. Though, you're my daughter. You shouldn't have to prepare your own food."

"Pressing 'add thirty seconds' isn't really preparing my food."

My mother gave a grunt of agreement.

"You shouldn't be serving others food," he said.

"You never answered me. How did you know about—"

He cut me off, smirking. "I did. I told you. I know everything, Vesper."

That shut me up. He spoke jauntily, but the words themselves carried with them something sinister.

If he'd known where I was, why hadn't he just come to me there? Why the secret invitation? Why all the shady maneuvering?

"Eat," my mother said, so I did. I sat there like an obedient child and ate my dinner. Even though I hated the taste of lamb, hated the texture, hated the idea of consuming such an innocent creature, which was pretty hypocritical considering I'd never had a problem with chicken.

I drank glass after glass of wine.

After dinner, the dancing portion of the evening commenced. Rosie was the life of the party, jumping around to Justin Timberlake, and Daft Punk featuring Pharrell. My father whisked my mother onto the floor at some point, and they danced close. Too close.

"Ew," I muttered into my wineglass.

"You should dance." It was Brody. He sat down in my father's seat.

"What, with you?"

"Well, uh . . ."

"Relax. I wouldn't dance with you."

"Because I'm married?"

I glared at him. "Because you lied to me."

"When?"

"You knew who my father was."

"No, I—" He took a panicked breath. "It was implied that you were important, but not that . . . I didn't know until my confirmation. Until I met him. Until I looked at him, and I realized . . ."

"You could have told me."

"When? You were already gone."

"Last night."

He leaned over, whispered, "You can't keep doing this to me, Ves. You can't expect me to choose between you and my faith."

"You already made your choice."

I looked to the dance floor and saw that Rosie was watching us, wearing a big fake smile. Her eyes gave her away, though. She was jealous.

Brody waved to her, shuffled onto the floor to meet her. He kissed her, and she wrapped her arms around his neck.

I knew then that it didn't matter who my daddy was. I had no allies.

It came on fast again, the urge to run. I didn't want to be there anymore. I wished I'd never come. I wished I'd been smart enough to stay away.

I pushed my chair back as quietly as I could. My body wasn't cooperating. The wine had exacerbated my nausea, and I was now so unsteady, I was afraid I couldn't make it to the door.

"Dance with me," I heard from behind me. "For old times' sake."

It was my dad.

The opening riff of "Sweet Child O' Mine" started to play, and next thing I knew, he was spinning me onto the dance floor. Everyone else cleared off, formed a circle around us. We had an audience.

"Your shoulders are stiff," he said, shouting over the music, which was too loud.

"I hate dancing," I said. "And being watched."

"You hate everything," he said. He seemed kind of proud.

"Do you think that's a good thing?"

"Do *you*?"

"No," I said. "Probably not."

"You're astute," he said. "You see things as they are. People for who they are. The world for what it is."

"Yeah, maybe," I said. I couldn't see the door, the lone exit, through the crowd of people surrounding us.

"The only thing you don't see clearly is yourself. Your power. Your place."

"My place isn't here, if that's what you're getting at," I said. "That, I'm sure of."

"Are you?" he asked. "I wasn't thrilled when you left. But I knew it served a purpose. You would see for yourself. The state of things. The world is ready to burn. And you, my girl, are the match."

"Don't. Don't get into this doomsday bullshit with me. Just save it. Please?"

"You've read the scripture. Whether you believe it or not doesn't change that it's going to happen. The final judgment. The end-times."

"Okay," I said, because what else? Satanists were obsessed with Armageddon; they looked forward to it, talked about it like it was Burning Man.

"Your very existence, your entire purpose, is validation of what you deny," he said, dipping me. The crowd gave an enthusiastic "Aww." "You are the harbinger of the apocalypse."

Bile clawed up my throat, and I was forced to swallow it down, or else spew it all over the dance floor.

I'd had too much wine.

I'd had enough.

Just finish the dance, I thought. *Just make it through the dance.*

"We are in the earth's expiring hours," he said. He spoke with authority, with conviction, and it scared me. Not because I believed it but because he did. He wasn't just some random manipulator who had convinced the members of Hell's Gate that he was their god, which wouldn't have been great but would have been preferable to his being genuinely batshit crazy. To his actually believing that he was the king of fire and brimstone.

It sank in that my father, who'd been this beacon in my childhood memories, was so twisted and ill, he might be dangerous.

It was never a good sign when charismatic men started talking apocalypse.

"Don't pretend you don't agree that it's a wrap on humanity," he said. "You've had the thought. I know you have."

He was right. I'd had that *exact* thought. About two months prior I'd watched a drunk woman eat a mozzarella stick off the floor at Shortee's and thought, *It's a wrap on humanity. We should just call it now.*

"It's time to call it," he said.

I pulled away from him.

"I know about that ledger you imagine inside yourself. The ancient-looking scroll where, with quill and ink, you tally up the incidents that subsidize your cynicism, your lack of faith in humanity. I know because I have a ledger, too. Only mine is real."

I couldn't believe what I was hearing. I couldn't. "I . . . I . . . I'm dizzy. . . . I'm going to pass out. I'm going to pass out."

"You're right to lack faith in humanity. It's done. Over. And if we wait any longer, there will be nothing left for us to inherit. Do you understand?"

"I need to go . . . lie down. I had too much to drink."

He grabbed me by the wrist, pulled me toward him. "You won't get far."

He'd never spoken to me like that before. With malice.

"What?" I said.

"You can't escape me, because I'm in here," he said, stabbing a finger into my chest. "And here." He then gently cradled my head in his hands. "There's no outrunning who you are, Vesper. No hiding. We'll be wherever you go because you'll be wherever you go."

He smiled, and my blood froze.

The song ended and the dance floor flooded, and I took slow steps back through the crowd, which had rushed, bowing and praising, to my father. In a daze—drunk and distraught—I staggered through the barn door, across the lawn, into the house, up the stairs to my room. I frantically gathered all my shit—my clothes, my wallet, my phone charger. I successfully ordered an Uber, which was a small miracle considering how far out in Bumblefuck, New Jersey, I was. It was arriving in twenty minutes. I had twenty minutes to make it out. Again.

The first time I left, I had walked two and a half hours to the bus station in the middle of the night. I was a few days shy of eighteen, afraid but determined.

Now, a few days shy of twenty-four, I was just as afraid, but without that honorable resolve. I wanted to get the hell out of there, sure, but I didn't know how to move forward with the burden of knowing the truth about my father—his involvement in the church, his delusions. He was a psychopath, and worse, my whole family believed him. Believed that I was the daughter of Satan himself. What was I supposed to do with that?

I descended the stairs, taking a final look at the portrait of the anguished man. I didn't find it scary anymore.

I held tight to the strap of my bag and opened the front door.

"Vessie."

Rosemary stood on the porch, between me and the steps down to the yard.

"Hey," I said.

"You're leaving?" she asked, eyeing my bag. "Why?"

"Is that a serious question?"

"You can't leave," she said.

"If you have a problem with it, talk to my dad."

She wouldn't move. I couldn't get around her. "But . . ."

"But what, Rosie? This wasn't a wedding. It was a fucking ambush."

"No! It *was* a wedding. *Is* a wedding. *My* wedding. And you—" She paused, collected herself. "I understand you might be overwhelmed. But all of this is good. Everything is as it's meant to be. And soon, soon, hellfire will consume the nonbelievers, and the earth will be ours."

"Cool. Have fun with that," I said, slurring my words a little. "Now let me through."

"I can't," she said.

I sighed. I was desperate to get her to move. Desperate for my time at home to just be over. To leave again, to put it all behind me, for good this time. So I said, "I kissed Brody last night. Actually, he kissed me. We kissed."

She didn't seem surprised, but she did seem hurt. Her eyes welled up, but she kept it together.

"You both needed the closure," she said.

"You don't want me here. You always wanted to take my place. Wanted my life. You got it. Now let me go. Please, Rosie. If you ever really cared about me. Please."

"It's all right, Rosemary." My mother stood near the oak tree, smoking her electronic cigarette.

"But, Aunt Constance . . ."

"If she wants to leave, she's free to go," Constance said. "There's no point in begging. And we can't force her, now, can we?"

Rosie pouted. "The party isn't over yet. And you just got here. Stay, Vessie. That's what I want."

"Did you know? About my dad?" I asked her. "Did you know?"

"I . . ."

"You know what? Doesn't matter. Good to see you again. I'm glad you're happy. I mean that."

She sniffled and then finally stepped out of the way.

My mother waited for me at the bottom of the steps, began to walk with me down the driveway.

"How could you not tell me?" I asked her. "About him."

"You won't accept any explanation I have to offer," she said. "So I'll go ahead and save myself the trouble."

"Fine. You don't have to worry," I told her. "You won't see me again. I'll stay gone this time."

"Is that a promise?"

I looked at her, marveling at her cruelty, her callousness.

"I don't want to hear from anyone either. I want to be left alone," I said. In the past, I wouldn't have been concerned about this, but now that I knew how "important" I was, it felt necessary. "I'll go to the cops. The press. I will."

I doubt I would have made that threat had I been sober and/or less upset.

"Mm," she said.

"Did you hear me?"

"I never wanted you," she said. "And, ironically, I could never act like I did."

My mouth hung open. She wasn't telling me anything I didn't already know, but to hear her say the words out loud, so unabashedly . . . Straight to my face. No guilt. No shame.

"Goodbye, Vesper."

"Yeah. Goodbye," I told her.

She stopped walking with me, didn't follow me to the end of

the driveway, where I stood waiting for Steve, my Uber driver, who, thankfully, arrived on time.

I ducked inside the car, meeting Steve's eyes in the rearview. He was a younger guy, probably around my age. Long sideburns and a collared shirt he'd probably thrifted for a retro hipster look.

"Big party?" he asked.

"Wedding," I said, shutting the door and locking it.

"Ah," he said. "You're going to the train station? Any trains running this time of night?"

"Guess I'll find out."

He did a K-turn and then we were driving, forty miles per hour down Donner Road. I waited for the relief to set in. For a feeling of freedom. But I just felt shitty. The shittiest I'd ever felt.

I knew there was no romance in a last look. Still, I wanted it. It was a big kind of want. That hunger for a satisfactory end. A neat cut.

I resisted the look. Kept my head straight, eyes forward.

"Was it fun?" Steve asked.

"Sorry?"

"The wedding—was it fun?"

"Oh," I said. "No."

He nodded, didn't ask any follow-ups.

I heard the *cluck-cluck-cluck* of the turn signal, and then we were on Route 6. It seemed a safe enough distance to look out the window, so I did. Only, I saw myself reflected in the glass. My face warped, gaunt, eyes dark.

Between the reaches of streetlamps, my reflection vanished. But whenever it reappeared, in that dull orange glow from the lamps, it was depraved. My face but not my face. Mine but not mine.

I was terrified, but there in the window, I didn't look terrified. I looked terrifying.

Who was I? Whom had I come from?

Why couldn't I have left it alone? Why did I have to go to that stupid wedding? Why did I have to go home?

I closed my eyes and dug my nails into my palms, white-knuckled it all the way to the train station. I made it there just in time to catch the last train.

I fell asleep on the train, face mashed up against the window.

I had a dream. A nightmare.

There was a man coming up the stairs.

He shouldn't have been there.

I was in my mother's house. She'd left me there.

I stood on the landing and watched as the man climbed slowly.

I saw him. His face. The intruder.

I struggled to breathe, out of fear, and because there was a rope around my neck.

No. Around the lamb's neck.

It stood beside me, staring up at me with sweet black eyes.

I woke up panting, scared. My own hands were wringing my neck. I was still wearing the necklace, my necklace. A fucking pentagram necklace.

Had anyone noticed? Had anyone seen?

I fumbled for the clasp. My fingers were too clumsy, my nails too brittle. I struggled.

Off. I wanted it off. Needed it off.

I clamped two shaking fists around the chain and yanked.

There was a loud, ugly clang, and the necklace fell into my hands. Clasp broken.

The necklace later found its way into a trash can at Penn Station.

Laid to rest where it belonged. In hell.

10

Kerri and I sat on my bed eating breakfast sandwiches at three o'clock in the afternoon. I'd texted her late the night before from the train.

I should have stayed estranged from my family.

Bad time, black sheep?

An understatement.

She didn't press me for details. The truth was, Kerri wasn't the kind of friend who was interested in your life, your history, how you were doing. She had main character syndrome. She used everyone around her as springboards, saw us all as opportunities to talk about herself. I was okay with it, mostly because I didn't care to talk about myself. I didn't really care to listen to her talk about herself either, but she was easy enough to tune out.

The breakfast sandwiches weren't to comfort me after a bad weekend with my family; they were an excuse to come over and chat about George, the new manager at Shortee's, Rick's replacement, who was apparently very attractive.

"He's technically my boss, but . . ." she said, and picked a poppy seed out of her teeth. "You know, you could probably come back if you wanted."

"If I wanted," I said.

"You still didn't start that other job, right?"

I'd applied to a few places after Rick fired me. Went on some interviews. I'd received offers to work at a TGI Fridays in a giant, sad mall that was mostly vacant, and at an upscale pub called Beeker's that had cocktails named stupid shit like "the Handsome Pharmacist" and "Sailor's Delight." I'd yet to respond to either.

"JK. Don't come back to Shortee's. Then George will fall in love with you instead of me."

"No, he won't."

"I guess you're right. You're hot, but your personality . . ."

"Yeah, thanks," I said.

"I'm just playing," she said, even though she wasn't.

"I don't know. Maybe I'd go back. Would be easier than starting somewhere new. Learning another menu . . ."

"I'll talk to George," she said. "Any excuse to strike up a conversation . . ."

Kerri stayed into the night. We watched bad reality TV, made microwave popcorn. She was a sufficient distraction. Not sure why, but I found it calming to be around someone whose biggest concern was when she would next get laid. It was a welcome shift to live in her world, where those were the stakes. Much easier than living in mine.

"What did your cousin's dress look like? Was it pretty?" she asked at some point. "Do you have any pics?"

"No," I said, sighing. "And it was . . . nice."

"I really like a traditional ball gown, but I think it'd swallow me up—don't you think?"

I shrugged, changed the subject. "Do you think you'll get new polos?"

"Oh my God. Should I ask George?"

Kerri left around midnight, and for perhaps the first time in my life, I wasn't relieved to close the door on company. I didn't want to be alone—not with my thoughts, not with myself.

I hadn't gotten back to my apartment until three o'clock in the morning. I immediately passed out and slept until noon, and then Kerri came. I hadn't had any time to sit in solitude, to sit with the events of the weekend. To accept that they had all really happened.

I decided I was most upset over the things I'd been wrong about. Thinking my father wasn't a part of the church. Thinking my family and the community I'd grown up in were generally good, loving people—despite being devotees of Satan. Thinking Hell's Gate wasn't a cult, when clearly it was, because it had a leader, who was my dad.

My pride was bruised. I felt stupid, which was worse than feeling hurt or sad or scared.

I also decided I didn't regret going to the wedding, because at least now I wasn't pining over a long-lost father, over Brody, over Rosie and Aunt Grace and a community that valued me for who I was. There would be no more what-ifs, no more missing. No more illusions. Maybe my ignorance had been easier, less painful, but it was still ignorance. Now I knew the truth, brutal as it was.

Still, I was bothered by my father's warning. *We'll be wherever you go because you'll be wherever you go.* Bothered by my mother flat out admitting she'd never wanted me. Could have done without those things. Their words seeped in. I couldn't unhear them, unknow them. They were impossible to extract or dismiss.

Fuck it, I thought. I was *done* done. They could enjoy their little Satanic apocalypse cult. Go full Jonestown for all I cared.

Having slept in so late, I wasn't tired enough to go to sleep now. I decided to unpack.

I unzipped my bag, turned it upside down, and shook, emptying the contents onto my mattress. There were the clothes I'd worn, crumpled. My toiletries—toothpaste, makeup remover. And then there was the picture. The photograph. The one from the nightstand in my childhood bedroom. The one of my father, his hand on my shoulder.

I could feel it in that moment. The sensation. The pressure. A squeeze.

"Nope!" I said, pacing, shaking free of an ethereal grip. "Nope."

Someone had gone into my room, taken the photo out of the drawer, and put it into my bag. They wanted to send me home with a souvenir.

Probably the same person who'd put the photo on my pillow, who'd brought up the glass of water, opened the window.

Probably the same person I'd seen up there when I stood under the oak tree.

Probably my father.

And the guy seemed to know a lot about me. Where I lived. Where I worked. What I thought . . .

Stop, I told myself.

I had to be misremembering. There were certain things he'd

said that he couldn't have said. That he couldn't possibly have said because he couldn't possibly have known.

There was his voice, there in the room with me. "I'm in your head. I'm under your skin. In your veins. Your bones are made of me."

I gasped, spun around. My apartment was empty. Of course it was. I brought the heel of my hand to my forehead, pounded lightly.

Maybe I should move, I thought. *Start over again. Far away this time.*

I sighed, went to the door, and locked the dead bolt.

When I turned back, that was when I saw it. The glint of silver. The necklace. The one I'd sworn I'd tossed into a New Jersey Transit garbage bin. It was there on my bed, among the contents of my bag.

Maybe I'd been so tired and inebriated that I'd confused thinking about throwing it away with actually doing it?

I grabbed the necklace, opened the window, ready to chuck it out onto the street, but the dazzle of diamonds and rubies made me reconsider.

I sat down on my bed, my hands clammy and trembling, the chain rattling. I let the necklace slide from my grasp onto the lump of sheets beside me.

I didn't know what to do with myself. Go for a run? Read? Watch a movie? *The Omen?* I laughed.

Considering I'd recently been informed that I was believed by some to be Damien, essentially, I wondered whether a viewing would be cathartic or damaging. I'd seen it only once. Constance had turned down an audition for a remake and I was curious about just how offensive it was to Satanists. The kid was sort of a drag, made babysitters jump off balconies, I think? I couldn't remember. He did have a 6-6-6 birthmark, which I was certain I did not have.

Pretty certain.

Next thing I knew, I was naked in the bathroom, frantically examining my body with a hand mirror, squinting at every freckle.

"This is stupid," I said. "You're being stupid."

I got into the tub and just sat there, head back against the tile, holding the mirror upside down, spinning the handle in a tight fist. I was too afraid to look at my own face. Afraid that I'd see only my mother, my father. Afraid that my self-image had been further tainted by the time with my family. Afraid that seeing them again had forever altered how I saw myself.

What else could I do to get away from them? What more to separate who I was from who they were?

Maybe I should convert to Christianity, I thought with a snicker, dragging my ass out of the tub and turning off the bathroom light.

I climbed into bed and pulled the sheets up over me. A mild breeze crept in through the window, and with it, a potent smell I chose to ignore.

The smell of smoke. And sulfur.

The next day, I got a call from Kerri asking if I wanted to come in to Shortee's for the dinner shift. She'd spoken to George, who was open to hiring me back after a brief trial run.

"Cool. Love to audition for my old job," I'd said. Though really, I didn't mind. I was happy to have something to do, happy for a return to normalcy. Plus, I was running out of savings and needed the paycheck. "Can I borrow a polo?"

I got to the restaurant at four fifteen, a little early. I met Kerri in the parking lot. She handed me one of her spare polos, one that had seen better days. It was too big, and it smelled like it'd been in her trunk for weeks. Musty with subtle notes of island coconut air freshener.

"Thanks," I told her, pulling it on as we walked around to the kitchen door.

"You're welcome," she said. "Missed you around here. You may be a bitch, but you get shit done."

"Put that on my tombstone."

"Glad to have you back," she said, opening the door for me. "*Your Highness.*"

"What?" I said, my voice breaking like a pubescent teen's.

"It's just a joke," she said. "I'm sorry. I thought you . . ."

"Oh, no. It's fine," I said, shrugging it off. Pretending I didn't hear my father's voice in my head. *Princess of Hell.* "It's fine."

"Wouldn't kill you to be nicer, though, right?"

"It might," I said.

"Hi, George! This is Vesper."

George wasn't what I was expecting. He was maybe five foot ten, sinewy, with a curly mullet and strikingly beautiful face. I was shocked by how good-looking he was, and that anyone blessed with that bone structure would opt for a mullet.

I figured he was in a band.

"Vesper," he said. "Heard a lot about you. Thanks for coming in on such short notice. Sonya called out, and now Toby has the flu. . . ."

"No problem," I said. "Whatever section. I'm game."

"Good attitude," he said. He might have been the only person to ever compliment my attitude.

"Vesper doesn't like bar, right?" Kerri said. "I'm good on bar. I have some regulars. I'm their favorite."

She was attempting to flirt, but George wasn't paying attention. He was examining his clipboard. "Okay, you can take bar."

"Great," Kerri said.

He gave us a nod and then disappeared into the office.

"Isn't he the hottest thing you've ever seen?" Kerri asked me.

"Meh," I said.

I noticed the line cooks staring at me. I smiled and waved.

They were not pleased to see me.

"I'm going to go check the shakers," I said to Kerri, eager to be busy.

"Be my guest," she said, taking her phone out of her pocket.

My shift was slow at first. I refilled all the salt and pepper shakers, wiped down the tables and chairs. But then things started to pick up. It was easy to slip back into it, the restaurant rhythm. I still had the menu memorized, knew what everything cost, where it all was in the system. Could punch in orders without even looking.

"What are you doing here?" Amy, the host, asked me at some point. "I thought Rick fired you for scalding a man's face with nachos."

"He scalded himself, but yeah, essentially, that's what happened."

She popped her gum in my face. "You've got three on six."

The night went on. I made decent tips. Counted out Amy. Counted out Mike, the bartender.

"We're going out after this," Kerri said. "You have to come."

"I don't," I said.

She whined, "Vesper. I need everyone to come so George comes. *Pleeease*. I got you your job back."

I wasn't typically big on coworker outings, but I realized I wasn't ready to go home. Wasn't ready to be alone. Wasn't ready to go back to my apartment to sit around and stare at my ceiling, pretend I hadn't stashed the photograph of my father and the pentagram necklace in my nightstand drawer because I didn't know how to get rid of them. I wasn't ready to battle insomnia, toss and turn while thinking back on my childhood, analyzing my memories in the harsh light of recent developments, wondering what was genuine and what treatment was informed by my parentage, by the fact that everyone at home thought I was the harbinger of the apocalypse. I couldn't bear it.

"Fine," I said. "I'm in."

"*Yaasss!*" she said. Then she cocked her head to the side, frowned. "Did you bring another outfit?"

I had not.

We went to a biker dive nearby, which was open until three a.m. The Black Stallion was the kind of place with more trash on the floor than peanut shells. It reeked of cigarette smoke, of body odor, of cheap beer. Every surface was sticky. There were an old-fashioned jukebox, billiard tables, darts. Junk hung from the ceiling—wagon wheels, barrels, antlers, license plates, a bear trap, a fake shark about four feet long with its painted teeth chipping. In the bathroom there was a condom dispenser covered in graffiti so crude, it was scandalizing even to me.

Though Kerri had asked me to come, aside from a brief wave of acknowledgment, she pretty much ignored me. I sat next to her at the bar, but her back was to me. Her primary focus was George, who had changed out of his polo into a grungy T-shirt that had probably already been ripped upon purchase. A pre-ripped tee.

I judged him for it. I figured between that and the mullet and the stupidly perfect face, there was no chance in hell he wasn't a giant tool.

But when Kerri got up to go to the bathroom and he slid over onto her stool to be next to me, I didn't shut down conversation. I wasn't really in the position. Because it wasn't enough . . . watching people and silently sipping my beer while making bets with myself about the next song someone would put on the jukebox. ("Back in Black" by AC/DC, or literally anything by Johnny Cash, or "Don't Stop Believin'"? All inevitable, but when?) It wasn't enough of a distraction, didn't fill me up enough. Because I saw the couple aggressively making out in the back corner booth as Brody and Rosie. It wasn't them; I knew it wasn't them, but I *saw* them. His hair disheveled, hers perfect, that beautiful strawberry hue.

And the man playing darts in a dark jacket—I was certain that if he turned around, he would have my father's face.

"Hey," George said, chewing on a cocktail straw.

"Hey," I said.

"Good hustle tonight. You'd consider coming back?"

"I'd consider it."

"I'll put you on the schedule."

"Cool," I said, taking my eyes off the man playing darts. I fidgeted with a napkin, folding in the corners to change its shape.

"You seem . . . haunted."

I snorted. "Haunted?"

"Yeah. Am I wrong?"

"I'm not some gothic heroine," I said.

"Really? Could have fooled me."

"Is this your way of telling me to smile?"

He shook his head. "Just making conversation. You're mysteri-ous. Anyone ever tell you that?"

"What are you getting at?" I asked.

He laughed a little, shook his head again. Took a sip of his beer.

"You know what's a mystery?" I asked, tapping his shoulder. "I was wondering. Did you buy this shirt ripped?"

"What?"

"Did you purchase this shirt pre-ripped?"

"Why would I buy a ripped shirt?"

I raised an eyebrow at him. In the act of doing it, I imagined my mother. She appeared before me, giving me the look I was giving George.

"You think I'm a douchebag," he said.

"I didn't say that."

"Yeah, you did."

I shrugged.

Kerri came back from the bathroom, but someone had taken the stool George had been sitting on, so there was nowhere for her to sit. She hovered behind us.

"Hey, guys," she said.

George didn't turn around.

"I'm gonna get another drink. Want anything?" she asked.

"I'm good," I said.

She narrowed her eyes at me. I knew she was pissed that I was talking to George or whatever, but as far as I was concerned, if she didn't want me talking to him, then she shouldn't have invited me. Tough luck.

"For the record, I'm not a douchebag," he said.

"Okay. I'll take your word for it."

There was a moment of quiet between us, and it permeated the bar. I realized there'd been a pause in the music, a lull between songs. And then . . .

The opening riff of "Sweet Child O' Mine."

I felt the blood drain from my face.

"You okay?" he asked.

"I'm going to go . . . get . . . air," I said, hopping off the stool and bolting for the nearest exit, moving as fast as I could with my feet sticking to the floor.

I pushed open a side door and spilled out into an alley. I could still hear the music, still hear Axl Rose singing, *"Reminds me of childhood memories, where everything was as fresh as the bright blue sky . . ."* And I could feel my father's grasp. I could feel his presence. The night smelled of smoke and sulfur, and the air sat heavy in my lungs. I could barely breathe.

"Vesper?" It was George. He'd followed me out into the alley. "What's up?"

"Nothing," I lied. I was in the midst of a panic attack, trying to play it cool. Trying and failing. "I just hate this fucking song."

"Fair," he said. "You sure you're all right?"

"Yeah, I just . . . I think I'm gonna call it," I said. "Uh . . . I guess, let me know when I'm on the schedule."

"You're leaving?" he asked. "You need a ride?"

I didn't, but since he offered . . .

I took a second to get my breathing under control. Then I said, "Sure."

"I'm this way," he said. He led me to the parking lot, to a big white van. "I'm in a band."

"Cool," I said.

"That's why I have the van," he said. "And for child abductions."

"Right. Obviously."

"Obviously." He opened the passenger door for me, and I thought about how he'd followed me into the alley to make sure that I was okay. I thought about how his company was saving me. I thought about Brody, about how long I'd carried a torch for him, without even fully realizing. I thought about our last kiss on the porch. I wanted the memory of it scrubbed from my lips. I wanted to move on. *Needed* to move on. I was finally ready.

"So, where do you live?" George asked.

I gave him directions, knowing that when we got there, I'd be inviting him up. I tried to think of a clever way to do it, but upon arrival, I just said, "You can park here. You won't get a ticket."

He nodded, pulled into a spot in front of my building.

"You want me to come in?" he asked, pulling up the parking brake.

"Yeah," I said. "Sorry, I'm not actually that mysterious."

He laughed. "Don't know about that. Is this cool? We do work together. Is that cool?"

"Cool with me if it's cool with you," I said. I wasn't sure if I liked him yet, but I wasn't sure that I needed to.

What I needed was not to be alone. What I needed was a distraction. Somebody new. Just somebody.

We walked in silence up the three flights of stairs to my apartment, and when I opened the door, I declined to apologize for the state it was in. Bed unmade, dirty clothes on the floor, jar of peanut butter left open on the kitchen counter.

"You live by yourself?"

"Yeah," I said. My phone buzzed in my pocket. I had a text from Kerri.

Did you leave with George?!?!

Another came through.

Like really??

Another.

What is wrong with you??? How could u do this 2 me???
You're legit the worst!!!

I sighed, put my phone facedown on the kitchen table.
Legit the worst.
"I like your look," George said.
"My what?"
"Your look. Your vibe. The hair," he said, sitting down on the couch.
"Thanks," I said.
"Would you ever consider being in a music video?"
"No, I wouldn't," I said. "Sorry."
"Really?"
"Camera shy," I said. "You want water? It's all I have to offer you. Maybe a single can of diet cola that's been in there since . . . Actually, I don't know when or how it got there."
"I'm all set."
"No? Don't want to see what happens if you drink the cola?"
"I think I have a pretty good idea of what would happen."

I laughed. Maybe I did like him. He had a sense of humor, the aesthetic of an eighties bad boy heartthrob. He sort of reminded me of Dylan James, the actor who had played Jackson Perry in the original *Death Ransom*, Constance's breakout movie. Jackson was my mother's—well, her character's, Kristal Link's—doomed love interest. Mr. Ransom decapitates him slowly with his hatchet while a restrained Kristal is forced to watch, helpless. Then the head is tossed at her feet, and she sobs over it. It was a stirring performance, I have to admit. But the Academy doesn't give Oscars to scream queens. Only trophies they get are severed heads.

Rosie didn't like to watch my mother's movies but would watch the parts of *Death Ransom* with Dylan James in them. She thought he was "dreamy."

Maybe this thought had some influence over what I did next.

I straddled George on the couch. He ran his hands up my thighs, up to my waist, up past my waist. To my neck. Then he kissed me.

It wasn't better or worse than the Brody kiss. Just different.

Good enough.

He escalated things quickly. My shirt was off. Then my bra. We both smelled like the Black Stallion, like Shortee's. Cigarettes and onion rings. But that weirdly added to the mood. Passionate filth.

My pants were off. I was on my back.

His pants were off.

"Shit," he said. "Do you have any condoms?"

"Nightstand," I said.

Like the diet cola in the fridge, the condoms in the top drawer of my nightstand also had uncertain origins. I figured they were probably fine.

He got up, and a second later I heard him say, "Whoa."

"What?"

I sat up on the couch and saw that he was holding the necklace. My pentagram necklace. My Hell's Gate collar. The one I seemed unable to get rid of.

"What's this about?"

"Uh, long story," I said.

"Are these real diamonds? Is this real?"

"I'm naked. Are we . . ."

"Right," he said.

He got a condom and came back to the couch. I lay there while it happened, trying not to think about how as soon as it was over he'd inevitably bring up the necklace again. I did what I could to get into it. I dug my nails into his back, pulled his mullet. He kissed my neck, which was nice. But I couldn't be present, couldn't be there in my body. I was too in my head. It was hard to climax when all I could see before me were swirling pentagrams. Fire and brimstone and childhood trauma.

He came, though. He stuttered; his breath got shallow.

"Goddamn," he said. He got up and went to the bathroom, and I put my underwear back on, threw on my Black Sabbath T-shirt. I drank a glass of water.

Do I feel normal? I asked myself. *Like a normal twenty-three-year-old? Like a normal person?* The answer was no.

I knew it always would be, and I was foolish to hope for anything different. *Hope is like candy,* I thought. *It's sweet in the moment, until it rots your teeth out.*

My past would always be my past. My family would always be my family.

So I'd never be fucking normal.

"Pentagram necklace," George said, pulling on his boxers. "Should I be worried? Are you going to sacrifice me? Drink my blood?"

He was teasing. He didn't know any better. Still, something in me snapped.

"Actually," I said, hugging my knees to my chest, "I was raised in a Satanic cult."

He laughed, but then he looked at me and his expression went grim. "You're serious?"

"Uh, yeah."

"You're not fucking with me?"

"Wish I was. Trust me."

He sat beside me on the couch. "Wait. What?"

"I was raised in a Satanic cult. I didn't know it was a cult. To me it was just . . . I don't know. Normal."

"Whoa," he said, leaning back, running his fingers through his mullet. "Really? I mean, I believe you. But damn."

I'd never told anyone before, so I was intrigued by his reaction. More curious than emotional about divulging my biggest secret.

"Like, ritual sacrifices in the woods and shit like that?" he asked. "Sorry. I'm trying to wrap my mind around it, but I want to be sensitive. That's . . . really insane. Are you okay?"

"Am I okay?"

"Yeah," he said, pulling my ankles to straighten my legs. He held them across his lap. It was a weird form of cuddling, a quick intimacy I hadn't anticipated.

"I don't know. Is anyone? Are you?"

He clicked his tongue. "Point taken."

"Families are complicated. I'm not the only one out here with shitty parents. Sure, mine are epically shitty. But . . ." I shrugged.

"Some people love their family. Other people . . . can't. I can't love mine."

"Do you still talk to them?" he asked. "Or is it that weird cult thing where if you don't fall in line, they pretend you don't exist?"

"The latter," I said.

"Damn. I'm not super close with my family, but we get along for the most part. I guess I can't really picture my life without them. Like, if I never spoke to them or saw them . . ." He sighed and squeezed my feet. "Must be hard."

"I don't know. It's not so much being without them that's hard. What's hard is . . ." I paused, unsure of how to articulate what I was thinking, what I was feeling. "It's me. The parts of me that are them. That were forged by them. Things they did to me, they said to me. Things I can't change, can't undo."

"Damage," he said. "They did damage. I'm not calling you damaged."

"Did you not hear the part about how I was raised by Satanists?" I asked. "I'm pretty fucking damaged."

He laughed. "I think you're pretty fucking awesome."

Maybe I'd never be normal, but maybe I could be happy.

He leaned over and kissed me, and I tasted the sweetness of hope. For once, I allowed myself to savor it, without worrying about what it might do to my teeth.

11

George slept over the night we hooked up, and in the morning, he took me to breakfast. We got French toast at the diner, shared a side of bacon and a sad fruit salad—which was, predictably, disappointingly, mostly honeydew. We drank hazelnut coffee. I wondered if it was a date. If a meal after you'd already fucked counted as a date.

I sort of figured the presence of maple syrup implied there were no regrets, at least.

We were midway through breakfast before he brought up Satanism again. I was almost relieved when he did, so I could stop anticipating the unavoidable *when*.

"I watch a lot of cult documentaries," he said, snapping the last piece of bacon in half for us to split. "But I've never met someone who was in a cult."

"Usually they keep us in zoos," I said, accepting the bacon. "Netflix and HBO and Hulu zoos. They give us branded bottled water, put us in cells that are actually conference rooms. Watch us through the glass. When they're ready, they bring us out to interview. Put us in armchairs, angled to the side a little. Ask us their questions. Take us back to the conference room to wait in case there's enough interest to squeeze out a second series."

"Not you, though."

"I can't be tamed."

"Of course," he said.

A waiter came by to pour us more coffee. I thanked them.

"We don't have to talk about it if you don't want," he said. "But it's hard not to be curious. With cults . . . it's not easy to get out."

"Not everyone wants to," I said. "Most don't."

"Yeah. It's brave, what you did. Leaving. I just want to make sure that you're, like, okay."

"Believe it or not, I existed before we met," I said. "I'm fine."

I realized by his face that I'd been too harsh, so I backtracked. I said something out of character. "Sorry. I appreciate your concern."

I wasn't sure if I meant it. Did I want him to be concerned about me? Maybe I did want him to care, but I wanted him to care about *me*. Me as a person, not me as an escaped Satanist.

But, thinking about it, how much of my identity was my past?

I was overcome with this urge to *live*. To stick up the diner, take all the cash in the register and get on a bus and another bus and a plane and a train and end up somewhere unexpected. To have random affairs with strangers, cover my entire body in tattoos. Drop acid in the desert, sun myself on the Amalfi Coast. To hike on a glacier, to see the northern lights. I wanted to live enough life to render everything in my past small and insignificant. But even still, I couldn't make it go away. I couldn't erase it.

I heard my father's voice again, as if he were there beside me. "There's no outrunning who you are, Vesper. No hiding."

"My dad was the leader," I said to George, who was sorting through the bowl of jams in search of a particular flavor. "I didn't find out until recently. He calls himself Lucifer. He thinks he's Satan."

George's lips parted as if he were going to speak, but instead he sort of just made this noise, a grunt, like he'd been punched in the gut.

"You know, it's almost like you've never had a girl tell you her dad claims to be Satan over breakfast before," I said.

"Yeah," he said, cracking a grin. "First time for everything."

"Happy to be your first."

He laughed, nearly spitting out his sip of coffee.

The waiter cleared our plates and George paid the check. He dropped me back at my apartment, kissed me on the lips.

"I'll let you know the schedule," he said. "I'll see you."

I nodded. He waited until I was inside before he drove away, which seemed like a gentlemanly thing to do.

It was promising that I'd told him the truth and he hadn't taken off, slammed on the gas, burned rubber. If I were him, I probably would have. One thing to date someone with baggage, but with my baggage? A whole other beast.

When I got upstairs, I found the necklace and the photograph of my father in the center of my unmade bed. Not where I'd left them.

I didn't think George would have set them there, but I didn't have any other explanation. At least, not one that I dared to entertain.

I put them back in my nightstand and got my laptop, ready to melt my brain with YouTube videos, fuck around on the internet for the rest of the day. Instead, I found myself watching *Death Ransom*.

I'd seen it so many times, I knew it by heart, could quote it in my sleep. Maybe it was messed up that I found a movie starring my estranged mother about a vengeful interdimensional grim reaper brutally killing teenagers to be so comforting, but whatever. Some parts were cheesy as shit, there were plot holes, some of the dialogue was cringe, and some of the kills were excessive, but there was catharsis in the screams, in the brutality that I knew wasn't real.

And the determination to survive in the face of such horror was something I admired. When Kristal Link stabs Mr. Ransom in the hand with her cool skull hairpin and gets control of his hatchet, kills him with his own weapon, that moment of triumph, *that* always felt real. Felt earned. Felt hopeful.

Sure, the victory is short-lived. Mr. Ransom comes back in the sequel. But maybe I found comfort in that, too. The devil you know.

I finished the movie, then took an escapist nap.

George didn't put me on the schedule until Thursday, so I spent two days languishing in my apartment. I did laundry, bought groceries, cleaned the oven, behind the oven, the fridge, behind the fridge. I binged a show that everyone on the internet loved. I hated it. I masturbated, and for the first time I thought of someone other than Brody. I thought of George, attempting to summon what he felt like on top of me, how he moved. How he smelled.

I granted myself permission to fantasize about a future. To dream of an existence beyond survival mode. I'd been so focused on the logistics of living—earning money, paying bills, paying

taxes, not running out of deodorant. For years, I think I intention-
ally neglected to aspire to anything else, maybe out of fear of failure, or of truly moving on. I had definitely neglected to confront
what I'd been through, and examine my emotional state. I'd suppressed all sentiment. I sort of had to.

My feelings had always scared me, felt dangerous. But maybe
I could open myself up. Not hammer down my emotions like I
was playing a game of Whac-A-Mole where the prize was profound apathy.

Maybe I could try.

And yeah, I hadn't always been the kindest or sweetest or bub-
bliest person. But maybe I could be different, be good. Maybe it
didn't matter who I'd been, or what I'd come from.

Maybe I could change. Prove to myself I wasn't who my family
thought I was.

Getting ready for my dinner shift Thursday, I put on makeup.
Mascara, lipstick. A spritz of perfume. Product in my hair to give
it some structure, some edge. I found a spare polo in the back of
my closet. I ironed it. I actually ironed it.

I knew Kerri was pissed at me, but I had tried not to worry too
much about it, hoping she might have cooled off. She hadn't.
When I got to Shortee's, I walked into the kitchen to discover
everyone glaring at me. The line cooks. The rest of the waitstaff.
Kerri herself.

She stood at the window, arms crossed, scowling.

"Hey," I said. I considered apologizing. If I was going to turn
over a new leaf and attempt to be a better person, a "sorry" seemed
like a solid place to start, requiring minimal effort. But before I
had the chance, she scoffed, turned her back to me, and stormed off.

She'd rallied the troops against me. Everyone loved Kerri; she was chatty and fun. Open. Kerri was very open. Too open, in my opinion. But what did I know? It worked for her. She was warm and likable; I was cold and unlikable.

I remembered something Rosie had said to me over the weekend. *I know you, Vessie. You're more like Constance than you like to think.*

I shuddered.

"Hey, Vesper," George said, poking his head out of the office. "Can I talk to you for a sec?"

"Sure."

I stepped into the office, and he closed the door. He kissed me, pressing my back into the wall. I wrapped my legs around him. It was a pleasant surprise.

He pulled away, and I nuzzled into his neck, smiling in spite of myself.

"I can't believe I'm into a guy with a mullet," I said.

"I can't believe I'm into the devil's daughter," he said.

I wasn't sure how the joke sat with me yet, but wanting to be warm instead of cold, I laughed.

"I did call you in for a reason," he said. "A less fun one than that."

"Okay," I said.

"Is Kerri going to be a problem?"

"What do you mean?"

"She's been acting weird, and I don't want her to—"

"Narc to corporate?"

He snapped his fingers and pointed at me.

"She has no proof of anything," I said.

He bit his bottom lip. "She tried to come in earlier. Said she needed to talk to me about something. I told her I was busy. Probably can't avoid her forever."

"If she brings anything up, just deny it."

"You haven't said anything to her?"

"Yeah, no. I'm not stupid," I said, though it really sank in then that hooking up with my manager whom my friend/coworker had a crush on was pretty fucking stupid. Why did I always have to make things so hard for myself? Why did I gravitate toward chaos?

Maybe I really am the Antichrist, I thought.

"I know you're not," George said.

"What?"

"Stupid. I know you're not stupid. I, like, didn't mean to put either of us in a tough spot."

"It's fine. But I should probably get out there," I said. "Longer I'm in here . . ."

"Right," he said, opening the door. "If you need anything, let me know."

I gave him a nod and headed out onto the floor.

Since Amy had been recruited to Team Kerri like the rest of the staff, I had a slow night. She avoided sitting parties in my section, so I pretty much just stood around. Kerri seemed to take some satisfaction in this, sporting a smug grin as she hustled back and forth from the kitchen. I didn't care. I could wait it out. She wouldn't be mad at me forever. She got a new crush every other week. And Sean would come back around eventually.

My shift dragged on. The dinner rush passed. Then came the late wave. Teens after practice. Single dads post–drop-off. Construction crews. Wine-night ladies. The bar was crowded, and at some point I walked past carrying a tray of boneless wings, and out of the corner of my eye I saw a man in a dark suit with silver hair. He was sitting at the counter, so his back was to me. I couldn't see his face.

While I was staring at the man, getting absolutely wrecked by dread, not paying attention to where I was going, I tripped on something. I barely managed to catch myself, to keep the tray of wings somewhat steady. There was some minor ranch spillage, but that was it.

Though I didn't fall, I did reap the attention of the entire restaurant. Not the man at the bar, though. His back remained turned.

I delivered the wings with a fake smile and a corny "That was a close one!" I hated myself for it.

I dashed back to the bar, but the man was gone. His stool empty, leaving a void like a missing tooth.

I had no way of knowing if it was my father or not.

My heart took off thump, thump, thumping furiously, so furiously. It felt like, sounded like, all the blood in my body was gushing out of my ears. I was queasy, and hot, and deathly thirsty, and all of a sudden, I couldn't breathe.

I ducked into the bathroom and hid in a dirty stall, silently pleading with my lungs, with my body, to just cooperate. To calm down. Staring at wads of soppy toilet paper surrounding my feet, I contemplated creation. I didn't make my body. My parents did. I came from them, from their bodies. It made me sick to think about. To live with. It was making me so sick.

I wanted to stuff my fist down my throat and claw out my insides. I wanted to peel away my skin. I wanted to crack my skull open like an egg, scoop the yolk. Lobotomize myself. I wanted to never think about my parents again.

But how could I forget them when they were everywhere?

Maybe George had been right about me. Maybe I was haunted. I didn't know how to exorcise myself.

This is why feeling is dangerous, I thought. *This is why hope is stupid.*

I opened the stall door and went to the sink, splashed some water on my face. I looked up and saw her in the mirror. Kerri. She stood behind me.

"Hey," I said.

She leaned a hip against the vanity.

"Look, Kerri, I—"

"When you first started here, I tried to figure you out," she said, circling behind me. "I thought you were just, like, a textbook pretty girl. Popular in high school, got away with everything because of your looks . . . I wondered why you didn't model or do pharmaceutical sales or something. You work hard, but you're not ambitious. You're snobby, and you're mean, but it's not, like, intentional. You don't even realize. You don't even care."

"Okay, Kerri. Can I apologize now? Because I—"

"Let me finish," she said, crossing behind me again, stepping between me and the door. "Sometimes I'd feel bad for you, like I felt bad for Rick. Like, wow, their lives must be so sad . . ."

Now . . . now she'd started to piss me off.

"Like, why is she like this? I didn't get it. And I felt bad when you got fired. I really did. Because I'm an empath. So I felt it." She put her hands over her heart. "The stuff with your family—it made sense to me. Like, okay, maybe there's something dark in her past. Maybe that's why she's not super friendly, has a wall up. But I didn't realize the extent of it. And now I get it."

"What?" I asked. "What are you talking about?"

Though I knew. I already knew.

I felt the knife in my back.

"I *told* you how I felt about George. When I was at your place comforting you. I brought you a bagel."

It smelled like piss and bleach and frying oil. And smoke. It smelled like smoke . . . smoke and sulfur.

"I was done with you. But now that I know, now that I have the full context . . . it makes sense."

"What context?" I asked.

"George told me everything. And, sorry, I'm not great at keeping secrets—you know I'm not," she said. "You grew up in a Satanic cult. No wonder you have no social skills."

I squeezed my hands into fists. I was angry at George, at myself for trusting George. Just angry, beyond angry. I couldn't stand the way that Kerri was speaking to me. Mocking me. She was pushing a bad button. "Kerri, stop."

She gave a little laugh. "Aww, honey. No judgment from me. I'm serious. But I've literally never met anyone who needs therapy more than you. You need to talk to someone."

"Kerri . . ." I said, her name sizzling on my lips.

"You should have told me. It explains a lot about you. Honestly, it explains everything about you. The other night when you left with George, I was, like, she's the devil. I had that thought. I—"

She took a step toward me and slipped in a puddle of what was hopefully water.

She fell forward, mouth open. She should have kept it shut—she really, *really* should have kept her mouth shut—because the sharp edge of the counter was waiting.

It was almost beautiful. Like a shower of pearls.

Only they weren't pearls. They were her teeth. Shattered, scattered in pieces across the bathroom floor. Some shards stayed stuck in her gums, which bled profusely.

Her hands reached up, as if trying to catch the blood, the waterfall. Her fingers made their way into her mouth, where they encountered the damage.

Her eyes went wide as billiard balls. She tried to scream, but there was too much blood. She began to choke on it.

Part of me was horrified.

And part of me felt nothing. Indifferent.

"*Heellpp . . . me . . .*" she stuttered, blood seeping. She leaned over, attempting to gather up her teeth, little specks of white on the floor, swimming in red. "*Helpp-ppp-pp.*"

I grabbed some paper towels and sank to my knees, getting blood all over my khakis, my polo. "Shit."

A customer walked into the bathroom, promptly screamed, and ran out. Amy came in a second later.

"Jesus Christ," she said.

Not quite, I thought.

"She fell," I said. "She hit the vanity."

Amy looked skeptical. She popped her gum. "Okay . . ."

"Can you call nine-one-one?" I asked.

"You call," she said. She pushed me aside so she could tend to Kerri. "Kerri, did you fall? Demon Bitch didn't push you, right?"

"Dude!" I said, insulted. But thinking about how she had fallen, how strange it was, and how violent the result . . . in that moment, I could no longer trust myself. I didn't know what to believe.

I stood up. My lungs seized. It reeked in the bathroom, and I was desperate for a clean inhale. Fresh air. I looked down and saw my clothes were soaked in Kerri's blood. I had to get out of there. I had to get out.

I opened the bathroom door. Customers were on their feet, staring. The woman who'd come in and seen us must have made a fuss. There was a crowd. An air of perverse curiosity.

"Okay, everyone. There was an accident in the women's bathroom. It's being taken care of. Everybody's okay." George had come out to make an announcement.

George.

I stormed past him, but he caught up with me, and somehow we ended up in his office.

"What happened?" he asked me.

"Well, Kerri came into the bathroom to tell me what I terrible person I am, and then she slipped because the floor's wet because I'm guessing no one's cleaned the bathroom today—way to stay on top of it, boss. Oh, and thanks for telling her about my past. Really appreciate you sharing my Satanic trauma with everyone."

"Vesper—"

"A staff meeting would have been more efficient, I think. Everyone all at once. Though I'm sure Kerri spread the word pretty quick."

He pushed his hair back from his forehead. "Fuck. I told her not to say anything."

"Really? That's your defense?"

"I didn't realize no one else knew. She came in here complaining, and I said she should take it easy on you because of everything you'd been through. I thought I was doing you a favor."

"Yeah. Big favor."

"How was I supposed to know?"

"Know what? That I don't advertise my unconventional upbringing?"

"We barely know each other, and you told me."

He had me there.

I couldn't blame him for my own bad judgment.

This was why I couldn't be open. Why I couldn't be warm. Could never be normal.

I pictured the massacre that was now Kerri's face. My stomach churned.

"You're right. I'm sorry. This is on me," I said.

"No," he said, rubbing his temples. "I'm sorry. This is my fault. This got messy because I let it get messy. I wasn't thinking straight. It's my bad . . . and I'm really sorry . . . but I think it would be best if—"

I hope I at least get another consolation margarita, I thought.

"It's fine," I said, cutting him off before he could fire me. I took off my bloodstained polo and threw it in the trash can. "Everyone here thinks I'm a freak now anyway."

"No one thinks that."

"Sure," I said, adjusting the strap of my tank top.

"*I* don't think that. I hope we can stay cool. Hang out again. I really am sorry about all this."

I wanted to accept his apology, to wrap myself around him. Go back to making out, imagining more breakfast dates at the diner, more late nights on the couch, my legs across his lap. Return to the hope I'd felt that night we slept together. But I couldn't.

"Vesper, I'm sorry."

"Yeah, I bet you are," I said, opening the door to the office and heading out into the kitchen. The line cooks stood and gawped at me through the window. I knew they knew. I could tell. Restaurant gossip travels fast.

I hate this place, I thought. *I hope it fucking burns.*

Flames burst from the stove, punching up toward the ceiling. The smoke was thick and black as tar; it rolled forth like a tsunami—a doom rumbling and ruthless.

Wait, I thought. *Wait, wait.*

One of the line cooks had the fire extinguisher. He sprayed the flames dead.

"What the . . ." George was behind me, aghast.

Everyone in the kitchen—the cooks, the waitstaff, bussers, dishwashers, George—all turned to me in unison, jaws slack.

"Yeah, that was me," I said, sarcasm disguising my dread. "Hellfire, right?"

I grabbed my bag from my cubby, kept my head down, and left, pretending I didn't hear George calling after me.

I didn't know what to do with myself. It was ten p.m. on a Thursday. There was blood on my khakis. I was too anxious and upset to go home.

Where can I go with bloody clothes and five dollars to spend? I wondered.

There was only one place.

Twice in one week, I thought, walking into the Black Stallion. *This is not a good week.*

The Black Stallion Saloon was not an ideal place for a young woman by herself. But I looked rough enough that I figured no one would bother me. I ordered the cheapest beer they had—two dollars—and sat at a small table that had only one chair. I bit my cuticles, chugged the beer.

I looked around at all the junk. The rusted license plates. The neon signs on the walls, all with dead letters, creating a language of nonsense. The fake shark that was suspended directly above me, made of plastic or Styrofoam or whatever. Its teeth bothered me because they reminded me of Kerri's teeth. How they'd cracked into jagged peaks. Because I'd wanted them to. Because I'd wanted her to shut up.

Stop, I told myself. *The floor was wet. She slipped. It was an accident.*

And that fire . . . *Also an accident. The cooks weren't paying attention.*

And a few weeks ago, the face scalding . . . *An accident. An accident . . .*

I remembered the sound of that guy's screaming, a tortured pitch. I remembered the smell of hot cheese and burning skin. . . .

How many strange misfortunes had I seen play out when I was angry? Not merely angry, but wrathful. At the wedding, my father had mentioned power. I'd never entertained the idea of power, because why would I? Why would I have believed that it was possible to make shitty things happen out of sheer will? How could I ever imagine the immensity of my badness? I hadn't even known who I was—who I *supposedly* was—until a few days prior.

I was eager to dismiss it all—I didn't believe in powers or magic or gods or any of that pixie-dust bullshit. I never had, and I refused to start because of my delusional father. I understood that belief was a slippery slope. If you wanted to believe in something, opened yourself up, suddenly you were seeing signs, assigning meaning, taking coincidences as proof. I wouldn't. I couldn't. . . .

I wanted to think about anything else, but my mind went straight to the strangest misfortune of my life. The intruder.

Of all my bad memories—the wide, wide selection—this one was the worst. It was the only scab I found too painful to pick, but in that moment I felt a deep, pleading need to reopen the wound, to root around in my pain. Because in that moment it became clear to me that there was something I'd missed back then, all those years ago.

I went dizzy with panic, and I went back to that night.

I was up in my room. It was late but I wasn't asleep. My mother was gone. Whatever. She was always away filming. Always leaving me alone in the house. I was used to it. I'd memorized its sounds. The clatter of shutters in the wind. The groans of the floorboards. The nervous scurry of critters in the walls, in the attic. The whistle of air infiltrating through a crack.

Though I knew these sounds, they still alarmed me. Of course, any disruption of quiet when you're a young girl home alone is unnerving. But they were familiar. I could identify and release.

But this night—this night, I heard a sound that was not familiar. It sat me straight up in bed.

It was the door creaking open. The front door. It wasn't subtle.

I could have sworn that I'd locked it.

The only other person with a key—aside from me and my absent mother—was Aunt Grace, and she wouldn't be dropping by past midnight.

No. I knew in my gut that whoever was coming into the house was not welcome. Their intentions were not good.

I stayed still as a statue, just listening to them. To the floorboards complaining under foreign weight. Whoever it was, they roamed aimlessly around the first floor, opening and closing cabinets, doors.

What were they looking for?

What were they after?

What did they want?

That was the worst question. Worse than What do they look like?

or How long until they get to me? *or* Do they have a weapon? *or* Should I try to run, try to hide?

I reached for my phone to call Aunt Grace, but I was clumsy in my terror, and it fell from my nightstand to the floor with a loud clunk.

And then I heard the intruder change course. I heard them start up the stairs.

Each squealing step confirmed my fear—the slow ascent of a dire threat.

I had my answer now. They were looking for me. They were after me. They wanted me.

I had nowhere to run. The only way out was down the stairs, and they were on the stairs.

This isn't happening, *I thought.* Please let this not be happening.

What a cruel thought—Let this not be happening.

I slid out of bed on jelly-coward legs, stumbling to the door to lock it.

What difference will this make? *I wondered.* If they've come this far . . .

I grabbed my phone off the floor and called Grace. There was no dialing 9-1-1 in Hell's Gate. The police were outsiders. Infidels.

She didn't answer.

The doorknob began to twist, and as I stood with my back to the wall, watching, I thought it ironic that my mother was off acting in a horror movie and I was actually living in one.

The knob shook. The intruder was frenzied.

They didn't just want me. They wanted me badly.

For what? *I wondered.*

Violence, probably.

My fingers found the hem of my oversized sleep shirt. It was so flimsy, the material. I felt dumb for not wearing armor. I was curious if everyone felt this way when they were in physical danger, when bodily harm was impending. Why didn't I wear a suit of armor? Where was my shield?

I supposed chain mail wasn't practical. I supposed shields were heavy. I found it a hassle to carry ChapStick.

And weapons? Was I meant to sleep with a knife under my pillow?

My whole life I'd been told to trust in the Lord, to "Hail Satan!" And I wondered if maybe I should have. Maybe I should have prayed more. Believed. Had faith. But even in such a state of peril, I knew it wouldn't have made a difference.

I was about to suffer violence, to die at the hands of a stranger in my own bedroom. And where was Satan? Where was my mother? My father? My family? The only person there for me was the one who sought to do me harm.

I thought, Maybe I should just go open the fucking door.

But I didn't need to. They'd already started to kick it down.

It was a bad racket. Loud, ugly thuds. A boot against wood. It took a few tries, but they got it.

He. He got it down.

A man I didn't recognize.

He was sickly pale, had a receding hairline, a large head. Very large. He was shiny. The moonlight reached in through the window, and he reflected it right back out. His features were nondescript.

We stared at each other for a moment. He seemed almost surprised, like he hadn't expected me. I figured then that he was probably one of my mother's rabid fans. A Constance Wright stalker. Of course. He probably had expected to find her, not a petite, disgruntled clone.

I got tired of waiting for him to do something. For him to hurt me.

"What?" I said to him finally. More exasperated than afraid.

He raised something up high over his head, and it glinted in the moonlight. I assumed it was a knife, but thinking back on it, I couldn't be sure.

"The daughter," he said. His voice trilled with fear, which was weird because he was the one who'd broken into my room in the middle of the night and was thrashing some kind of weapon around at me—a teenage girl.

He took a step forward. He held the knife, or screwdriver, or whatever, out in front of him. He approached me weapon first.

"No!" I was stern in my delivery. Authoritative. I wasn't pleading. Ever since the man had entered my room there had been no real fear on my end. There wasn't bravery either. Not exactly. I just no longer felt I was in any danger.

I don't know why.

But it was clear from what happened next that I was right.

"Stop," I told him, and he did. The man stopped moving forward. He turned pea soup green and made a noise like a cat whose tail had just been stepped on.

Then he turned around and sprinted out of the room.

I assumed he must have had a change of heart. That he couldn't actually go through with the violent fantasy that had brought him up the stairs and into my bedroom. Maybe he was disappointed that I wasn't my mother. Maybe he drew a line in the sand when it came to kids. Breaking and entering? Sure. Unless there are children involved!

Didn't matter. Whatever the reason, I didn't care. He was leaving.

But he wasn't going quietly. He continued to whimper, make that manic-cat sound.

I couldn't help it.

I wanted to know why.

So I followed him. I stepped out onto the landing and watched as he hurried down the stairs, arms flailing.

He must have heard me coming, because he looked over his shoulder, and as he did, he lost his balance. He tripped.

There are two ways to fall down the stairs. One leaves bruises. The other kills you.

The man pitched forward, not backward. That was the first clue as to which type of fall it would be. He didn't break his fall. His arms got tangled behind him somehow, so his face hit first. There was a crunch that I'd soon realize was his nose breaking. He slid down the rest of the way to the second-floor landing. The momentum flipped him onto his back. His pale melon head was now marred with a big red indentation. His nose was in different places, interrupted by a peak of white. Bone poking through skin. I'd never seen a face in such disarray.

The man's eyes began to swell. Through the rapidly expanding mounds of flesh I saw two dark pupils shoot toward me, to where I was at the top of the stairs.

"Forgive me . . ." he said. He sounded so pathetic. It made me angry. He was in a hell of his own making, and he deserved to be there.

"Forgive me. . . ."

"Uh, no," I said, possessed by a bratty defiance.

He grunted, attempted to stand, which was a mistake. He was concussed, unsteady. He windmilled his arms, trying to get balance, stay on the landing.

"Ah, ah, aahh!"

He spun back and fell, and from my vantage point I couldn't really tell what broke when, but I knew things were breaking. The damage wasn't quiet; it never is. Not that kind of damage.

He was getting bludgeoned by every step, and by the time he hit the bottom, either he was already dead, or it wasn't the stairs that killed him; it was the final impact.

The silence that followed was chilly. Unpleasant.

I wasn't relieved by the man's misfortune; I didn't take any satisfaction in the viciousness of his fall.

*I also wasn't relieved that the danger was gone. The danger had made
me feel something. A vulnerability that was pure and uncomplicated,
unlike what I felt around my mother, what I felt waiting in vain for my
father to come around, what I felt in mass. I appreciated this danger-bred
vulnerability. The clarity of it. The simplicity.*

*I heard my phone ringing up in my bedroom, probably Grace calling
me back. Or maybe Brody, who was an insomniac like me. I ignored it
and, instead, I went down the stairs. I went to see what had happened
to the intruder, to the man who gave me a taste of what it felt like to be,
for a moment, innocent and unashamed.*

*His body lay in a heap beside the clown planter / umbrella stand,
beside Bart's bell jar. His neck was broken in a manner so gruesome, so
vile, I was compelled to reach out and touch him. Touch where I could see
the protrusion of spine. Where his head was yanked in the wrong direction. His limbs were splayed in such a way that he looked spiderlike or
like a starfish clinging desperately to the side of a fish tank. I knelt down
to see his face. His eyes were just two purple bruises. He, of course,
wasn't breathing. But he also wasn't still.*

*"Still as the dead" is just an expression. The freshly dead twitch. No
one tells you that. That, you have to discover on your own.*

"Vesper!"

Grace stood in the doorway.

"Oh, honey!" she screamed. "Are you okay?"

*"He broke into the house," I said. Calmly, very matter-of-fact. As I
heard myself speak, I wondered why I didn't sound more upset. Why I
wasn't more upset. "And then he fell down the stairs. He's dead."*

"What did he say?"

It was a weird question, but I didn't clock it at the time.

I understood now what I couldn't then. The intruder hadn't
been a superfan stalker. He hadn't been there for my mother at all.

He'd come for me. Because of who he thought I was. It wasn't a knife he wielded. It was a crucifix. Because of fucking course it was.

Because he believed I was evil.

He died believing I was evil.

And I couldn't help thinking he might have been right.

I tipped my glass back, waiting for the last drops to come to me.

A certain song began to play, and when I set my glass down I found another on the table, this one frothy, full. And suddenly, the bar smelled of sulfur and smoke.

I was no longer alone.

12

Wh-what are you doing here?" I asked him, my voice trembling.

He pulled a chair out from somewhere and sat down across from me. "That's how you greet your beloved father?"

"How did you find me? How did you know I was here?"

He laughed, shook his head.

I put my face in my hands. "No, no. I do not need this right now."

"Have to disagree," he said, sliding the beer toward me. "I think it's obvious that you need me. It's okay, Vesper. You're allowed to need your dad."

"You have a lot of nerve saying that to me."

"Come on, now. I know I wasn't around much, but I'm very busy. I have a lot of responsibilities. The universe implodes without me."

"Sure."

"I brought something," he said, reaching into his suit pocket. My whole body tensed; I was afraid he'd whip out a giant pentagram in the middle of the bar. But it was a pack of cards. He tipped the deck out onto the table and started to shuffle.

"Really?" I said.

"Like old times, yeah?" He was a skilled shuffler. When I was a kid, I'd watch in awe. I asked him to teach me, but he never got around to it. "Gin rummy?"

He didn't wait for me to answer; he just dealt, lightning quick. He placed the top card faceup in the center of the table, set the rest of the deck beside it. The king of spades.

"Shall we?" he asked, picking up his cards.

As part of my commitment to a "fuck you, Dad" attitude, I considered refusing to play, but if I'm honest, I wanted to. I'd always loved playing cards with my father.

I picked up my hand, fanned it out. They were shitty cards.

"Your turn," he said, grinning.

I studied him for a moment. He hadn't aged at all; he looked the same as he had when I was young, when I would just stare at him across the table, exactly like I was doing right then. I would just marvel at him, at the power of his grin, and the way it made me feel immortal. He was so *cool*, so charismatic. He wasn't like anyone else in Hell's Gate. Even Aunt Grace, and Rosie, and Brody, and kids at school whom I liked . . . a solid 50 percent of their personalities was their faith. More, for some. But my father was unburdened by worship.

I couldn't hold my adoration of him against myself. He'd amassed hundreds of staunchly loyal supporters who were ready to follow him to hell and back. He was that magnetic.

"Are we playing or not?" he asked.

"Don't rush me," I said. I picked up from the deck. Ace of hearts. I had the six of hearts and the ten of hearts, and no other aces. I discarded it. "All right. All you."

He picked up, and then put down a set. Three sixes. Six of spades, six of diamonds, six of clubs.

"Wow. I see what you did there."

He laughed. "Just playing with the hand I was dealt."

"Oh yeah. The everyman's lament."

He discarded the two of diamonds.

"What do you want, Vesper?" he asked. It was the question that kept haunting me. That I had heard my own disembodied voice ask me when I was up in the bathroom that night I returned home.

Why did I still think of it that way? As *home*.

No matter how it betrayed me, what it did to me, what it'd already done, it would always be home.

My mother's farm. Virgil. The people who lived there. Hell's Gate.

Home.

More home than any apartment I'd ever had. More than Shortee's, which I figured was probably for the best.

I picked up the king of hearts. The suicide king.

"Vesper? Still with me?"

"What do *you* want?" I asked. "You don't need to pretend that you care about what I want. We both know you don't. Let's cut to the chase. What do you want from me? Why are you here?"

"I'm here for you. To be here for you. You're coming around on things," he said. "I knew you would eventually. Took longer than expected, though. And now—now we're tight on time."

He pointed to the wall, where there was a Kit-Cat Klock identical to the one in my bedroom back at home. I hadn't noticed it before.

"Time for what?" I asked, putting down my six to his set. "Just out with it. Just say what you need, what you mean. What is it with religion? Takes three hours to say one fucking thing. Now you're telling me we're tight on time. The audacity."

"Apple doesn't fall far," he said. "Does it?"

"Don't give me that."

He leaned forward, elbows on the table. "What happened to your friend in the bathroom—do you honestly believe that was an accident?"

"How do you know about that? That *was* you, wasn't it? You were there, at Shortee's. You're following me."

"Answer the question."

"I . . . No."

"No, you don't believe it was an accident?"

"No. I mean, yes. Of course it was," I said. I went to take a sip of my beer and noticed my hand was shaking.

"And that strange man who broke into the house? He just . . . fell down the stairs? All on his own?" he asked.

"Yeah, he did," I said, ashamed of my uncertainty, the lack of conviction in my voice.

"He did go there to kill you. You do know that, yes?"

Hearing it out loud, I experienced instant, acute nausea, a Russian doll of a panic attack. I felt completely unmoored.

"It's the truth. That man thought he was saving the world. He'd left Hell's Gate after you were born, afraid of what was coming. Know where that got him?"

I took a breath. Attempting to conceal how distressed I was, I said, snidely, "Let me take a wild guess. Hell?"

"He'll be falling down those stairs for eternity. There's no relief for him when he feels the crank of his neck, because he knows his eyes will open again, and when they do, he'll find himself back at the top. Damnation. A suiting punishment for his earthly crimes."

"Yeah, definitely," I said, slamming my cards down. As far as I was concerned, the game was over. "That whole thing was so messed up. And it's on you. You and Constance and everyone. You put me in danger by spewing your bullshit."

"Why are you so afraid of accepting the truth? Everyone wants to be special, Vesper. And you are. All these people," he said, gesturing around to the bikers and random hipsters and doleful divorcées. "These people are extras. Walk-ons. You and me? We've got leading roles. We didn't choose this for ourselves. The universe chose for us. It isn't easy, but it isn't meant to be. I would rather have been playing gin rummy with you than—"

"I'm going to stop you there," I said, standing.

"Sit," he said, with such authority that I did. I sat right back down.

"What is good? What is evil? Right? Wrong? Do you know?"

"I . . ."

"You're of me. I *know* you. I know you better than you know yourself. I know what you feel, what you've always felt, this sense you were different, this sense you didn't belong. It was never about the church, about Hell's Gate, or the world outside it. It's because you are different. You don't belong."

"Thanks for the pep talk, Dad."

"Do you want to belong?"

I didn't know. I couldn't answer.

"I have a theory," he said, leaning back in his chair and crossing his legs. "That this, what's happening right here, right now, is exactly what you want. What you've always wanted. You left Hell's Gate, but you didn't go far, did you? Both times. Didn't make yourself hard to find. You wanted someone to chase after you. You claim to be against the faith, but you want someone to tell you what to do. Even if it's just so you can say 'No, no, not that.' You need the push and pull. You need Hell's Gate. You need your family. You need me. Because you're nothing without us, and you know it. And you don't want to be nothing. You crave power."

"That's not true," I said, though it took me a little too long to say it. The doubt in my voice too obvious. "Don't . . . don't project your shit onto me."

He laughed, but it wasn't his usual laugh. It was condescending.

"What you want is to see suffering outside yourself. You want a reckoning. You want swift and violent retribution. You want pain for those you're certain deserve it, because you're tired of questioning whether you deserve your own. You've buried this want so deep that you don't even realize it's there. You don't even recognize it when it comes to the surface."

I wanted to tell him that he was wrong. I wanted to argue. But I had no argument.

"You dream of it. Of punishment. When you're asleep. When you're awake. Those casual fantasies of violence. I know. I have them, too," he said, leaning across the table to be closer to me, taking my hand. "I can show you how to turn those dreams into reality. How to control it. Your power."

"Yeah, no, thanks," I said, gathering up the cards, stacking the deck neatly.

He slammed his fist down on the table. The cards slid around; my beer spilled. I felt his anger like a hand on my neck. But it didn't last. It was there and then it was gone, and he was smiling at me. "Why don't you go put on a song? Go on, Vesper. Go pick a song."

"Uh . . ."

"Like old times. Picking records. We used to love to do that— remember?"

"I remember."

"Well, we don't have all night," he said. "Go put on a song. *Tick-tock, tick-tock.*"

He pointed to the Kit-Cat Klock on the wall. Its eyes abruptly stopped moving, like the eyes of the clock in my bedroom had. They focused on me.

My heart thrummed in my throat.

"Go on . . ." my father said.

I stood up, tripping over the leg of my chair.

I thought about leaving, running for the door, but I realized it didn't matter where I went. How fast or how far. It was all coming to a head.

Everything felt heavy, my lungs filled with bricks.

I swayed in front of the jukebox. I didn't have it in me to flip through the selections. I made a lazy choice, the first song that came to mind. "Sympathy for the Devil."

When I turned around, the cards were still on the table, soaking in spilled beer, but my father was gone.

"Dad?"

I scanned the bar, checked the bathroom. He wasn't there. It was pretty pathetic that his leaving could still surprise me. I should have been relieved that he was gone, but I wasn't. I was abandoned, alone in the midst of an existential crisis in a shady dive.

I went out front for air, and to see if he was there, if he'd gone outside, knowing I would follow. There were a few tatted-up dudes smoking by the door. They didn't seem pleased by my presence. Or maybe they were too pleased; I couldn't tell.

I stepped out to the parking lot. From the corner of my eye I caught something moving, and I turned just in time to watch a figure disappear into the alley.

Without any thought, I pursued.

"Dad?"

The alley was all shadows. The light next to the side door blinked off and on, off and on, off and . . .

"Dad?"

There were footsteps, fast approaching, but I couldn't tell from where, which direction. I spun around, and in the strobing light I could see someone, but not who they were. I couldn't distinguish a face.

I was alone in a dark alley with a phantom.

"Dad!" I called out again.

"Aren't you angry?" It was my father's voice, but it wasn't my father with me. The light flickered on, and I could finally see who it was.

"George?"

"Vesper," George said. He seemed dazed.

"What are you doing here?" I asked him.

"I brought him here," my father said. "He was your boss. He took advantage of you. Then he fired you."

I didn't know if George could hear him, too. He wasn't reacting.

"George? What's up? What's going on?" He didn't respond. He just blinked at me.

This is weird, I thought. *I don't like this.*

"He's just as guilty as Kerri, don't you think?" my father said. "Why does he still have his teeth?"

This is bad. This is very bad.

"You should get out of here," I said to George.

The light went out. Went on again. George's eyes were glassy.

I reached out and touched him. He felt familiar. Smelled familiar. It was him, but it was like he was in a trance.

"I did like you," he said, his voice eerily hollow. Robotic. "You were fun to fuck."

"What an ugly thing to say," my father said. "You're going to let him get away with it? With saying that to you?"

"I . . ." It was embarrassing, to have George say that, and to have him say it in front of my dad. . . . The shame made me want to disappear, but the anger . . . "Dad. What's happening?"

"I'm showing you. I'm teaching you."

"Teaching me what?"

"Who we are. Who you are."

"I don't—"

"Why don't you tell Vesper the truth, George? Be honest with my daughter," my father said. He appeared behind George and put a hand on his shoulder.

"You weren't worth losing my job over," George said to me.

I didn't care deeply for George; I wasn't sentimental, wasn't crushed that he wasn't madly in love with me or willing to fall on his sword, quit so we could be together. Still, it hurt to hear. And it was fucked-up that he was the one in a position of power and he'd emerged from the situation unscathed. It was his fault. He had been careless with me, with my secrets.

An hour ago, I'd been fine to let it slide. But now . . .

"What should we do to him?" my father asked me. "What should his punishment be?"

The thought was there; I didn't need to search for it. *Destroy his hands. He can't work with broken hands. Can't play music. Can't touch anyone, even himself.*

George fell to his knees, as if in prayer. His back hunched, arms extended. His hands splayed out on the pavement.

My vision went blurry; sweat poured down my face as I was suspended in the final moments of being who I thought I was before inevitably becoming someone else. Someone I wasn't sure I wanted to be. I thought of a caterpillar getting its last glimpse of light before it closes its cocoon. Do caterpillars think, *No, let me stay this way forever*, or do they think, *Eh, fuck it?*

I was beyond panic. Beyond sadness. Beyond confusion. Beyond shame. All I felt was anger. Wrath.

I recognized it this time. The need for swift and violent retribution.

The horrendous sounds of bones snapping echoed through the alley, along with George's screams.

My father stood behind him, smiling, reveling in his misery. But he wasn't touching him. What was happening to George's hands—it was wholly unnatural.

It was . . . it was *me*.

"No!" I shouted, staring down at my own hands, which were hot and shaking.

The noises stopped. The bones. George's screaming. He crumpled to the ground. Fainted.

My father's slow applause rang out. Crisp, measured claps. "Nicely done."

"What just happened?"

"Exactly what you wanted to happen. This is who you are. What you're capable of." He hovered his hand over George's limp body, and George flipped over onto his back. "I kind of want to set him on fire. They'll all burn soon enough, but I'm impatient."

He snapped his fingers and then there was a flame in his palm.

All I could do was gasp.

"You don't feel sorry for him, do you?" He sighed, and the flame extinguished itself. "He won't remember anything when he comes to, if that's what you're worried about. Not that it matters."

I stared at my father. At Satan.

I'd been wrong about everything. He was real. It was real. All real.

I struggled to process the events of the evening, the series of violent incidents, of grim epiphanies . . . but I'd grown up hearing such wild, fantastical shit about hellfire and Satan and all that our Lord and Savior was capable of. Life eternal. I'd grown up living in a house full of Hollywood horrors, had consumed scary movies, stories of psycho killers and monsters and vengeful ghosts. I'd go on to reject it all, sure, but it was still part of me. When you're young, you just absorb your surroundings. Absorb, absorb, absorb, like a tiny, stupid sponge, and then your bones grow around it, skin stretches to fit it. So it was all there still. It wasn't new. I didn't need to use any imagination. All I had to do was accept.

And as I was rapidly metabolizing all this, I could finally recognize that the line between believing and not believing in something is so precariously thin. We hold fast to our convictions, reject even a whiff of persuasion, boldly declaring it an impossibility, maybe in part because we know it isn't. We're all so easily swayed, such sheep. Why give a shit about anything? Why not just lie down in the grass?

I was tired of resisting. I was ready to surrender.

My dad had been right. I just wanted someone to tell me what to do.

"Ready? Let's get out of here," he said, pulling me in close. He hung his arm around my shoulders. It felt good to be embraced in this way. It felt good to allow myself to be held, to be led. To just once allow myself to be someone's daughter. Even if it was his.

The night was so clear, so pretty. The sky batted its lashes at us.

"Look at the moon," my father said. "Almost ripe for the picking."

We stepped around George. Left him there, with his hands mangled so badly, they barely even looked like hands. My father guided me across the parking lot, to where a vintage muscle car was parked across two spaces.

"Is this your car?" I asked him.

"Every car is my car," he answered, opening the passenger-side door for me.

Even in the vulnerable state I was in, I had enough sense to pause before I got in. Question whether I was being an idiot, following a floating pie off a cliff because I was hungry. But I guess I didn't have enough sense to walk away.

"Or did you want to drive?" he asked. "You can go as fast as you want, Princess. No rules."

"That's okay," I said. "But I'll take a cigarette if you have one."

He nodded, pulled a pack from his suit pocket, and handed me one. He lit it for me.

"Thanks, Dad." I took a drag, and the smoke felt like nothing in my lungs.

I didn't really want to be anywhere, so I figured I might as well just go with him. I slid into the car. He hopped into the driver's seat and revved the engine.

"You will be absolved of everything," he said. "Your past. Your pain."

I had zero ability to determine whether there was any truth to what he was saying, because my concept of reality had just been shattered. He could have told me that the Easter Bunny was the mayor of the fourth circle of hell and also my second cousin, and how could I justify my doubt?

I was defenseless. I'd been whittled down to the bone.

"You'll see," he shouted over the whip of wind as he sped out of the parking lot. "It's time. This is the way. The only way. Look around, Vesper. It never ceases to amaze me how much they all take for granted. These outsiders—they can't comprehend how close they are to the end."

"I don't know about that. Have you ever been on Twitter?"

He didn't acknowledge me. He was too busy monologuing.

"The heat is rising. The planet is melting. Right now there's a skeletal polar bear taking its last gasping breaths." He paused to wheeze, a menacing demonstration. "And as everyone argues over what to do about it, argues over whether or not it's happening, and as those who do believe drink out of their paper straws or buy a pair of pants made out of recycled water bottles so they can feel good about themselves, so they can sleep at night thinking they're part of the solution, and as those who don't . . ."

We pulled up to a stop sign. He pointed to a mountain of trash on the street corner.

"As all that happens"—he paused to do the wheezing again—"that polar bear starves and dies, bones swallowed by a growing sea. But wait, *wait*. Wait for inflation. Wait for corporations to line their pockets, to buy up all the houses and rent them back, a return to serfdom. I can't stress enough how *boring* it is to watch history repeat itself over and over again. A rerun of the same episode every night. Greed, greed, greed, greed, greed. The wealth gap broadens. The rich eat. . . ."

He grabbed my arm and pretended to gnaw on it.

"The poor starve. The rich ask, *Why are you hungry? If you were just like me, you wouldn't be hungry.* They have their portraits done. Let history remember the rich. Let their houses stand. The castles to visit. The videos of celebrities giving tours of their multimillion-dollar homes for *Architectural Digest* while wearing pins in honor of war-torn countries that are really just to say, *I would give none of this up for them.* Wait. Wait. Wait to see which pale man has the most eager fingers. Who presses that button first? Who presses it next, in retaliation? Boom! Nuclear annihilation!"

I let my cigarette go, watched the ember fly into the night.

"It's time to start over, Vesper. It's time to burn it all down and rise from the ashes. Me, you, and the faithful."

I found it interesting that those who believed themselves righteous only ever cared about those who agreed with them, and were keen to let those who didn't suffer whatever brutal fate. There seemed to me an inherent hypocrisy in faith itself. I wasn't sure there was any way around it.

I didn't know how to exist anymore. The world was too complicated to navigate, and I suspected that it was in part because of me. I was bad, born bad, and therefore responsible for all that was bad. What hope was there? I couldn't find any. Couldn't fathom. I thought the world would be better off without me, and I without it.

I rested my head on my father's shoulder. He was warm. Always warm. Unlike my mother, whose presence was a bitter chill.

When I was a kid, my hair was a nest. I was feral, frequently unsupervised. I liked to roll around in the yard, hang out with the animals in the barns. Being dirty made me feel free. It also got my mother's attention. She would drag me upstairs to my bathroom, tear a sharp-toothed comb through the knots of my hair. If I ever complained, told her it hurt, she would say, "You did this to yourself."

And even though it was painful, even though she wasn't gentle, wasn't nice, I relished that time, because she was *there*.

It was so fucked-up. I was so fucked-up.

Maybe Constance was right to hate me. Maybe she saw me for what I really was. An evil, destructive force. A villain.

I looked up at my father.

"I love you," I told him, because I wanted to hear him say it back. Because I needed him to.

"Love you, my girl."

And I wanted, more than anything, to believe him.

13

Constance sat on the porch steps in her black robe, drinking a glass of red wine, smoking her electronic cigarette.

My father pulled up in front of the house, turned off the car, the radio. I lifted my head from his shoulder.

"Constance," he said. "I've brought you a gift."

My mother took a look at me and then finished her wine.

My father jumped out of the car, strode up to her, and kissed her on the forehead.

"I don't have any of my stuff . . ." I said, stepping out of the car in a stupor. The house lorded over me, leaning slightly, like at any moment it might tumble over, fall on top of me, reduce me to guts.

"You don't need any stuff," my dad said. "Let's go in."

My mother sighed and stood up, opened the front door. She let my dad in first. Before stepping over the threshold, he paused to give her another kiss, this one more intense. I'd watched my mother kiss men in movies, but to watch her kiss my father was different. It was gross.

He went inside, whistling.

"So much for staying gone," my mother whispered to me as I stepped up to the door.

"Sorry to disappoint you yet again," I said.

She grabbed my arm, but not in the typical way. There was no deadly vise grip, no nails sinking in. No force. No anger. No violence. It was gentle.

Our eyes met for a moment, and her gaze carried none of its typical withering severity. It was a thing of great power, her stare. Sometimes when she'd look at me, I'd hear the *Jaws* theme play in my head. My toes would curl, body wilt under the weight of such dread.

But the way she looked at me then was so terrifying that I was certain my soul had succeeded in momentarily abandoning my body. Because she looked at me with what seemed like pity. She looked mournful.

Sad.

It was startling. Concerning.

"Should I pour us drinks?" my father called from inside. "Constance, more wine?"

"Yes, please," she said. Then to me, "Are you going to stand there all night?"

"Guess not," I said, stepping inside.

I was greeted by towering flower arrangements. They crowded the foyer. At first, I thought they might have been left over from the wedding, but that had been days ago, and they looked fresh.

"What are these for?" I asked.

"The party," my dad said.

"What party?"

"It's a surprise," he said. "Come, come."

My mother slipped past me, holding out her wineglass for my father to refill.

"I think I'll go to bed," I said. I sounded distant. Meek. I was bloodless, beyond drained, and I realized I was standing in the exact spot the intruder had died in, and having confronted my memory with fresh context, I felt pretty shitty about it.

It really dawned on me then that, directly or indirectly, I'd caused his death. Didn't matter if I'd meant to or if it had been self-defense. He was dead because of me. And sure, he'd shown up with a crucifix and bad intentions, but could I blame him?

And then there was George, and Kerri, and that nacho guy, and whoever else . . .

I had this immense guilt, this shame I didn't know what to do with, how to live with. What do you do when you find out you're evil incarnate?

Lie down. I just wanted to lie down.

"Vesper?" my dad said.

"I don't feel well," I said. "I . . . I don't want anything else to drink."

There was a long pause.

"Have some water. Something to eat."

"No, thanks," I said, starting up the stairs. "I'll see you in the morning."

I climbed up to the second-floor landing, and I saw that my mother's door was wide-open. The light was on, and there was a sewing mannequin, or dress form or whatever, perfectly framed by the open door. It had some pins sticking out of it, but otherwise it was naked.

Intrigued, I tiptoed down the hall and poked my head in.

There were swatches of fabric on the vanity, on the floor. Ribbons and lace. Threaded needles set on saucers. The antique sewing machine my mother had left to collect dust in the basement had been carried up, placed on a wooden table. It was clean and appeared to be in working order.

I couldn't remember the last time my mother had sewed.

Actually, I could.

She'd made my dress for my twelfth birthday / first communion. In Hell's Gate, when you turned six you received your pentagram necklace. When you turned twelve you made your first communion and drank the blood of fallen saints, which was just red wine—or so I'd assumed; now I couldn't be so sure. When you turned eighteen you were confirmed. After that you were all set to carry on until you died.

My communion dress had been elaborate. Lace and bows and puffy sleeves. A long skirt, short veil.

I wondered what my mother was up to, what she was sewing and why.

I wondered what my dad was talking about when he mentioned a party.

I remembered then that my stupid birthday was coming up. I was turning twenty-four in three days. I hadn't celebrated my birthday in years, not since I left the church.

Are they throwing a party for me? I wondered, anxious as a bunny sensing an approaching mower.

I hoped not. I was absolutely not in the mood.

Could I smite them if they did? Go in with a soft touch? Threaten a paper-cut punishment if forced to wear a conical hat?

I looked at myself in the vanity mirror. I was sallow. Gaunt. My skin was dry. I was dehydrated again. Or maybe it was all that hellfire scorching me from the inside.

I couldn't decide if I should laugh at the insanity or cry at the tragedy, so I did neither. I turned around, ready to put myself to bed. I saw it on my way out, out of the corner of my eye. A red satin pouch on my mother's nightstand. It was open, and from it spilled what, at first, I thought might be little gems.

On further examination, I saw they were teeth.

More specifically, my teeth. My baby teeth.

Either that or some other kid's baby teeth were on my mother's nightstand.

"Ugh," I said.

There were only a couple there. I was too horrified to count but was pretty confident they weren't the full set.

What had she done with the rest?

Also, how had she gotten them in the first place? Satanists didn't have the tooth fairy—which was one thing I could get behind, since leaving teeth under your pillow always seemed pretty fucked-up to me. Whenever I lost a tooth, I gave it to Grace. She'd give me a small trinket in exchange. A plastic spider or a glow stick or a disposable camera. I couldn't fathom why Grace would save my teeth for my mother. I couldn't imagine Constance accepting them with anything but indifference.

Maybe they weren't real teeth? Maybe they were prop teeth? Whatever they were, wherever they'd come from, did I really want to know?

I found it ironic that for so long all I'd wanted was to explore my mother's room, and now here I was, gagging at teeth.

I thought, *Maybe that's all life is. Wanting something until you get it.*

Then something else caught my eye. A comb. It had tangles of hair caught in it. Too light to be my mother's, too wavy. It looked like . . .

My hair?

"Uh . . ." I didn't want to touch them, not the comb, not the baby teeth, and I don't think I would have if not for the fact that they rested on top of what I suspected was a photo album. A red leather-bound album with a brass pentagram clasp. I'd never seen it before. I wondered if there were pictures of me inside. If my mother had actually cared enough to curate the memories, save them to look back on.

I bit down on my bottom lip, and swiftly pushed the teeth and comb aside to get to the album. Then I made a quick exit. I carried the album up to my room, which had been tidied, sheets cleaned, bed made. Cannibal lamp on, glowing faintly, disgustingly.

I locked the door and sat on my bed with the album balanced on my thighs.

For some reason, I was hesitant to open it.

What did I hope was inside? Sweet pictures of my parents holding baby me, my cheeks pink and chubby? Photos of us all together, looking happy?

I wondered about their relationship. It was clear there was something between them. Love. Attraction—yuck. It was hard not to be curious. Their story was my story.

It's natural to want your parents to love each other—makes your existence feel justified. Like you were *created* instead of being something that happened.

I figured I was probably created—from context clues such as being told I was the harbinger of the apocalypse. What that entailed exactly, I wasn't sure. I didn't want to think about it.

I turned the album on its side, fingered the clasp. It popped open.

It wasn't an album. It was a book. Ancient pages slipped into laminate sleeves. The writing had faded, was barely legible. There were those colorful little Post-it arrows next to some passages. Constance always kept them around; she used them in her scripts. And I guess scripture, too.

I skimmed the page.

". . . Blood of the lamb, the blood of the new and eternal covenant, which shall be sacrificed to purge the world by fire . . . There shall be no mercy but by the lamb."

Charming, I thought. *Some light bedtime reading.*

I shouldn't have been surprised, shouldn't have been disappointed that it wasn't an album, that there were no photographs, no memories. That there was no affection, no trace of me in her life, in anything she owned, she coveted. That once again my mother put Satan before me.

I set the book aside, kicked off my shoes, and changed out of my blood-spattered khakis. It occurred to me how strange it was that my mother hadn't commented on my gnarly appearance. Then again, she must have known what I was capable of. And other people probably did, too. Or at least had an inkling.

I climbed into bed, curled my knees to my chest, and bit at my fingers.

I'd already considered that nobody in Hell's Gate loved me for the reasons I'd wanted them to; nobody loved me for *me.* They loved me because I was Satan's daughter, the harbinger. But I hadn't considered that they might not love me at all. They might fear me.

The adoration was to appease me.

I laid my head down on the pillow and stared at the book. I imagined what it would be like if my parents were just some normies. If I were just an ordinary girl stumbling through her twenties, figuring out who she was, free of expectation, of Satanic history, of apocalyptic doom. I granted myself permission to visit a universe where I wasn't an evil hell baby, to fantasize about a world that wasn't under threat of ending.

A world where I could get dinner with my parents at a place like Shortee's. Eat chicken fries and watch sports and gossip about our neighbors. Kerri, whom I wouldn't know, who would have all her teeth, would sing me the birthday song along with a few other sorry-looking servers. They'd applaud at the end, and I'd wonder, *Gosh, is this more embarrassing for me or for them?* And I wouldn't know the answer, which would be *For them.*

My dad would say, *Make a wish!*

And I would. It'd be an innocent wish. Like getting into grad school, or acing that interview, or finally taking a trip out of the country, or—I don't know—winning the lottery.

I'd blow out the lone candle on the lava cake, and my parents would kiss my cheeks, get emotional. And I would feel so lucky to be alive, clinking spoons with my mom and dad before devouring the cake. I'd have plans with my friends later to go out to some trendy bar with arcade games. Rosie would be there with festive sprinkle cookies she made herself, just for the occasion. Brody, too, and it'd be fine; we'd be cool, because I'd be dating somebody else. Not George, someone better, and we'd be in love. We'd kiss and play pinball and take shots, and he'd tell me how glad he was that I was born, and I'd know that he meant it. I'd believe him.

In this universe, there would be no need to imagine other lives, other worlds, alternate dimensions, parallel cosmos, other versions of me leading vastly different existences. No need to fantasize.

That's how happy I'd be.

The next morning I woke up to a sadistic headache.

The sun lasered in through the window, neon yellow.

There was a racket downstairs. Too many voices to identify any. They tangled together, a mystery chorus.

Whoever the voices belonged to, they were in constant movement. They took things with them. Picking things up and setting them down. Heavy things that made heavy sounds. Doors opened and closed. A kettle whistled. The oven bleeped. Something was ready. It was time.

I rolled over onto my side and pulled the sheets over my head.

There's always this brief moment after you open your eyes, when you're still in sleep's maw, and you don't remember any of the shit that's wrong in your waking life. It's only breathing and blinking, a sweet peace before the hammer comes down.

And it comes down hard every time.

I felt like I'd dug a spoon tunnel out of my cell only to come up in the prison yard. I felt like I'd escaped the killer in the first movie only to be murdered in the opening ten minutes of the sequel.

I didn't want to get out of bed.

You should cry, I told myself. *You're upset. Cry. Prove you have a soul.*

I'd never had a real zest for life, but I lived. I set my alarm. I bought books that I intended to read. I bathed and ate and took vitamins. Now I wasn't motivated to do any of that. Living didn't seem like such a great idea. My whole existence was destructive.

Cry, goddamn it! I demanded, I begged.

I felt genuine despair. I felt more emotion than I had in years, but I still couldn't do it. Couldn't cry. Not one salty tear.

There was a knock on my door.

"Star?" Grace came shuffling in.

I peeked out from under my sheets.

"Look at you, bug in a rug," she said, sitting on my bed. "How're you doing?"

"Bad."

"Aw, sweets. You need something? You want breakfast?"

"I guess."

She stood up. "You got it. Oh dear."

She picked up my khakis. "I can get these cleaned up for you."

"You can just throw them out. That's blood. That's not coming out."

"It'll come out," she said with a wink. "Come down when you're ready. Don't mind the commotion."

"What's it for?" I asked.

"The party!" she said. She left before I could ask any follow-ups.

I slowly shifted my weight to the edge of the bed, and let gravity do the rest. I pulled out of my dresser a pair of stiff jeans and a summer camp T-shirt that had *Faith Eternal* written in loopy script across the front, with the image of Baphomet on the back.

Wasn't my favorite shirt, but I was too lazy to search for one I liked better. Besides, I was pretty sure I wouldn't find one. All the clothes in my room belonged to some stupid girl I used to be. I was jealous of her obliviousness. I was angry at her and I felt sorry for her.

I went to the bathroom, splashed some water on my face, and headed downstairs.

There were more flower arrangements in the foyer. The megatable setup from the rehearsal dinner was back. It was in the process of being set with plates and silverware, giant goblets. They weren't from my mother's collection, at least as far as I knew. They looked medieval.

"What's going on?" I asked a woman who was placing a baroque candelabra in the center of the table.

She turned to me, smiled, bowed her head, and said nothing.

"Grace," I said, stubbing my toe on a crate of glassware. "Grace?"

"In the kitchen, Star!"

She stood at the kitchen counter wearing a red bandanna.

"When did you put that on?" I asked her.

"I'm going out to the garden. Need some fresh veg."

"Am I in a time loop? The wedding was last week," I said, sitting at the island.

She presented me a plate with an egg that looked too soft. I didn't want it. I no longer wanted to be the kind of creature to eat the young. I was bad enough already.

"The wedding *was* last week," she said. "Beautiful, wasn't it? Rosie and Brody are so happy. You'll see them soon."

There was a crash in the parlor.

"What happened?" Grace called out. "I'll be right back."

"Wait—"

"Right back," she said.

She disappeared into the parlor.

I poked at my egg with a fork. The yolk bled.

I thought of Kerri's broken mouth. All that blood.

I had no appetite.

"Don't touch that again," I heard Grace say. "Constance will have your head."

She flurried back into the room. "Your mom and that precious statue."

"Mr. Ransom?" I asked.

"Yeah, yeah," she said, opening the dishwasher. "You know she's got the other one now, too. The reboot guy."

"Reboot Ransom?" Instead of one hatchet, Reboot Ransom wielded two. The black trench coat was swapped for a leather jacket with a high collar. Instead of covering his face with gauze, he wore a balaclava. The general consensus was that he wasn't as scary or badass as the original. The reboot had been a big failure. Constance had had only a cameo.

"He's in the basement. She doesn't have anywhere to put him," Grace said, holding a butter knife up to the light to determine its cleanliness. "Which, thank the Lord."

"Speak of the devil," I said. "So, uh, what is all this? Why won't you answer me?"

"It's for the party," she said, her voice jumping an octave. "You haven't eaten your egg. You want something else? Toast? Water? Coffee? Juice? You feeling all right? You want some Advil? I could get you some more of those electrolyte pills."

"Uh, sure," I said. My throat was dry, head pounding.

"Gotcha," she said, darting off.

I took her absence as an opportunity to investigate. I went into the parlor, hoping to run into someone I could bully—nonviolently—into telling me what this party was. But the room was empty of people—except for Mr. Ransom, if he counted.

"Welcome to your nightmare," he said.

"Thanks. Glad to be here." I reached for his OFF switch.

There were flowers all around the parlor. Taper candles. There were coasters. Also not my mother's. Hers had dancing skeletons on them. These were plain ceramic.

"Got your medicine," Grace singsonged. She appeared behind me. She shoved a glass of water into my left hand and two pills into my right. One was a greenish gel cap, an Advil. The other was white, ovular, about the size of a penny. It looked different from the electrolyte pills she'd given me the week prior, but I didn't think much of it. My head was roaring, so I lifted my palm to my lips, deposited the pills, and washed them down with the water.

"Thank you," I said.

"You should have another glass. Eight a day!" she said. "And maybe get some more rest. Want to be fresh for the party."

"What party?"

"*Your* party," she said. "*The* party."

"Yeah, I was afraid of that. Look, thanks, but I'm not in the mood to celebrate my birthday."

"It's going to be the night of all nights," she said, cupping my face in her hands. "You'll see. Praise Him. What a gift He's given us in you."

I sighed. "Aunt Grace . . . did—did you ever really care about me?"

"How could you ask that? Of course!" She went ghost pale. She looked terrified, and it broke my heart. She was afraid of me. "I love you. You know that. I've always loved you as if you were my own daughter. You're so special to me, Vesper. To all of us."

"Because of my dad? Because I'm . . . I'm this evil fucking freak? I don't want you to love me for the reasons you love me. Or fear me. Or whatever. I don't want it, Grace. Please. I don't want it like this."

"Vesper. We all only want what's best for you, which is for you to come into your own. Embrace who you are and what you were meant to do."

"Which is what, exactly? Start the apocalypse? I'm not about it."

"The world is already burning," she said, a sobering shift in her tone. Grace rarely ever got stern. "Would you have us burn with them? Out of stubbornness? Out of spite?"

She collapsed onto the couch behind her, buried her face in her hands. She let out a sob.

"All we ever did was love you. Provide for you. And you left us. It was so painful to lose you. Such a hard time. So much worry."

I might have felt guilty if I weren't busy being so dizzy.

"But the hard times are over now," she said, her voice warping, face blurring.

I staggered back, pulling at the air as if it might save me.

"No more suffering," Grace said.

The room shuddered around me, and then vanished in a snap.

14

There was no birdsong, and I wondered why. I wondered, *What do they know that I don't?*

"Vesper. Vesper, wake up."

It was Rosemary. She wore a shimmery gown, and there were flowers in her hair.

"I'm awake," I said, as my eyelids languished. "I am."

Rosie said something else, but I was distracted by the pounding of my heart. A loud, pugnacious beat.

And again I wondered, *What does it know that I don't?*

My skin was a hapless sack holding in the rest of me, heavy and unwieldy as wet sand. I felt separate from myself, like there was some assembly required. Just the thought of movement was wearying.

"I don't feel right," I said, the words scraping my throat.

"Sleepiest sleepyhead," Rosemary said, tugging the covers from my grasp. "I know you don't care about being late, but as you know, if I'm not on time . . ."

She trailed off, or I stopped listening.

My heart carried on, waging war against my sternum.

"Wait until you see the dress," Rosie said, recapturing my attention.

"What dress? Rosie. Help me."

"I am helping you," she said. "You're groggy. Have some water."

She handed me a glass. One of the black ones from the kitchen, with the spiderweb-patterned rims. It was a struggle to drink, to grip, to swallow. The water was tepid, had a strange aftertaste.

My vision blurred, eyes went in and out of focus.

"That better?" she asked, pressing a cool hand to my cheek.

"No," I said. "It's warm."

"I can open the window."

"I meant the water. And that window is impossible to open."

I went to set the glass down on the nightstand, and I noticed the friendship bracelet that Rosie had made me over a decade ago was back on my wrist. Had she found it on my dresser, tied it on me as I slept?

"I can open it," she said with a wink. She walked over, and with a quick yank, in spilled fresh air. The ripeness of August. "You see, Vessie? All things are possible through the Lord."

Is she fucking joking? I wondered.

She smiled at me with every one of her big white teeth.

And then things went hazy again.

"Glory, glory to the faaaa-ther. Glory, glory to the faaaa-ther . . ." Rosie sang as she dressed me, pulling the laces of the corset tight.

My head lolled. A glittering stream of drool slowly trickled down my chin.

"Was I out?" I gurgled, wiping my face with the back of my hand.

She didn't answer.

I was completely disoriented. I was sitting up at the foot of the bed. Hadn't I just been lying down? And what was I doing in my room? What was I doing *home*? I couldn't remember. I panicked.

"Hey," I said. "What am I even doing here?"

"You came home, silly," she said.

"I left." I couldn't stand, couldn't get away from her. My head felt heavier than the rest of me. "I left again."

"And you came back again. You'll always come home, Vessie. It's where you're meant to be. Now hold still." She went on tying me up, tying me in. *"Glory, glory to the faaaa-ther! Our Lord is hell's true king."*

As she finished her little song, my confusion faded, and I remembered exactly how I'd gotten there. I remembered everything. Kerri. George. The Black Stallion Saloon. The muscle car. The soft, runny egg. The pills.

"You drugged me," I said, my tongue like a slug in my mouth.

"What?" Rosie said. "Look. Look at this dress. Look at *you* in this dress."

She pulled me up to stand, and it was instant torment. A brutal pain at my side, under my left breast. "Ow, fuck!"

"Dollar in the swear jar. Here, look." She dragged me over to the mirror.

I was a monstrosity.

I'd never seen a more ridiculous dress. The bodice was covered in intricate beading. Pentagrams. All pentagrams. The bottom was layer upon layer of crimson tulle. The sleeves were also tulle. They gathered at the elbow, then puffed out again, cinching at the wrist with slim bands of beaded pentagrams.

"One more thing," she said, crowning me with a goofy beaded headpiece. She squealed in delight. "What do you think?"

"I look like a Satanic *Star Wars* princess," I said. I was starting to feel more myself, wrangle my thoughts.

"You look like the Princess of Hell," she said, beaming.

"You dressed me?" I asked, running my fingers over the expanse of fabric. "Hold on. What did Grace give me? Why do I feel like this?"

"You must be *sooo* exhausted," she said, leading me back to the bed. I sank onto the mattress, and she knelt in front of me. "I want you to know how sorry I am about the wedding. I hate how we left things."

I pressed my thumbs into my forehead, massaged the tension there.

"I can't imagine how it's been for you. And, you know, it wasn't just you they kept things from. I was in the dark, too. I really didn't know the whole truth until after you left. I swear."

"Okay," I said. The discomfort was both acute and elusive.

"There was so much I didn't understand before," she said, resting her chin on my lap like a puppy. "I would pray on it. Pray and pray. I would pray for you. I've always prayed for you."

"Thanks," I said. "Rosie, I don't feel good. What did Grace give me?"

"Your body needed rest," she said. "It's ready now."

"Ready for what?"

"The party," she said, standing.

"Right. Is it a costume party?"

She giggled. "Of course not. It's your birthday party."

"It's not even my birthday," I said. "My birthday is . . ."

I realized I didn't know what day it was. I didn't know the time. Late afternoon, based on the sun. I checked the Kit-Cat Klock, but its hands pointed to midnight, which couldn't be right.

"What time is it?" I asked.

"Time for us to go downstairs," she said. She smacked her lips. "We're probably already late. But I did want to take a moment with just us."

She pulled a tube of lip balm out from somewhere. She held it up, showing me it was birthday cake flavored. She applied some to herself, then leaned over to put some on me. "Appropriate for the occasion."

"Rosie, you're not hearing me."

"No, I know," she said. "I do hear you."

"I don't feel well. At *all*."

"You'll feel better soon," she said. "We all will. I just want things to be okay between us. I forgive you, and I hope you forgive me. You know how much I love you. You're my sister, my best friend."

"Then help me out of this dress," I said, clawing at the seams.

"What?"

"You heard me. Get this dress off. I don't want to wear this. I look like a vampire bride. I look absurd."

"You look beautiful."

"I don't want it on. It's not *me*. And it's itchy. And hot. I'm so uncomfortable. It's so hot. Is it hot in this room? Is it the room? I feel like I can't breathe. I can't breathe!"

"Shh, shh. You're okay," Rosie said. "Remember that summer it was so hot, we tried to dig our own pool in the backyard?"

"Yeah, we were super-dumb kids."

"No," she said. "We had big dreams!"

It was what I loved most about Rosie. Her optimism. I always envisioned my heart as something hard and rough as a peach pit, an unyielding core. But Rosie could make it feel soft enough to cut clean through.

I wanted to hug her. I wanted us to be dumb kids again.

"It could have worked. That's how all pools start, right?" she asked. "A hole in the ground."

"Sure," I said, distracted by an itch at my hairline. I went to scratch, and the headpiece slid out of place. Rosie reached over to adjust it.

"Your hair isn't long enough, so I can't clip it in," she said. "There we go. You ready?"

"I don't want to go downstairs. I don't want this on my head. I don't want any of this."

"It's dinner," she said. "Aren't you hungry?"

"No. I feel like flaming garbage."

"Everyone's here for you," she said, giving a little sigh. "Please, Vessie? It's going to be great, I promise. Please?"

I was once again reminded that she had never asked for any of this either. She had been born into it, same as me.

"Fine, I guess," I said, resigned. "Help me up."

"Yay!" she said, clapping twice before lifting me off the bed. I flopped into her arms like a rag doll. I could barely stand; I had no idea how I was getting down the stairs. Especially not in all that tulle.

"My side really hurts," I said, pointing. "Right here. Is that the dress? Is there a pin?"

"Mm. Yeah, maybe," she said, lifting my skirts to facilitate movement. We got to the stairs and started our descent. I was breathing like I'd just run sprints. It was slow going.

"I really can't change into jeans?" I asked. "It's my party, apparently."

"When are you ever going to get a chance to wear a dress like this again?"

"Hopefully never."

"Constance made it," she whispered in my ear. "For you."

"When?" I asked, examining the intricate beading. "Why? For this? How did she even—"

"There they are!" Brody stood at the bottom of the stairs. He wore a suit that was likely the same one he'd worn to his wedding the week before; he was a perpetual groom.

"Hey, babe," Rosie said, and gave him a quick peck on the lips.

For some reason it made me think of George, and I felt my mood tip into a vat of acid.

"You look beautiful," Brody said. He was talking to Rosie. He caught himself. "You both do."

I snorted. It was the only response.

"Happy birthday," he said. "There's champagne."

"Think I'd prefer bleach," I said, tripping over my hem to get by.

The house had been completely transformed. Red velvet draped over the walls, covering the creepy pictures, the portrait of the screaming man from *Cemetery Tales*. However the fabric had been adhered—with tacks or tape or nails or whatever—was concealed behind bronze garland, long, shimmering vines of it, of metallic leaves and berries. Pentagram ornaments hung from the garland. Each pentagram was unique. Some were solid gold. Some bejeweled, encrusted with rubies and black diamonds. Others stamped iron, forged in fire. Others delicate blown glass with rainbow iridescence.

The only light was candlelight. There were so many candles. Tea lights and votives and tapers. Giant red pillar candles with wax dripping slow and steady, like blood from a slim, deep cut. The candles burned on glass plates, on slabs of stone. They flickered wildly, waved from ornate candelabras perched around, placed on any and every open flat surface. It seemed a fire hazard, but I figured no one who prayed for hell flames to swallow the world had any real concern about that.

The kitchen smelled of rich meat, of animal fat. There were hors d'oeuvres placed in pentagram patterns on wide silver platters. I had no appetite, but I couldn't help it. I had a compulsion to ruin. I grabbed a mini quiche and stuffed it into my mouth, disrupting the symbol.

It was still obviously a pentagram, still easy to identify. Mission failed.

The quiche was gummy and painful to swallow. My throat was killing me.

There were crystal bowls filled with halved figs and pomegranate seeds. Hideous innards.

Have to hand it to nature. For every beautiful thing it offers us, in the hand behind its back it holds something truly repulsive.

There were bottles of wine lined up on the counter, what seemed like an excessive amount. But there were a lot of people. They were everywhere, dancing around me, conversing—hush-hush, words lost beneath the steady sing of violins.

Wait, I thought. *Who the fuck is playing violin? And why?*

The party was a fever dream, and whoever planned it had done it without any consideration of me. Well, kind of. I recognized that my family, that the entire community . . . that this was how they saw me. This was who they thought I was, what they thought I'd be into.

I'd always been better at identifying what I didn't like than what I did. All I could think then was *Not this, not this, not this. Anything but this.*

I stepped into the parlor. Mr. Ransom had been hidden behind a tall wooden room divider, pentagrams carved into each panel. I figured my mother wouldn't permit anyone to move him but had conceded to his concealment. But why? For what reason?

Happy birthday! Happy, happy birthday, Vesper. Happy birthday. Vesper, happy birthday. Vesper! Vesper!

The voices sounded so distant, but the people were close. Their collective breath made the air seem wet, like I was swimming. Or like I was drowning. I saw Jane and Ant. I saw Brody's parents; they stood with Birdie and Bea, who wore matching outfits, red dresses with black ribbons around the waist. I saw faces I recognized and didn't recognize and it was as if I were seeing them all through frosted glass, or as if I'd gotten Vaseline in my eyes. The people could have been ghosts in their translucence, in the wispiness of their wishes for happiness on a day that I wasn't certain it was, as they said my name, which somehow, right then, didn't seem to belong to me.

I hadn't chosen it for myself. It had been chosen for me.

It belonged to the version of me they all wanted. That they thought I was or hoped I would become.

They were confused.

Or was I?

Vesper, Vesper, Vesssppperrrr, Vesspperrrr.

I knew they weren't ghosts, the misty beings swarming me in the parlor. They proved their physical form through touch. Fingers caressing my arms, my face. Light prickles that paled in comparison with the chew of pain at my side, the buzzing in my head, like my skull was crawling with hungry flies. There were too many sensations to focus on just one.

I turned toward the window, and I saw the reflections of candles, hundreds of flames, in the glass.

Or beyond the glass.

"Are there people outside?" I asked.

Vesper, Vesper, Vessspppperrrr. Vesper!

"Vesper."

It was my mother.

She was dressed almost as outrageously as me. Only, she could pull it off. She was an actress; costumes were her thing. She wore a gown of black feathers, a black fascinator with a birdcage veil.

"How many crows died to make that dress?" I asked, aloud, by accident.

"As many as possible," she answered.

"Oh, Star! Look at *you*!" Grace was also in a crazy outfit. A red-and-black-checkered pantsuit. Everyone was dressed in red and black. I was picking up on a theme. "Carl, look at our Vesper."

"What a beaut," Carl said, patting me on the back. He did it too hard, and I crumpled forward. "Careful, there."

There was a screaming at my rib cage, a burst of warm agony.

"You all righty, Vesperino?"

"No!" I said, but I was in so much pain that I was incapable of volume, so the word was indistinguishable.

"Vesper, would you like a drink?" my mother asked. "Grace, Carl, would you get Vesper some champagne? A shame to be walking around empty-handed at your own party."

"Of course!" Grace said. "Carl, shall we?"

"Wait," I said, but they either didn't hear me or pretended not to.

I turned to Constance, about to tell her that I suspected my aunt had slipped me something, and that I felt like I was in a shitty sur-realist film, that I was sick and incapacitated by a pain I couldn't identify, that I hated the party, and that I really fucking hated the howling violins, wherever they were, and that the dress was heavy and itchy and suffocating, and that all I wanted was to go lie in bed and close my eyes but I was too afraid because I didn't know what was happening, and the people who were meant to love me and keep me safe I no longer felt I could trust. But the way my mother looked back at me . . . I knew she already knew all of this.

And she didn't care.

Her expression was blank, still as a photograph. A beautiful void. It was the face she'd always worn on red carpets, in interviews. A face of practiced, intentional nothing.

Staring up at my mother's cold, dead expression, I understood just how alone I really was.

I'm alone, I thought, repeating it in my head like a grim mantra. *I'm alone. I'm alone.*

I shared blood with this woman beside me. Her body had made mine. And that should've held meaning, and it did. It mattered the most . . . and not at all. There was this attachment that I seemed unable to saw through, a bond of nature that logic failed to amputate, but she didn't seem to feel it. Nobody there felt it, not like I did.

It was abruptly, dreadfully clear to me that I was still fucking *desperate* for these people to see me, to love me, and they couldn't. They wouldn't. They looked at me and saw someone else. They loved someone else. This doppelgänger I couldn't control, couldn't conquer, who stood where I stood, moved when I moved, sounded just like me.

It was obliterating. And it made me feel insane. It made me want to claw out of my skin, abandon my body. I didn't want it; it was part of them, and I didn't want any part of them if they didn't want every part of me.

It hurt too much.

"Here you go," Grace said, placing a champagne flute in my hand. I couldn't grip it. It slipped right through. "Whoopsie! I'll get that cleaned up."

"Where are the violins? Who's playing these violins?" I asked. I tipped toward the window, pressed my forehead into the pane of glass, hoping it'd be cool. It wasn't. "Are there people outside?"

"Almost time, don't you think?" Constance asked.

I turned around. She was talking to Grace.

"Just about," Grace said. She was hunched over, picking up glass—the champagne flute that I'd dropped, that I'd broken. In her palm was a shimmering collection of shards, deceptively beautiful in the candlelight. "Should I gather everyone to the table?"

"Yes," Constance said. "Leave the mess."

Grace nodded, carried the glass off into the kitchen.

"I'm not hungry," I said. "I don't want dinner. I want to lie down."

"Don't be rude, Vesper."

A familiar refrain. *Don't be rude. Don't be smart. Don't be cute. Don't, don't, don't, don't.* Always telling me what I shouldn't do, shouldn't be.

"I'm not a bad daughter," I said, because I was apparently too loopy for foresight. Had I given it any thought, I'd have just shut the hell up, because there was no point in arguing with my mother. No point can be proven if no point will be taken.

She sighed. "Then go sit at the table. Your father will be at the head, and you to his right."

The violins exacerbated a ringing in my ears. I moved through the foyer. Bart's bell jar had been covered in black velvet. I reached for it, wanting to rip it off, set him free, but my fingers couldn't grasp anything. They were too weak.

I turned the corner into the dining room. The megatable burst with flowers and candles and platters of food, all wedged between elaborate place settings.

My dad wasn't at the table yet. I didn't know where he was. The dress was so heavy, so difficult to move in, like I was bathing in tar. And the space between the chairs and the wall was so narrow, thanks to all the decorations—the draped fabric, the flowers, the candles. I experienced a moment of grave panic, realizing that if the dress caught on one of the candles, I'd be literal toast. But then at least I could watch the dress burn. I'd like that part.

I wasn't sure how long the walk was taking. Time had gone gooey. I sensed I had an audience but couldn't be bothered to look.

Finally, I made it to the head of the table, and sat myself in the chair to the right. Not that I cared, but it was apparently my birthday, and yet my dad needed to be at the head of the table. I wondered if it was his call or everyone else's.

There were roast chickens with glistening skin. Whole snapper wearing thin slices of lemon and generous sprinklings of dill, surrounded by potatoes crusted with fat flakes of sea salt and crushed black pepper. Bowls of mushrooms sinking in brown gravy, carrots and leeks with rosemary and thyme. Long baguettes that appeared slippery and eellike thanks to the butter slathered on top.

It was a feast, and the sight of it, the smell of it, instigated my nausea.

There were a glass of ice water and a glass of milk at my place. Also, a goblet filled with wine. I chose the water. It was one sip— and the swallow was agony. My throat was raw. Like I'd been gargling with razor blades. Some water dribbled out of the side of my mouth.

"Come, everyone!"

My father. I didn't see him come in, but there he was, sitting beside me, gesturing for everyone to take their seats.

"Vesper," he said, touching my face with the back of his hand. His rings were cold, nipped my cheek. "Happy birthday."

"Thanks," I said, struggling to set my water down.

He took the glass, did it for me.

"I'm sick," I told him. "There's something wrong. But you already know that."

"No, Vesper. Nothing is wrong," he said, taking my hand and pressing my knuckles to his lips. He waited until everyone was seated, and then he stood, raising his goblet, which was larger and more opulent than the rest. It was ridiculous. "I look around, and here are the most faithful. The most devout. Sitting at this table and just beyond these doors."

Holy shit, I thought. *There are people outside. How many? The whole village? And what are they doing? Just standing there holding candles? Do they get any food?*

"Years. Centuries. Ages of worship . . ." He was a skilled public speaker, my father. So captivating. "And now the hour is upon us. Let us grant humanity a quick, merciful end. Let us purge the earth of rot and start anew. I am the liberator, here to bring light to the darkness, cast it out with fire."

He paused, and everyone applauded. It was horribly loud. I closed my eyes, and when I opened them I noticed my vision was distorted. Small, wormy shadows scurried across my view. There was an encroaching orangey hue steeping the edges of the scene.

I felt increasingly faint. With each passing second, my waking presence was more precarious.

Who will save me now? I wondered.

No one. No one.

"I present to you this feast in honor of my daughter, my joy. A gift to us all," he said, looking down at me with such pride and adoration, I forgot myself. In that moment, I would have fallen at his feet. "To Vesper."

They all raised their goblets of wine.

Should I raise mine? I wondered. *Toast myself?*

Here's to me, the sorriest girl in the world.

"Now. On this divine eve of the apocalypse, please enjoy this last meal before the reign of hell."

A "Hail Satan" chant ensued. I didn't participate. I was a little hung up on the whole "last meal before the reign of hell" thing.

Oh, I thought. *Shit.*

This wasn't just a birthday party. This was an apocalypse party.

"Let's eat!" my father said, sitting.

Clergymen entered carrying more trays of food. Smoked pork ribs, mashed yams with garlic, baked clams, a wheel of honey-drizzled brie nestled inside a wreath of crusty bread. No one was shy about helping themselves. No one except my mother, who left her plate empty as she guzzled wine.

I took a sip of my own and found it tasted funny. The texture was off, too. It stung my aching throat.

"Go on, Vesper," my dad said. I looked over at him. He was eating something different. Whatever was on his plate was strange, gruesome. It looked raw. Like raw meat. Or the pulp of a ripe plum. "This is a celebration. This is all because of you."

"What's this wine?" I asked, but I think I already knew the

answer. I suspected it wasn't wine at all. I swirled it in my glass. It was thick. Too thick.

"Isn't it nice, to be together?" He took a delicate bite of his mystery dinner. The sight of it deepened my wooziness. All around us, the candles burned, casting frantic shadows. "Are you happy? You've been wandering, searching for purpose, for meaning. And now you're here. Where you're meant to be, about to fulfill your purpose."

"Fulfill it how? By doing what?" I asked. "I can't do anything right now. I'm about to pass out. What then?"

"You're strong," he said. "Can't you feel it? Our time is now."

"Our time is now," I repeated. "The night is blackest of black." His brow furrowed.

"*The Black Hallows Coven Investigation*," I said. "I thought you were quoting—"

He shook his head, confused.

"It's from the movie. Lady Verona. Her character says it." I pointed to my mother, who hid behind her goblet.

"Oh," Lucifer said with a quick laugh. "I've never seen it."

"What do you mean, you've never seen it?"

"My days are consumed in shadow. I am a purveyor of retribution. I deal in terror and misery. The last thing I want to do in what little spare time I have is engage in more horror."

"But she's your partner," I said. A tension permeated the atmosphere. I was taking a tone with my father. I was taking a tone with the devil. "It's her work."

"Vesper," my mother said at a warning pitch. I couldn't tell whether the warning was for his benefit or for mine.

"They're good movies," I said, which wasn't entirely true, but that was beside the point.

"She understands," he said. He turned to Constance. "Don't you?"

She nodded. "Of course, my love. My Lord."

But I detected bullshit. She was lying. She was hurt. It hurt her.

"You should watch," I said. "We can watch together."

His expression shifted for just a moment. Turned wicked.

"And this house," he said, and clicked his tongue. "Once I can live here on this earth, I'll deal with this . . ."

He gestured around.

I hated that house. I'd *always* hated that house, hated my mother's horror memorabilia, her clowns and rat tea sets and cannibal lamps. But it was *her*. It was who she was. And the house belonged to her. She'd earned it.

I didn't know how it happened, how I was somehow compelled to defend the person who had arguably caused me the most pain.

"I like the house as it is," I said.

He didn't respond, didn't acknowledge. Just cut another tiny fraction of the dark mess on his plate. It was such a small portion, he probably could've finished it in two bites. But he was savoring it. Taking his time.

My mother's plate remained empty. She tapped her nails on her goblet, the same fidgeting I'd seen her engage in before my father's arrival at the wedding. Was she anxious? Impatient? Upset? If she was, this was as close as she would ever get to showing it. I wondered then if she was inherently unfeeling, or if she'd trained herself to suppress emotion as I had. She wouldn't meet my eye, and for the first time in my life, I felt sorry for her. She had been born into the faith, too. Indoctrinated.

And my father . . . what was the nature of their relationship exactly? I stared at him, my wheels turning. If he was Satan, that meant he wasn't really human. That meant he was old as shit. And Constance had been young when she had me. She'd been . . . she'd been my age.

I was again distracted by the thing on his plate, wondered what it was. Was it red or purple? I couldn't really tell in the candlelight, and my throat was so sore, it was distracting me from the plate, and the throbbing in my head was distracting me from my throat, which was distracting me from the queasiness, and the blurred vision, and the shrieking violins, and the people standing outside— *why, why?*—and the enervating ache of my body, the pain. I was in so, so much pain.

And then there was my mother, sitting across from me, not eating, only drinking wine that wasn't wine. And beside me, to my right, was Rosie, whom I hadn't noticed until just then, resting her head on Brody's shoulder. He sat beside her, on the other side. He kissed her forehead, and it was sweet and nice and innocent, but nothing about the night was innocent.

These people all thought it was the apocalypse. They thought the world was about to burn, that billions of people were about to die, and they were living it up, stuffing their faces, drinking lamb's blood. Smiling. Laughing.

But how could I judge them? I was among them.

"I remember when you were born," my father said. "You screamed."

"Yeah," I said. "All babies do."

"Not like this," he said, and licked his lips. "Not like you. From the moment you arrived in this world, you didn't want to be here. I've always found that interesting."

"What?" I said. "What are you talking about? What's even happening? What do you want from me?"

"You really didn't do your homework, did you? How much scripture did you skip over?"

"A lot, I guess."

"You will open the seal tonight. It can be opened only once every six years, and only by you. You were too young at six, too young at twelve. At eighteen you left. I thought about bringing you back, but I'm soft on you, kid. I decided to give you more time. But now there is no more time. Any longer, the world will be too far gone."

"What do you mean, open the seal?" I asked. He cut into what was left of the pulp on his plate, releasing a geyser of dark red juice. "And what is that? What are you eating?"

"Vesper," my mother said, again in a warning tone.

"What? What do you *want* from me? Please, just tell me."

My father took the napkin from his lap and dabbed at the corners of his mouth. He then folded the napkin, set it down across his finished plate.

It must've been a signal, because everyone else immediately followed suit.

"The feast is over," my father said, standing. "It's time. Follow me into the darkness, and I will lead you into the light."

Another "Hail Satan" chant broke out, a chant that apparently no one knew how or when to end, because it just kept going and going and going. My dad offered me his hand. I stared at it.

"No," I said.

He grinned, his eyes sparking. "You have nowhere else to go."

It was cruel and it was true.

"Trust me," he said. "I'm your father."

As if being my father meant my trust in him should be implicit.

"Dad—"

"I'm your favorite person. You said so yourself, remember? And you're mine."

He was reaching into the past, mining it for sentiment. Using it to manipulate me. It wasn't fair.

"That's not fair."

"It's true. I love you more than anything else in this world. My girl. Come. Let me take care of you. Isn't that what you want? Let me."

What choice did I have? I was too sick to run. And he was right. I had nowhere else to go.

Whatever evil Antichrist powers I might've possessed, I couldn't summon them. I didn't have the strength, and didn't really know how, and besides, what was I going to do? Unleash my hell telekinesis on a family member to get out of starting the apocalypse, or whatever the fuck was about to happen? I didn't want to hurt anyone else. I hated what I was capable of.

Sitting at that table, I wasn't wrathful or thirsty for vengeance, just vulnerable and scared. There wasn't really a good option for me, at least not that I could think of on the spot.

I gave my dad my hand and he pulled me up. There was an uncomfortable warmth spreading from my torso. I hobbled forward, got out from behind the table. My mother followed behind. Then Rosie and Brody, Grace and Carl. The High Priest. It was a procession.

My father opened the front door for me. He leaned in close, whispered in my ear. "There's no need to be afraid, Vesper."

And for a second, I believed him. I felt relief. But then he added, "You should know by now. Your fate is sealed."

He nudged me out the door, and I tripped onto the porch.

Outside, there was a sea of people in dark robes holding candles. Members of Hell's Gate. I suspected every member of Hell's Gate. They were all chanting, *Hail Satan, hail Satan, hail Satan.* I wondered if the breeze would carry the chant on its back. I wondered if people in neighboring towns would hear. Pause to listen. I imagined fear dawning on their faces.

But what did it matter? What could they do?

The crowd parted, and we walked through it, hand in hand.

"Breaks my heart," my father said. Maybe he was whispering in my ear, or maybe his voice was inside my head. "How much time you wasted running. You could never quite figure out how to *be.*"

We were passing under the oak, and my foot caught on a root. I stumbled, and my hand tore free of my father's grasp. I clutched my side and found it wet. The fabric was soaked through. I peeled my hand away. My palm was red. I was bleeding.

"Dad . . ."

"I think you've always known, on some level, that you were a vessel of doom."

"I'm bleeding."

"Such fierce resistance to your purpose. You've made everything so hard for yourself."

"Lucifer."

"I do love you," he said. "But I wish you wanted this, like you were meant to. Would have been easier on all of us."

"I'm bleeding," I said, this time with more urgency. "It's bad."

"We're almost there," he said. "It's almost done."

I glanced over my shoulder, and there was a horde of people

behind us. I tried to pick out faces. Rosie's. Grace's. Brody's. My mother's. It was too dark.

Where's the moon? I wondered. *Where are the stars? Do they know what's about to happen?*

The barn door opened itself, and my father escorted me through. I whimpered when we got to the winding steps down to the cathedral.

"I can't make it," I said. "I need help."

"I'm helping you," he said. "I'm helping you."

He picked me up. He carried me. Carried me as I bled.

"That's my girl," he whispered.

I went light-headed, lost consciousness, vanished into a memory.

"That's my girl," he said. *I'd just beaten him at cards. We sat at the kitchen table, sharing a bowl of pitted cherries. "No more letting me win."*

I used to lose on purpose, because I thought he'd have more fun winning, and if he had more fun, he'd come over more. But he'd confronted me about it, and I came clean.

"You're very clever," he said. "Almost as clever as me."

"Almost," I said. "Maybe someday."

He slipped a cherry into his mouth. "Maybe someday what?"

"I'll be as clever as you."

He laughed, and, oh, the rapture of making my father laugh.

"What?" I asked. "What's funny?"

"Nothing," he said, shaking his head. "I love you, my girl."

"Love you, too."

"Yeah? You promise?"

"Promise."

"And you promise you'll always love me? And listen to me? And do exactly as I say?"

"Yes. I promise that, too."

"That's it, Princess," he said. *"That's it."*

How could I have known then? How can anyone know when ruin wears the disguise of love?

15

I swayed at the altar. Lucifer kept his arm around my back. The crowd filtered in. They all wore hooded robes. They were indistinguishable from one another.

They must have set their candles down somewhere, because they weren't holding them anymore. *How were these logistics coordinated?* I wondered. *Why wasn't I, harbinger of the apocalypse, the big cheese, looped in?*

And, more important, *How much blood is too much blood to lose?*

"I'm losing blood," I told Lucifer. Who knows if he could hear me over the organ music, which even under these circumstances was a bit much? "And you don't even care."

"You don't need to worry so much, Vesper," he said. "You're only half-mortal."

I should've been happy to hear it, since I was bleeding out, but I was really, really not.

"Ah—" I gripped my leaky side. As I crumpled forward, the beaded headpiece slid off me and onto the floor, down the aisle.

"Bring her crown," Lucifer said to the High Priest.

"Crown?" I asked. "Wait, where's my necklace?"

"You don't need it. It'll only get in the way."

"The way of what?"

I was wedged between dire panic and total resignation. I'd always assumed I'd know what to do if I was in real danger, figured I'd have some instincts. I think everyone makes this assumption about themselves. And maybe some people do have those instincts. They can crawl through the woods to safety while bloody and bludgeoned, trick their kidnappers, fight off their assailants. Some people have that in them. Not me, though. Not then.

The High Priest set a crown on my head. A tall Satanic tiara with diamond pentagrams all around.

I must have looked like a bloody, demonic pageant queen, like I belonged in one of my mother's movies. A final girl.

Except I didn't have that staunch determination to survive.

I could barely motivate myself to keep my eyes open.

Maybe I should've just listened to my father, my family. Gone along with Hell's Gate. After all, how far had my defiance gotten me? But if I surrendered myself to them right then, opened the seal . . . then what?

"Behold, the little horn. The great key," the High Priest boomed.

The crowd roared in response.

The aisle seemed miles long. I couldn't run. I couldn't make it. The scene faded in and out. In and out.

"Thus upon us is the hour of hell. The doors to the kingdom shall be opened, and its fires shall spread. The sun will go black. The sky will split. The world will be ravaged. And we, the chosen, shall rise from the ashes to build a perfect world in His image."

I was still struggling to wrap my mind around how any of it was real. But I didn't have the luxury of time to wrestle with doubt, to analyze the supernatural or the logistics of hell or whatever, because if it really was legit, the fate of the world was at stake. Like, right then. At that exact moment.

The fate of the world was in my sticky, bloody hands.

Shit.

"Behold the Lamb," Lucifer said.

The adrenaline arrived like fireworks.

What have I done? What do I do?

"Behold the Lamb," Lucifer said again.

It was only after he repeated it that I realized he was referring to me.

I remembered my mother's book. *"Blood of the lamb, the blood of the new and eternal covenant, which shall be sacrificed to purge the world by fire."*

Oh, I thought. *Oh no, no.*

He walked me forward.

"The time has come to reap, the earth ready for harvest. We who overcometh shall inherit all things." He was droning on and on, and I could hear what he was saying, but it was like I was underwater. Everything was warped.

My legs gave out and I nearly collapsed, catching myself on my father's arm. There was a communal gasp.

He looked down at me, his expression void of concern, of empathy. Of affection.

I didn't recognize him anymore. He looked completely different. Frightening.

I noticed a slim silver chain partially concealed by his collar. On it, I saw a charm just peeking out from behind his top shirt button. It was a small gem.

No. I realized. *A tooth.*

It was a small tooth. A baby tooth. Easy to recognize because I'd just seen some baby teeth at my mother's bedside the night before.

He brushed me off, gestured to the High Priest. Two clergymen carried over a large gilded chest. They set it down on the altar. Opened it.

It appeared empty.

"I have consumed the body of the Lamb and provide its rib as an offering to the legions of hell. Flesh of my flesh, blood of my blood." He removed something slim and white from his suit pocket. He lifted it high over his head, a garish presentation.

A bone. It was a bone.

A rib.

The scream died in my throat.

It was a staggering, soul-devouring horror. A boundless, unfathomable terror.

My hand trembled as it ripped at my bloodied dress. I needed to see. I needed conformation of the grisly suspicion, what I already knew in my gut to be true.

I shrieked, tearing at the dress with all my strength until I got to the gauze underneath, which was completely soaked through with dark blood. I gingerly peeled it back, and the sob that escaped me was tragic. The sound of pure anguish. Of true heartbreak.

Stitches. There was a line of messy stitches at my side. Puckered skin leaking. A butchering.

The cacophony of my wailing filled the cathedral.

It's what he was eating at dinner. My fucking rib. A piece of me.

I couldn't form words. I couldn't take my eyes from the wound.

"Vesper," Lucifer said, a brutal edge to his voice. He put a hand on my shoulder and I immediately batted it away.

"Don't touch me!" I screamed. I turned to the crowd, where the rest of my family hid in the safe obscurity of their robes. "You drugged me. You took my *rib*."

"You are the Lamb. My Lamb," he said, unremorseful.

I screamed again. A bloodcurdling, unearthly scream.

I squeezed my eyes shut, summoning, summoning. When I opened them, the crowd pulled back their hoods in unison.

My mother sat in the front pew. Grace beside her. Rosie. Brody. They appeared unmoved. They all looked to their Lord. They didn't look to me.

Approaching Constance, I tripped over the hem of my dress, landing hard on my knees. My crown fell at my mother's feet.

"What's *wrong* with you? How could you do this to me? To your own daughter?" I asked her, tears blistering my face. The horror mutated to anger. Rage.

I'd been right to leave, and so stupid to come back. But how could I have known? How could I have believed my own family was capable of such depravity? How could I have lived with the grief of knowing that the people who brought me into this world had done it so they could carve out parts of me against my will?

"You're my mother," I said, indignant. "You didn't need to want me or even to love me, but how could you not protect me? Not save me from this? Mom?"

Her mouth fell open. I hadn't called her Mom in years, not since I was little, and I thought maybe there was some promise of emotion, of remorse. But then she turned her cheek to me.

"Fucking shameful," I said, stumbling to my feet. I addressed the crowd. "You don't deserve to inherit *shit*. Maybe you should be the ones to burn tonight."

"Vesper," Lucifer said, holding out a flat palm like he was training a feral dog. "Come here."

He reached forward and grabbed me by the neck.

"I'm not opening any goddamn seal," I said. Hot fury broke over my skin. A searing sweat. All this anger that I'd kept tucked away—I must have known it was dangerous. I must have known that if I were ever to crack the shell of my indifference and release the full force of my wrath, it'd be nuclear.

"Vesper, enough. You're embarrassing yourself," Lucifer hissed in my ear. He had his left hand pressed to my wound so I couldn't move. "Now, hold still while I slit your throat."

There was a whole new wave of terror, of devastation.

"Behold the Lamb," he said to the crowd. "Behold my sacrifice, which I make for you, so that the seal may be opened."

The glint of a dagger entered my peripheral vision.

I realized he was actually going to do it. He was actually going to kill me. Going to slit my throat. And they were all going to let him. They were all going to sit there and watch.

"You were meant to do this willingly," he said, holding me more tightly as I attempted to wriggle away.

"I hate you," I spat.

He raised the dagger to my throat.

"You don't mean that. You'll see. Your blood will open the seal and you will be reborn by hellfire. But then we won't have any real need for you, so you should try being nice."

There was a great rumbling of the floor beneath us. He dragged me back as the marble disintegrated to dust. In its place was now a giant stone pentagram. It bowed at the sides. A basin.

A place for me to bleed. To die.

"In," he said.

"No. *No.*" I willed him to let me go, but nothing happened. I had no power over him.

And it was too late. He put the blade to my skin, and I felt just how sharp it was. I stepped into the basin, stealing a final look at my mother, who stared into her lap. I wondered if it was because she couldn't bear to watch me die, or if she couldn't be bothered.

It's sad that the moment I finally realized I was so much better, so much more, than the people who had brought me into the world was the very moment I was forced to leave it.

"My flesh, my blood, my kingdom," he barked. "For eternity."

He yanked the blade back, and at first it went easily, as if my skin were warm butter. It stung, but it didn't hurt as badly as I'd imagined dying would. But then it got rough.

What's in a neck? Veins? Muscle? I'd never given it much thought until then, as I felt whatever it was getting sliced through, destroyed.

My blood spewed everywhere.

I watched it. My life spilling out.

This is what it is to see your life flash before your eyes. Not a montage of pretty pastel memories. Just a violent stream of blood.

There was a very loud, very distinct *snap*, followed by a dreadful gurgling.

I thought about all the damage I'd done, everyone I'd ever hurt. Had they deserved it?

I asked myself, *Do I deserve this?*

I couldn't breathe.

I was shivering, cold. So cold.

My head leaned back, and it was far. Too far.

The cathedral smeared into nothing. There was darkness, and there was quiet. But there wasn't peace.

No peace. Only a stirring in the ashes.

16

I woke to the smell of fire. Smoke. Burning.

To the sound of it. The salivating of flames.

My eyelids were too heavy to open.

I reached for my neck, but all I could feel was heat. The gentle caress of . . . something?

A gasping breath jolted me into full consciousness.

I was alive. I was alive.

I was . . .

On the cathedral floor. Behind me was a giant sinkhole, a fucking volcanic void.

I'd have screamed, but my throat . . .

My fingers found the wound, but all that was left of the total annihilation was a faint scar. A slim raised line with a rough texture.

I blinked. Somehow, until that moment, I'd failed to realize that I was on fire. Engulfed.

"Behold!" It was Lucifer. He stood beyond the sinkhole lava void, arms outstretched. "The miracle of hellfire. Let it replenish! Let it cleanse the earth!"

I'm on fire. I'm on fucking fire! I thought. But the flames . . . they didn't hurt. They kind of . . . tickled?

I got to my knees, staring at my flaming hands. I pulled them into fists, and the flames were extinguished. I opened my palms again, and they ignited.

"Uh, what?" My voice sounded different. Husky. Like I'd smoked for fifty years.

"Rise, Daughter. Join me. Let us release the legions of hell together," Lucifer said, smiling warmly, like he hadn't just killed me. "Come, Vesper. Take your place."

I looked back to the rest of the cathedral, to the crowd swaying, chanting, speaking in tongues, arms raised in worship. They were very enthused either about my resurrection or about the flaming sinkhole. Brody and Rosie held each other. Grace stood on a pew, hands clasped together in prayer. And then there was my mother. Her body was still, her face blank.

She finally looked at me. Our eyes locked. And she just shook her head, a nearly imperceptible no. Left, right.

Maybe she could sense what I was about to do and was discouraging me from doing it. Maybe that was what was to be gleaned in this brief, wordless moment between us. Or maybe she'd had a change of heart after watching me bleed out, and was telling me *not* to join my father, to choose differently than she had. Whatever message she was trying to convey, it really didn't matter, considering the me who gave a shit about my mother's love and approval had died a few minutes ago.

I rose to my feet. I didn't feel sick anymore. I actually felt pretty solid.

I felt alive.

I opened my palm and summoned a flame, an exciting new feature. I turned toward the fiery abyss, tilted my head to the side in contemplation of how exactly I should go about dealing with it. I pushed my palm toward it, shooting a steady stream of flames. At first it didn't seem productive. Fire into fire. But then the cathedral began to groan around us.

"What do you think you're doing?" my father asked.

"I opened the seal," I said, peering over my shoulder. The chandeliers were swinging. "Maybe I can close it."

"Vesper."

"I'm busy."

"Vesper, stop this. Come. Join me."

"Why would I do that? You just killed me. You cut me open. Twice! You ate my rib."

"I made your body. It's mine to take from," he said. He lifted the chain from behind his collar. "I keep you close to me always. Your teeth, locks of hair. They've allowed me to walk freely between realms. And your rib—"

A flare of anger came, and I didn't punch it down, didn't shy away from it. I allowed it to grow. I fanned the flames.

The cathedral shuddered. The walls. The ceiling. A statue of Baphomet fell, broke apart. The horned goat head rolled toward us and tumbled into the pit.

Tense murmurings rippled through the crowd.

Lucifer's top lip curled.

"I can't change that I'm your daughter. I can't control what I've inherited from you," I told him. "But you can't control that either."

I burned. The resentment. The sadness. The love. The hurt. I released it. I let the tears fall hot and free. Finally, finally. I let it go. I let it all go. I let it burn.

The entire cathedral quaked. The stained glass, those horrific images that had made me squirm as a kid—they shattered, one after another, in a perfect circle of destruction around the room. Glass sprayed like confetti. People screamed, ducked under smoking pews.

"Vesper!" Lucifer said, his voice deep and menacing. But I wasn't scared. I knew he couldn't do anything about it, about me.

That's the thing with damage. It can't be undone. He couldn't fix what I was breaking.

Our gift was destruction.

Pentagrams flew off the walls, whipped through the air like Frisbees. They were getting sucked into the sinkhole, which festered like a wound. Giant blisters of a lavalike substance simmered up, burst open, revealing large insect creatures with hard shells and translucent wings. Demons? The legions of hell?

Didn't matter. Their attempts to fly were instantly thwarted. There was too much fire. Their wings caught, and they fell right back into the pit.

It was so heinous. So riveting.

Coming from the void were these distant cries of suffering that I could hear even over the screaming in the cathedral, over the tipping and burning of the pews, over the organ, which was in the process of collapsing in on itself.

The floor cracked beneath my feet.

"Need I remind you that you have no love for humanity? Think about what you're doing. The world has never shown you any kindness, and it never will," Lucifer said. "You *want* to see them all burn!"

"No, I don't. You do." And it was the truth. Maybe the world was a rotten place full of self-serving assholes. Maybe I'd had bad luck with people. Maybe I was the problem; maybe I wasn't. It didn't matter. I wasn't willing to condemn them all to a cruel fate, because, I knew then, it just wasn't who I was. I wasn't hateful. I wasn't evil. I wasn't my father's daughter.

I was tired of being bitter, tired of my cynicism. It had never saved me from heartache, never insulated me from hurt. It had only made me miserable. Maybe I wanted to be the kind of person who, in spite of everything, still chose to have a little fucking faith. To have some hope. Not to give up.

"You're not saving the world," Lucifer shouted, face red with fury. "You can't. They're the walking dead."

A prayer book slid down the aisle into the pit, and I could see that the floor had tilted. The incline got steeper by the second.

"All you'll do is doom everyone," he said, dodging the pulpit as it tipped into the hungry, gurgling hole. "This is selfish."

"Yeah, well," I said, knowing he was full of shit, "I've never been a team player. Must get that from you."

The first pew went. Slid right down, got swallowed by the pit. I turned to see the crowd running toward the doors. It reminded me of Penn Station, that mad dash.

Except that the pitch of the floor was making things difficult. They climbed over one another, clawing in desperation. I thought maybe I should feel sorry for them, but then again, they'd all just watched me die. With enthusiasm.

Maybe they belonged in hell. But I didn't want to be the one to put them there.

I looked to Lucifer, and he was sneering. "Either you finish what we started, or they'll all fall down."

I thought about what Rosie had said to me on the porch swing the night before her wedding. *"I never knew how to help you."* I didn't know how to help them. How to save them. And they hadn't cared enough to save me.

"This isn't my decision. It's theirs. It's yours," I said. "And it's already been made."

And so it began.

It was Grace first. On her back. Legs and arms up, flailing.

Grace, who used to sing to me while I brushed my teeth, so I would know how long to do it for. Who let me pick out gum while waiting in line at the grocery store, any flavor I liked, every time. Who made me those chocolate chip banana pancakes. Who drugged me so I could be carved up for dinner. Who served me up on a platter.

She made no noise when she went. It was over the edge and into the pit. Just like that.

Carl followed. He was not quiet. He tried to scramble away. Unsuccessfully.

They all went. All the people who had watched my father hurt me and said nothing. Done nothing. Let it happen.

Brody and Rosie, clinging to each other. My first love and my best friend. I wondered. How could the boy who had kissed me for the first time on the porch steps when we were eleven, and for the last time just a week ago, and a million times between—how could he watch me screaming in pain and do nothing? And Rosie. *Rosie.* How many nights had we spent giggling in blanket forts, making funny pinkie promises, and sneaking Oreos from the kitchen? How could she dress me up for my execution?

She made a small cry in the final moment before they fell. Before the pit took them both.

"Look at what you've done!" Lucifer stood on a pile of cathedral wreckage. I could barely see him through the flames. He couldn't hop the chasm to get to me. It was too big. Too wide.

"This isn't on me. They made their sacrifice," I said. "I had to make mine."

"You've destroyed it all."

"Kind of my thing," I said, and blew out the flames sputtering from my fingertips.

Behind me there was a crash that caught his attention, so it caught mine.

Constance.

My mother stood upright, somehow. She unclipped her robe at the collar, let it fall. She stood still and regal in her black feather dress, despite the walls literally crumbling around her. She didn't flinch. Didn't scream. There was no trace of panic, of fear, in the face famous for it.

She took a step forward, and I could hear the click of her heels above the chaos. A sound that had always terrified me. Thrilled me. Maybe even comforted me. Because even a cold, cruel mother seemed better than no mother at all. I ached to understand her, and there'd been some small part of me that hoped that someday—someday—I might. But it occurred to me in that moment that now I never would.

She walked toward the pit like she was on a red carpet. Chin up, shoulders back. Not smiling but not frowning. Neutral. Appeasing. Pretty. Purposely withholding.

Everyone else, the rest of Hell's Gate, plunged gracelessly to their fate. Not my mother. I figured I could stand steady because I was the source of the destruction, but how my mother managed was beyond me.

She came up beside me, looked at me. She grabbed my hand and slipped something into it.

A hairpin. The skull hairpin from *Death Ransom*.

She leaned in close. She sighed, then whispered, "Draw blood."

"Mom?"

She didn't say another word before she fell.

The cathedral shook with grave insistence, and one of the wrought iron chandeliers plunged from the ceiling, landing with a grievous thud. I almost lost my balance.

I threw myself back from the pit, tripping over the flame-crisped tatters of my dress.

"If we're all going to hell," Lucifer said, "you're coming with us."

All I could think was, *Hard pass.*

That and *Shit, shit, shit.*

I hadn't gotten my rib eaten, my throat slit, fucking *resurrected*— some fun things I knew I was going to have to confront at a later date, TBD—to end up trapped in hell with the people I was eager to get away from.

I skirted around the fallen chandelier, jumped over the husk of a burned pew, over pools of broken glass. I wasn't really running; it was more climbing, but there wasn't much to hang on to. The cathedral was on the verge of complete ruin.

"Vesper. Vesper!"

Don't turn around, I told myself. *Don't look.*

But the need was too strong. I let my curiosity win.

I looked.

My breath jammed. From where I was, the view was so ghastly. I could see straight down, straight into it. And the atrocities in the pit, which appeared to me through the fire and brimstone and spouts of lava . . . they bored into me, scalded my mind. Within the depths of the pit was the most depraved misery. True hell. My understanding of evil broadened so rapidly, I felt as if my brain were being drawn and quartered.

"Let me go!" I screamed. "It's over. It's done. We're done."

Lucifer now stood on top of the altar. He gestured to me, and my feet slipped.

"Come home, Vesper. Come home. Where you *belong*."

"No!" I started sliding down. I grabbed onto a pew.

"Have you forgotten who I am, baby? You don't get to say *no* to me," he said. "When I look at you, I don't see Constance Wright. I see myself. I think you look just like me."

He dropped his head abruptly, adopted a limp, spineless posture. The seconds ticked away, my palms sweating, my grip on the pew now hazardously loose. His shoulders began to twitch. His suit tore at the seams. He was steaming. Seething. And his skin. It dripped off in perfect spirals, like he was an apple being peeled. His head snapped back, and I could see his face. His pupils expanded, and blood soaked the whites of his eyes.

I recalled my own dilated pupils.

Shit, I thought. *What if I really do have my father's eyes?*

His cheeks sank in. Blemishes appeared; wounds popped open like the beaks of hungry baby birds. His teeth and gums rotted yellow. His hair thinned, went wiry and white. He was *ancient*.

His former skin writhed in a pile at his feet, his suit along with it, leaving him in nothing but a leathery hide hanging loose from his bony hips.

He didn't look like a cartoon devil, or like Baphomet, or like any image of Satan I'd ever seen. He looked like a weak old man.

But also like pure evil.

He laughed. It was an appalling sound, his vocal cords corroded. He curled his thin lips back to show me the decay of his mouth.

This is it, I realized. *This is his true face.*

I couldn't unsee it. I still can't, though I wish—I wish—I could. I wish I only ever knew him as I did in my childhood memories. As the handsome, charming man who showed up with little gifts. Such adoration between the two of us. Those simple days playing games, sharing snacks, choosing records, him letting me set the needle down—neither of us knowing who the other was yet. Safe and happy in our assumptions, our projections.

He reached down and pulled up his skin. There was a nauseatingly wet noise as it came back together.

While he was reassembling, I refocused. I'd found it, clicked into that final-girl mind-set, that staunch determination to survive in the face of such horror, and I knew I needed to close the seal, end it all for good. But how?

My upper-body strength was pretty pathetic, but I beckoned what little I had to pull myself up, climb away from the pit. I closed my eyes and willed the seal shut.

Enough, please. Let this be over. Let them be out of my life. Let it stick this time. Please. Let it stick.

I thought I had been ready to be done in the past, but I wasn't. Clearly. I wasn't ready until that moment. Finally ready to put them behind me. All the good memories . . . Rosie and I learning to French-braid each other's hair, Brody and I stealing away between classes to make out in the supply closet, Carl carrying me on his shoulders during our annual trip to the apple orchard, Grace tucking me into bed with a quilt she'd made for me. Getting to watch one of my mother's movies for the first time. Looking out the window and seeing my father coming up the driveway.

I imagined these good memories falling into the pit. I imagined them burning.

There was a distant rumbling.

"You'll never be rid of me," Lucifer said. He'd returned to his previous form, looking sharp in his suit.

I gripped tightly my mother's hairpin. Kristal Link's hairpin, the one she'd used to defeat Mr. Ransom, to save herself.

Draw blood, my mother had said. Her last words to me.

If my blood had opened the seal, maybe my blood could close it?

I flipped onto my back.

"I'll still be here. I'll always be here. Watching. Waiting," he said. "And they will be, too."

He gestured down to the pit. To hell.

"Someday . . . someday you'll come home again. When you're reminded that no one out there can give you what you need. You'll always come home to me. Daddy's girl."

I let him have the last word. He needed it more than I did.

In a quick movement, I stabbed the hairpin into my palm. I squeezed. Let the blood trickle down. Let it meet the lips of the void.

I expected an uproar. A loud, fiery end.

But it was nothing like that. It was swift and it was gentle, and it sounded like liquid being slurped through a straw.

The hole folded in on itself. The flames fizzled. The earth encroached. There was a whirl of dust and smoke, and Lucifer stepped into it, and then he was gone, and then, where there'd been a giant pit leading straight to hell, there was nothing but dirt.

And I was alone in the cathedral.

The walls keened, and I understood that the place was still about to collapse.

My palm was bleeding pretty badly. I couldn't ignite it, couldn't burn the injury away. I ripped some of my dress off and wrapped it. I crawled out, cutting my limbs on glass the entire way.

I moved to the music of my own breath, ignored the slabs of ceiling falling around me.

"I'm going to make it," I said to myself, because I had no one to reassure me. I had to. It had to be me. And I realized that was okay. There was no shame in it. It was fine. It really was. "I'm going to make it."

I climbed up the first set of stairs on all fours, passing through the arched doorway, using the red velvet curtain to pull myself upright. The winding staircase was too steep, and I was so exhausted.

But I had to keep going.

I clung to the walls, dug my fingers into stone.

I was bleeding a lot, but it didn't really faze me. Not after how much I'd already bled.

I stumbled, and my kneecap clipped a step. I could hear the bone chip. It echoed.

I winced, clenched my teeth.

"I have to keep going," I said. "I have to keep going."

It was too dark to see how far I'd come, how far I had left to go. I had no fire in me then. I couldn't light my own way. All I could do was climb.

There was a hint of fresh air.

A hint of light.

I threw myself forward, tripped through the door into the barn, reeled outside.

It was disgustingly humid, but I didn't care. I didn't care. It was the most beautiful night.

Bright stars. Big moon. Loud crickets. Sweet grass. A breeze against my skin.

"Hell and back!" I shouted. I caught a tear with my tongue. "Hell and back."

My voice still sounded strange. Raspy. I wondered if it would ever go back to what it had been. I felt the thin scar at my neck.

Permanent damage.

At this thought, the ground shuddered beneath me, and the barn caught fire.

It went up quickly.

I couldn't help but watch. It was mesmerizing. Catastrophic.

I slowly lowered myself to the grass. It didn't take long for the barn to burn to the ground. A mountain of ash hiding the ruins of Hell's Gate.

The flames petered out eventually. I picked pieces of glass from my hands, my shins, my forearms. I traced the scar from the incision made for my rib. I realized I was going to have a lot of scars.

It is what it is, I thought.

There was a sudden rustling behind me. A presence. I went rigid.

Maybe everyone experiences it differently, the sensation of hidden eyes.

I whipped around.

The eyes that met mine were black, and round, and innocent, set in a small, sweet face.

A lamb.

It had a pink nose, floppy ears. It opened its mouth and bleated at me.

"Hey," I said.

It bleated again. We were in conversation.

"Rough night?"

It approached me.

"Yeah. Me, too."

It came up beside me. It was a little dirty, kind of stank. But who was I to judge, covered in blood and ash, reeking like barbecue?

"You know, I think it's my birthday," I said. "And the happy Shortee's happy birthday to me, hey!"

The lamb was silent. Unamused.

"All right. You want to get out of here?"

It didn't answer, but it didn't need to.

I gathered the strength to stand. I scooped it up in my arms, and I carried it into the night. Carried it away from that place, toward a future I had to believe was better than hell.

EPILOGUE

Now

The working title of the movie was *Hell's Ingenue* but the studio released it as *Devil Love*. The early reviews have been unforgiving.

Still, it was hard to get a ticket for this advance screening, hosted at the longtime home of the subject of the movie, soon to open its doors to the public as a "deliciously creepy" museum / B and B. A must-visit for any hard-core horror fan. Rumored to be haunted by the ghost of its famous former owner.

I'll see about that.

Constance Wright's ghost is one of the many rumors about the farm, about Virgil, the mysterious abandoned village once occupied by a Satanic cult. Did they up and leave, not bothering to pack anything, to hide the trail of their devil worship? Was it a mass-suicide situation? Nikes and Flavor Aid. Did they die in the barn fire? If so, where were the bodies, the bones, the teeth?

Maybe Satan *had* come for them.

A few ex–Hell's Gate members, including Jane's sister, Lily, went on TV, rode the latest wave of Satanic panic. The Constance Wright connection was a big get, and the outlets didn't exactly shy away from exploiting it or exaggerating my mother's role in the cult.

"It's possible she was manipulated like the rest of us," Lily said during one of her interviews. Maybe in the Hulu docuseries, the one I got all high-and-mighty about, telling my therapist I wasn't interested in watching, then proceeded to binge all of in one sitting, because I couldn't help myself, and because not knowing what was said was usually worse than knowing. I had to be vigilant for any potential mention of me. "But I don't think so. I think she liked having her position."

I'd considered reaching out to Lily at one point, thinking she might be someone I could talk to. Relate to. But I was always too afraid she'd sell me out. And for a while, I'd been trying to stay away from the past, not to seek it out. Not to pick at the scab.

She'll be here tonight, though. She was a consultant on the movie.

The bus bumbles along Route 6. Most of these people know one another, are in little groups. I sit alone in the first row, head down, hair pulled in front of my face. I've found the short, icy blond bob has been my best disguise. Some long bangs to hide the eyebrows. These days, I hardly ever get the comparison.

The actress cast to play my mother looks nothing like her. She had a big role in a prestige TV drama a few years back, but her career stalled after that. This movie was meant to be a comeback, but so far, her performance has been panned.

The bus turns onto Donner Road, and everyone whoops and hollers, high-fives, fist-bumps. There's a lot of excitement on this bus. I'd say everyone on this bus is about as excited as one can be while on a bus. Everyone except for me, obviously. I reach for my neck, the black velvet choker I wear to hide my scar. I play with it, move the clasp around.

This bus ride was included in the price of the ticket, transporting us from a mall parking lot in Morristown out here to the sticks. Part of the "experience."

"There it is!" someone says.

I haven't been back here in years. Not since . . .

Again, I feel the scar at my neck. A nervous tic.

The bus pulls up, parks behind several other buses. Since I'm first row, I'm first out.

It's the barn that draws my attention. Rather, the lack of it. How strange the farm looks without it. The remains—the ash, the bolts, the nails, and whatever else survived the fire—were all cleared away after some sorry UPS driver took a wrong turn and ended up down here, discovering the wreckage. He said it smelled like dead bodies, but that was likely just from the remnants of the feast, which had rotted and attracted vermin. This was almost four months later. It had all been sitting there awhile.

Where the barn used to be is now a patch of struggling grass. There's a section that's roped off, a sign beside it. I walk over to read.

The oak tree still stands. When I pass by, it seems to bristle with recognition.

No. It's just the breeze. The steamy breath of summer.

The ropes surround the winding staircase. There are about five visible steps before rubble blocks further access. The sign reads:

> It is believed these stairs may have led to an underground place of worship, but several experts have said it's too dangerous to excavate. We may never know what hellish asylum lies beneath this spot or the details of the Satanic debauchery that occurred there. Is this

where Hell's Gate met their fate? Trapped underground
with their secrets? Listen closely. Maybe you can hear
their screams. . . .

Cool.

"Does the movie address the daughter thing?" I hear someone say.

There's a group of people coming up behind me. They're
young. Teenagers.

"It should," another says. They peek over the ropes at the stairs.

"Sick. So sick."

"Dude, no way these are real."

"The daughter is just a rumor. The movie is meant to be fac-
tual. Based on true events."

"True events," one of them scoffs.

"These stairs are definitely real. They look old. Like . . . like
castle steps."

"Been to a lot of castles, Em?"

"Shut up. You know what I meant."

I put my head down and move fast, weaving around the horde
of teens without letting them see my face. I walk toward the
house, compelled by an all-powerful nostalgia. I climb the porch
steps, listen to their familiar groan.

The house no longer smells like my mother. Her musky aura
is gone.

Bart isn't, though.

"Hey, Bart," I tell him, rapping my knuckle on the glass.

"Excuse me. There's no touching," says a hawkish woman sitting on the stairs. They're roped off behind her.

I bite down on my tongue so I don't tell this lady, *This is my house.*

"Ticket?" She stands, begins to come down. Her heel clips a step funny, and she's about to fall.

I give a quick, silent plea. She steadies herself, clinging to the banister.

Was that me? Shit. No way. I've been careful. *So* careful. No incidents for years now.

Those stairs, man.

I take out my phone and she scans the ticket QR code, then puts a red paper bracelet around my wrist. It goes with the theme of the event, and therefore is patterned with pentagrams. Clever. Classy.

"You can move around the first floor in the areas that are open. No going behind the ropes, no touching anything. The screening starts at eight thirty. That's in"—she checks her watch—"about twenty minutes. You're going to want to get a seat."

"Yeah," I say. "Thanks."

I drift into the parlor. Mr. Ransom stands in his corner spot. He's on, lifting and lowering his hatchet, spewing catchphrases.

"Welcome to your nightmare."

"Nice to see you, too," I mumble, moving past him.

The people who got the house at auction paid something crazy for it. Five million? Six million? Furnishings and memorabilia included, of course. They made clear from the get-go that they were going to keep it as it was, turn it into a spooky experience.

They kept their promise. It hasn't changed much. Some things were stolen in the aftermath, once word got out that the place had been abandoned but before law enforcement got wise to what they were sitting on. A few pieces of art. The anguished-man painting. Constance's jewelry. Things that could be carried.

"Imagine living like this."

Several groups trickle in behind me. They're older. They probably knew who my mother was before, knew her from her work, unlike those kids outside, who undoubtedly discovered her through the scandal.

"I think it's cool," someone says. "Halloween twenty-four seven."

"Only she was actually *living* Halloween. Not, like, pretending."

"What do we know?" says a guy dressed up like Jackson Perry from *Death Ransom*. I forgot this event encouraged costumes. I've been lucky enough so far to be spared from seeing any. "It's all speculation. No one really knows what happened."

"Well, not according to the people who were in the cult."

"Is Lily Sterling here? Have you seen her?"

Their chatter drives me out of the parlor and into the kitchen.

Nostalgia nips at me here, too. The table, the counter. Where I sat across from the people who mattered to me in my first life. The people I banished from this one.

"Where's the popcorn?" someone asks.

"All concessions are outside."

I look out through the kitchen window and see the setup out back. A huge screen. Rows of folding chairs. A large food truck serving movie snacks. A stand selling merch. Several portable toilets. They've relocated the evil scarecrow from *Farm Possession II: Revenant Sickle* to accommodate the seating. He's now positioned next to a stand dispensing hand sanitizer.

It's surreal to see the yard like this.

"Fifteen minutes 'til showtime!" someone shouts. "Fifteen minutes!"

"We're having everyone take their seats," says the woman from the stairs. The ticket lady who almost ate it.

"Do we get to come back in the house after? I'm still looking around."

"Did you book an overnight stay?"

"Yes." A lie. It was another four hundred dollars on top of the ticket, which was one ninety-five plus tax. I still can't believe I spent two hundred dollars to visit my own house.

If I'd wanted, I probably could have come forward. Laid my claim to Wright Farm. Sometimes when I'm up early to work a double at the diner, I regret not cashing in. But then I'll look in a mirror, or have an itch, and I'll be reminded of the small pink scar on my palm, or the long one across my neck, or I'll be in the shower and my fingers will slip across the one at my side, which is not quite as wide but is twice as thick, and I'll remember why I've done the things I've done.

I'll remember how far I've come and I'll feel a sense of pride.

Hell and back, I'll tell myself. *Hell and back.*

I'm not who I was, and it just isn't worth the scrutiny I'd invite by outing myself.

"If you booked an overnight stay, yes, you're allowed to come back into the house. But that's a red bracelet. Red bracelet means you have a regular ticket."

"My boyfriend booked the room," I say, already too deep in the lie.

The woman snorts, and I take a breath before my mind goes somewhere it shouldn't.

"Then you'll need to come back with him."

"All right, then," I say. She's obnoxious, but she's just doing her job. Can't hold that against her. Maybe she loves enforcing rules because it gives her some semblance of control. Maybe outside of work and after a margarita, she's actually the most fun person on the planet. Never know.

"Miss, you really should go find a seat."

"Okay," I say. "Thanks."

She ushers me out through the front door. I roll my eyes at Bart, but he doesn't acknowledge me.

I follow the little arrows around the side of the house to the back. I pick up a "free" popcorn—included in the price of admission. There's beer but it's extra. The ticket checker was right to encourage me to get a seat. Most are now taken. I have my pick of the undesirables. Right up front. Next to a guy dressed in a very elaborate, very disturbing Blood Thirst costume. Next to a couple in full Kristal Link / Jackson Perry cosplay, hard-core making out. Or next to a guy in a generic Spirit Halloween devil costume. Red spandex. Cape. Horns. Pitchfork.

If only that guy knew what Satan really looked like.

No one would wear that costume.

I see others in the crowd in Satan wear. Pentagram earrings. T-shirts modeled after the ones found around Virgil, the ones Hell's Gate kids wore to summer camp, with *Faith Eternal* written on the front and Baphomet on the back. These versions have breast pockets, come in different cuts and colors.

It's strange to have your real-life horrors commodified. But I don't lament such things; I don't feel I have the right.

Besides, there's so much to suffer. If someone is really so fascinated by Hell's Gate that they want to purchase and wear a T-shirt, then hey. Their fascination probably occupies space they don't want to afford to something else. Maybe something painful to them.

I decide to sit next to Blood Thirst.

"Nice job on the costume," I tell him.

"Hey, thanks!" He's got a pretty cheery demeanor for someone in such a vicious getup.

There's no dimming of the lights, since we're outside. The trailers start. I eat all my popcorn. Swat away mosquitoes. Anxiously bite my nails.

I don't know what to expect from the movie, marketed as part horror-icon biopic, part straight horror. I don't know how biographical it can be, considering how little is known about my mother. Maybe it'll surprise me. Maybe not. I do need to be prepared if it's going to stir up the "daughter rumors." If it gives the internet sleuths fresh fodder that'll complicate my life, the one I've worked so hard to build over these last few years. Jeopardize my new identity, my new name.

And yeah, I could have just looked up spoilers online or gone to a regular-ass movie theater in a few weeks, but I'm not really here for the movie, am I? At least, not just for the movie.

Oh, it's starting. It's starting.

It opens with young Constance on the farm, skipping around, humming to herself, her hair in pigtails tied with black ribbon. It was shot here, on location. Well, partially. The rest of Virgil had already been sold off to investors to bulldoze and turn into a fifty-five-plus development by the time the movie got green-lit.

The barn doors open all by themselves. A shadowy figure emerges. Cut to title card, scored with screeching violins. It picks up with Constance as a young adult auditioning for *Death Ransom*.

The casting is bad. The acting is bad. The dialogue is *bad*. The movie doesn't know if it wants Constance to be the hero or the villain. Is she a victim of a charismatic master manipulator who calls himself Lucifer and claims to be the devil? Or does that make her character weak? Is the more feminist take to put her in the driver's seat?

The director, screenwriters, actors, producers, whoever . . . they couldn't decide. They also couldn't decide if the movie was supposed to be camp or not. Sometimes it doesn't take itself too seriously; other times . . . there's laughter when there shouldn't be laughter.

I watch the crowd watching. They seem confused but entertained.

I suspect this is going to go on to be a cult classic.

The irony.

The story line follows a young starlet caught between her ambition in Hollywood and her love of Satan. The depiction of Satanism is predictably egregious. Yes, lambs were sacrificed, but the members didn't fall to their knees to lap up the blood like animals.

I shouldn't be defensive after what they did to me, but this is how it is. I'm allowed to feel what I feel about my family, but when it comes to strangers . . .

"I thought it was supposed to be scary," says the guy dressed as Blood Thirst next to me. He's checking his phone. I can see he's on Twitter. Probably tweeting, *I thought it was supposed to be scary #DevilLove.*

I'm not featured as a subplot, but I am a twist at the end. Maybe there's a baby. Maybe Satan is real. Maybe this baby is the Antichrist. Maybe the Antichrist is out here among us. *OoOoOoo.*

Spoiler alert—she is! Picking popcorn kernels out of her teeth.

Thanks to the overall quality of the film, I doubt this baby tease will lend any credence to the conspiracy theories. If any-thing, its inclusion will feed the skepticism, further insulate me from Reddit detectives.

The credits roll, and there's hesitant applause.

Some rando holding a microphone steps in front of the screen. "What did we think?"

Another sad round of applause.

"Yeah! Let's keep the good times rolling!" This is all so pathetic that it's actually kind of sweet. They're trying. "We've got a spe-cial treat for you. Let's welcome author and former Hell's Gate member Lily Sterling!"

This gets the crowd going.

Lily struts out, waving like a motivational speaker. She looks good. She was always prettier than Jane, had normal-sized teeth. She wears a power suit; her hair is blown out. She looks rich. She is rich. Satan sells.

"Hi, everyone," she says. She gets a warm reception. Warmer than the movie did, at least.

There's a quick setup. Two folding chairs. The rando sits in one chair, Lily in the other.

"So, I have a few questions for you, and then we're going to get into some audience questions."

This should be interesting.

"I think what most people want to know is, how much truth is in the movie? How accurate is the depiction of life in Hell's Gate, and of Constance Wright?"

"The thing about it is, it's complicated. There's a lot of truth in the film. A lot of truth."

She and I used to steal from her mother's secret stash of ciga-rettes and smoke them on the porch whenever Constance was

away filming. She'd talk about the places she wanted to visit—
New York City, Los Angeles, Paris, Ibiza—and I'd think, *She
doesn't want to be here either.*

I'm happy for her. I am.

I really am.

"I can't speak to what went on between Constance and Lucifer.
Lucifer—I only met him once, at my confirmation ceremony,
which I talk about in my book, *Beyond the Gate*, which is out September fifth. He wasn't a figurehead; he was mostly working behind the scenes, pulling the strings. We had the High Priest, who
was the head of the church, but everyone knew Constance was in
a position of real power."

She crosses, uncrosses, then recrosses her legs. Jane used to do
the same thing. Neither of them could ever get comfortable in a
chair.

I wonder if Lily mourns her sister, her family. I wonder if she's
here to listen, press her ear to the ground to check if she can hear
them calling her name from hell.

The mosquitoes won't leave me alone. I turn around to look at
the house, and at what's just beyond it.

"Would going back truly be helpful to you?" my therapist had asked
me. She knew basically everything, except that Satan was real,
that hell was real, that I was the Antichrist and had supernatural
powers, which included, to my knowledge, spite violence and fire
hands. Instead, I told her that I had anger-management issues. We
worked on those.

"Honestly, I'm not sure," I'd said, fidgeting with a certain infa-
mous hair accessory.

"If you're looking for closure—"

"I know, I know. I just feel like it's something I need to do."

"Was any part of the film hard for you to watch?" the rando asks Lily.

"Yes. These were all people I knew," Lily says. "I knew Constance Wright."

"What about her daughter? There's been a lot of speculation over the daughter, whether she existed or not, if she was Lucifer's or maybe Josh Keen's, Constance's *Bloody Midnight* costar who she was linked to in the nineties."

I sit up in my chair.

Lily clears her throat. "If she is alive, I want to respect her privacy."

I'm pleasantly surprised by this. Then again, her response might not be about respect. It might be about fear. Even if Lily doesn't believe in Satan, hell, et cetera, and even though she left, who's to say she's completely free of superstition? If part of her doesn't wonder . . .

"So she's real?"

"And she's here tonight!" she says, and I swear, I black out for a second. "Just kidding! Sorry, sorry. No, again, I touch on it in my book, but it's not my story to tell. And I get why people are so intrigued by the concept of her, but I think to focus on that, and even Constance, to an extent, is to miss the greater picture. What Hell's Gate was, how it corrupted. The innocent lives it claimed. Sorry—"

She reaches into her Birkin for a tissue, pats at dry tear ducts.

Think I'm all set on this.

"Excuse me," I say, climbing in front of Blood Thirst. I do the awkward shuffle down the aisle so I can get out.

It's astonishingly easy to slip back inside the house, under the rope, up the stairs. The place is empty, unguarded. The ticket lady must be out back, listening to Lily. She is pretty compelling.

I know I'm procrastinating, but I can't resist. I go up to my room first. The third-floor landing is the same. Same rat tea set. Same books.

My door is wide-open, which is unexpected, strange. I step inside. The room's been rearranged. There are two double beds. The dresser is gone. The Kit-Cat Klock remains. And the cannibal lamp. Of course the cannibal lamp perseveres. It sits on the night-stand between the beds. It's not my nightstand, not the one I had. I walk over, swipe my hand across its surface. There are a notepad and a pen, both branded with a logo—the outline of the house in flames. There's a laminated card with the Wi-Fi password, but nothing else.

I open the drawer. Inside it are a spare phone charger, a remote for the flat-screen TV the new owners hung across from the beds, and that's it. I open the closet and find none of my clothes. The mirror is still there, and the hanging rod. A few lonely hangers.

I didn't expect any of my shit to be here, but it's still weird to see the place without it.

I go down to the second floor. Blood Thirst's mask is where it's always been, reliably scaring me senseless. The case it's in is bolted down so no one can steal it. I don't know why anyone would want to, it's so utterly terrifying. I shudder as I pass by.

My mother's room is locked. Go figure. I press against the door to listen for guests, the people who paid hundreds of dollars to rent this room and attempt to commune with Constance's ghost.

I don't hear anything, so I pick the lock with my hairpin. *The*

hairpin. I keep it on me at all times. Took me a while to understand why.

I push the door open. The furniture is the same, the velvet
drapes, pentagram chandelier. But it's not my mother's room anymore. The bed is made up with plain white linens. Her books are
gone. Her parlor palm. Her perfume bottles and makeup and jewelry all missing from the vanity. Her absence is palpable.

The sound of applause drifts in from outside. The interview
must be over. I'm running out of time.

I leave the room, closing the door behind me.

The memorial stone is less about honoring their memory than it
is a tasteless roadside attraction. It's enormous, twice as tall as me
and as wide as a sedan. It's carved with pentagrams and devil
horns and flames, engraved with my mother's name.

IN MEMORY OF CONSTANCE WRIGHT
AND THE MEMBERS OF HELL'S GATE.
WHEREVER THEY MAY BE,
MAY THEY BE AT PEACE.

It's about a five-minute walk, positioned between the farm and
Donner Road, on the far side, its placement strategic so that you
can get a photo of it with the house in the background. It's surrounded by bouquets of dead flowers and odd trinkets—cheap
jewelry, smooth pebbles, messages in glass bottles, plastic dou-
bloons, pentagrams, stuffed Baphomets.

I take a breath and ready myself to add my contributions.

The hairpin. My pentagram necklace and the photo of me as a kid with my father's hand on my shoulder—which were both there waiting for me when I went back to pack up my old apartment. I should have gotten rid of them then, but I didn't. I couldn't. These things are all I have left of my family, my first life. I've held on to them for years, as I've held on to guilt and grief. For too long. I'm ready to leave them behind. To have my peace.

I take a last look at the photo. I don't see myself in it anymore. Just an innocent, naive little girl in the grip of a selfish, narcissistic parent.

Someday you'll come home again. You'll always come home to me. The last thing he said to me.

But I know I'm not here for him. I'm here for me.

I look over my shoulder to make sure that no one's around, no one's coming, then incinerate the photo in my palm, let the ash fall among the dead flowers. I toss the necklace down on top, a stunningly beautiful piece of jewelry that bound me to a nefarious cause.

Just the hairpin now. I turn it over in my hand, run my thumb over the skull, its grooves so familiar to me, the feel of it a strange comfort.

There's so much about my mother that I'll just never know. So many questions left unanswered.

How do I forgive her? How do I forgive any of them? How do I forgive myself?

Maybe they deserve to be where they are. Maybe I did what I needed to do. It's impossible to know.

What I do know, what I've learned the hard way, is that we don't get to choose our parents or the circumstances we're born into. We can't change our blood. But it shouldn't determine our fate. It doesn't. We still get to choose who we are, who we want to be.

I made my choice. And it was the right one.

I'm really not so bad.

I lower to my knees and gently set the hairpin at the foot of the stone, and here, close to the earth, and what's underneath, I hear whispers. Voices.

I hear my mother. I swear, I hear her.

"Vesper," she says. "Go now. Don't look back."

I rise to my feet. As I turn away, with the stone, the house, the farm, all behind me, with the road ahead, I notice a certain smell. A smell that ignites nausea, immediate dread, the hammering of my heart.

Can't be, can't be. But . . .

I wonder why the crickets are so quiet. I wonder what they know that I don't.

Doesn't matter. I'm leaving. I'm going.

And this time—this time—I won't look back.

Acknowledgments

To Lucy Carson, I will always be completely awestruck by your talent, skill, creativity, and enthusiasm. You're extraordinary, and you're the hero in the story of writing this book. You had me at Shortee's. Thank you.

To Jess Wade, it's such a joy and honor to work with you. Thank you for your insights, your hard work, and your understanding.

To the absolute stars at Berkley: Danielle Keir, Jessica Plummer, Gabbie Pachon, Katie Anderson, and the whole team. I hope you know how grateful I am.

To my parents and my family, I appreciate everything you've done for me. This book is, thankfully, a work of fiction. For the most part. Also, a friendly reminder that I get my sense of humor from you ☺.

To Deanna and Lauren, for being a second family to me in my formative years, and for all the fancy food.

To the brilliant writers I'm lucky enough to know and call friends, thank you for being there. To Courtney, for listening to me pitch this idea way too many times and still picking up the phone.

To Nic, for your support, and for installing all the skulls in my office.

And to the readers, thank you for coming along for the ride.

Author photograph © Nic Harris

Rachel Harrison is the national bestselling author of *Such Sharp Teeth*, *Cackle*, and *The Return*, which was nominated for a Bram Stoker Award for Superior Achievement in a First Novel. Her short fiction has appeared in Guernica, Electric Literature's Recommended Reading, as an Audible Original, and in her debut collection, *Bad Dolls*. She lives in western New York with her husband and their cat/overlord.

VISIT RACHEL HARRISON ONLINE

Rachel-Harrison.com

🐦 RachFaceLogic

📷 ♪ RachelHarrisonsGhost

Ready to find
your next great read?

Let us help.

Visit prh.com/nextread

Penguin
Random
House